D0968209

WATER

NEW SHORT FICTION FROM AFRICA *edited by* NICK MULGREW *&* KARINA SZCZUREK

SHORT STORY DAY AFRICA

2015

NewInternationalist

CONTENTS

INTRODUCTION 7

INTRODUCTION

Security. Commodification. Conflict. Scarcity. Put water before any of these words and you begin to understand the social, economic and political climate into which Short Story Day Africa sent the 2015 call for stories.

Water can be divisive, acting as a border and a source of conflict between us and our neighbours, but it unifies us too. At any given time, between 50–70% of the human body is made up of water. Water flows through us, rejuvenating and cleansing our cells before returning into the systems that sustain humanity. Through water, we become part of our neighbours.

The twenty-one short stories in *Water: New Short Fiction from Africa*, reflect Short Story Day Africa's survival ethos: to subvert and reclaim. Reclaim the place of the short story. Reclaim a space for nonconformist writing. Subvert ideas about what it means to be a writer in Africa. Subvert ideas about what makes a story African.

Our call for stories was answered by 456 writers from all over Africa and the diaspora. The twenty-one we chose to publish pay tribute to the versatility of the genre and its relevance to contemporary fiction, not only in Africa, but worldwide. Ranging from the lyrical to the prosaic, the stories draw on respected traditions and like an undertow pull them into the present in riveting ways.

Of the winning entry by Cat Hellisen, the judges said: "'The Worme Bridge' stood out for us with its brave story and clear, distinctive voice; it's a wonderfully dark exploration of the water theme. The story works effortlessly to construct another kind of reality while grounding itself in the real world. The writing is compelling: the reader is drawn into this family and the strangeness that overtakes them. We found this a powerful piece of writing that continues to haunt the reader afterwards."

Second place went to Alex Latimer for 'A Fierce Symmetry', which "wonderfully observes the theme of the competition, has an admirably sparse style, interesting content and a strong voice"; while third went to Mark Winkler for 'Ink', which was "imaginative and evocative", and reveals its "unfamiliar world in a vivid yet delicate way".

A special mention was reserved for Fred Khumalo's story 'Water No Get Enemy', in which water is a pretext for the denunciation of the betrayals and brutality experienced by young freedom fighters in the Liberation Army camps in Angola.

The theme has been interpreted in most exciting ways in the other stories included in this anthology. Bodies of water are settings for pieces like Efemia Chela's exquisite 'The Lake Retba Murder', in which the corpse of a local woman is found floating in the picturesque, pink-coloured lake; or Mary Okon Ononokpono's historical 'Inyang', which retraces the importance waterways played in the slave trade.

Water as myth and a force of nature features in Wesley Macheso's 'This Land Is Mine', when a devastating flash flood becomes an agent of change allowing the narrator to begin a new life away from the confines of patriarchy and tradition. Through urban legends, historical figures and mythical mermaids, Christine Coates portrays the physical and psychological violence perpetrated on women in her 'How We Look Now'.

The scarcity and inaccessibility of water as well as the politics involved are considered in Louis Greenberg's intriguing and linguistically innovative 'Oasis'. It is one of a few stories which play with elements of speculative fiction, magic realism or fantasy. The most daring of these is the incredible 'Mother's Milk', in which Dayo Ntwari creates a fantastical, futuristic world that is a fascinating reflection of our times.

In 'The Tale of the Water Carriers', Pede Hollist takes us to Sierra Leone, where the country's resources – water only one among them – are in the greedy hands of the corrupt few while the most vital – human potential – is lethally exploited.

Perhaps the most surprising at first, but not in retrospect, are the stories which approach water as an indicator of mental vulnerability, as manifest in Louis Ogbere's unsettling 'Were', Megan Ross's powerful 'Traces', Siyanda Mohutsiwa's disconcerting 'And Then We Disappeared into Some Guy's Car', Wairimu Muriithi's touching 'Love Like Blue', and Donald Molosi's subtle 'Beetroot Salad'. Also in this vein, grief is finely explored in connection with drowning and loss in Alexis Teyie's heart-wrenching 'Mama Boi', Florence Onyango's 'Nyar Nam' and Chido Muchemwa's 'Finding Mermaids'.

Passing water has also been addressed in the most original manner in Mark Mngomezulu's 'Urgency' and Thabo Jijana's 'Native Mayonnaise', not the only stories in the collection to capture the suspense and engaging humour of oral storytelling.

The Short Story Day Africa team is grateful for the assistance of volunteers who helped us with the slush pile. These passionate African fiction lovers are important to the project not only for their willing contribution of time and energy, but for their enthusiasm to help create a sustainable and thriving literature on the continent, for the continent.

The reading and assessing process is a blind one, the stories judged on merit alone. Sixty-seven engaging, beautifully written stories remained after the slush pile was whittled down. When we first began with *Feast, Famine & Potluck*, we only had sixty-eight entries. To now receive that number of publishable stories is a testament to the brilliant writing the continent has to offer and to the growth of the Short Story Day Africa project.

This year, with funding assistance from ANT ProHelvetia, Short Story Day Africa was able to run Water Flow Writing Workshops in Botswana, Malawi and Zimbabwe. Whereas entries to the Short Story Day Africa Prize from these three countries have not been forthcoming in the past, the workshops resulted in several from each in 2015.

To the African writers telling African stories with African readers in mind: Short Story Day Africa salutes you. Be brave. Keep writing. We will continue working to create a platform for your stories and getting them into the hands and minds of readers with the help of our publishing partners: Hands-On Books, Cassava Republic and New Internationalist.

KARINA SZCZUREK AND RACHEL ZADOK

9

A Fierce Symmetry

Alex Latimer

*T*wo bodies arrived at our house a year apart. The first was my mother's, in an ambulance, for us to see. My aunt came into my room. I had my head resting against the wall and my eyes closed. She sat on my bed.

"Do you want to see her?"

"No, I don't."

"Are you sure? I'll come outside with you and we can just see her and say goodbye."

"I don't want to."

"Okay."

The ambulance left a few minutes later. I heard it roll back out of our driveway and into the street, then turn down the hill past the Joan Harrison Swimming Pool.

A week later I was standing on a chair, looking for a practice golf ball in the pocket of a golf bag on top of Dad's built-in cupboards. I was excused from school for the week and bored with daytime television. Behind the suitcases was a tin that I didn't recognise.

Inside was a paper bag that held coarse, dry sand. I unrolled the top and felt it with my finger. I sniffed it too. I took a second to realise it was my mother's ashes and I put the lid back quickly, as though I'd let her ghost out.

We sprinkled those ashes in the sea the next day. We drove out before sunrise in our grey-blue kombi to Igoda Beach, with flowers, the tin and some matches. We didn't talk in the car. We ate shop-bought muffins and stared at the sun rising in the side mirrors. Igoda Beach is endless. The sea is always rough and dark there, and the dunes are steep and tall and edged with thicket. We walked down to the sand in single file and crossed the shallow river mouth. Dad led us along the shore until the car was a speck in the morning haze.

"Here," he said.

The four of us rolled our trousers up to our knees and waded into the surf and we each threw some of that sand into the water. Then we tossed roses like javelins into the foam.

"The sea is connected everywhere," Dad said. "It doesn't matter where you go, she'll always be with you."

He asked if we had anything we wanted to say, but it was too hard to speak and we stood quietly, our feet numb from the cold, our rolled-up trouser hems damp with frothy swell. We retreated up the side of a sand dune, with the whole ocean laid out in front of us, and made a pyre of the newspaper we'd carried the flowers in, and the empty paper bag. They burned reluctantly and the wind whipped the ashes away while we sipped on juice from boxes and watched as a fisherman passed by far below. He stopped to look at the washed-up roses.

Twelve months later the second body arrived.

I was lying on the same bed, trying to reach a letter that had slipped down into the dusty space beneath it, when my middle brother ran into my room.

"Do you want to see?"

"What?"

"Come."

I followed him; my eldest brother trailed after.

When we came out of the kitchen door, the garden gate was open and we could hear a bakkie idling in the driveway. Dad was clearing pot plants off the cement table.

"Make space," he said, shooing us.

Four men came through the gate, carrying the body wrapped in a couple of hessian sacks. We knew what it was – Dad had told us it was coming – but the arm that protruded from it seemed too human and we were unsure for a moment. It was a fingerless hand, pink and cupped and clawing.

"Where do you want it?" one of the men asked, and Dad showed them across the courtyard to the table. They laid it down and I could see for the first time how long it was and I caught its smell. Fatty and meaty.

Dad would not peel back the hessian to let us see the whole creature: it would only attract flies. Instead he sent us to fetch things from the garden: the zinc tub from below the washing line, the one we used to wash the dog in; bricks from the pile below the cherry guava tree, sixteen of them; firewood, wherever we could find it.

We carried armfuls of jacaranda twigs and old pine off-cuts from beside Dad's workbench.

Then we watched him stack the bricks into little columns, two high and two deep, and arrange and re-arrange them to counter the uneven paving. He rested the zinc tub on the pillars and tested his construction for stability, pushing down hard on the rim with his palms so that his feet lifted off the ground.

"Can we see it yet?"

Dad didn't answer.

"Where's the dog?" he asked, lying on his side on the paving, holding a match against the crumpled newspaper. "Is the gate closed?"

"Yes."

"Just check if she got out."

We began our search in the living room, calling for our Irish terrier, and looking under tables and beds. I found her at the bottom of the garden cowering under the leaves of a delicious monster. I took her by the collar and checked her muzzle. She'd hidden away like this once before and Dad had found her foaming at the mouth – a dead raucous toad beside her. She vomited a lot that night, but she survived.

"I found her," I said when I got back to the courtyard. "She's fine." The hose was hanging over the lip of the tub, gurgling, and Dad had the kitchen scissors in his hand.

"You all ready?" he asked.

He cut away the hessian and, snip by snip, revealed the carcass of a female Bengal tiger.

She looked uncomfortable. Her front left leg stuck out sideways, while the others were tucked in towards her body. Her tail was curled down between her legs and she was stiff – locked into place, the same nervous position she'd been in when she'd collapsed from the tranquilliser.

"Died during a routine check-up. Anaesthetic was too strong," Dad said.

I used to visit the zoo a lot, so I'd seen this tiger when she was alive. But I saw now that half of her was fur and fat and charisma – and the people at the zoo had already trimmed all of that away. Here she was without her skull or her teeth or her claws or her flesh. She was a headless Sunday chicken carved down to the bone, good only for broth.

"You two, take that side. Us two will take the front."

We lifted the tiger up off the table, crab-walked to the tub and lowered her into the rising water.

We spent the afternoon feeding the fire until bubbles like Fanta appeared on the bottom of the tub. They multiplied and the water boiled and we watched her turning to soup. Her bones changed colour in the heat: first pink, then yellow and beige. The heat liquefied the fat that had rested between the tendons and bones, and it rose to the surface as a layer of waxy foam. It smelled like bad lamb pies. The hot water relaxed her completely and at last she lost her cowering pose and took the shape of the cauldron. Her protruding paw sank slowly into the froth.

The neighbours came to look over the wall, and they were polite and understanding, as people are when they are dealing with the mild insanity of the bereaved.

"I hope you don't mind the smell," Dad said.

"Oh, no. It's not so bad. What's in the pot?"

"A tiger. The one from the zoo died."

"Oh, shame."

"I'm going to re-build her. Wire the bones together."

"And where's the head?"

"The zoo kept it, and the skin too. For a rug, they said."

"Oh, okay. Well, we'll keep popping our heads over to see the progress."

They never did.

We left her to boil for days. The last thing Dad would do before bed was lay a few thick logs on the fire to sustain it during the night. And in the morning, we'd rekindle the ashes and get it blazing before we left for school, our hair smelling of smoke, our clothes saturated with the smell of animal.

In class for "How Was Your Weekend?", I stood up and told everyone about our tiger. After I sat down the boy after me made up a story about how his cocker spaniel had hijacked their ride-on mower and driven it into the swimming pool. The tiger was better as a secret anyway.

The next Saturday over breakfast Dad told us to let the fire die. He hadn't stoked it the evening before and the ashes were cold. The tub was lukewarm when we touched it.

The bones had loosened and disconnected and sunk to the bottom. Dad found a coat hanger in the shed and he bent it into a long hook and fished around in the stew with it. He hooked her pelvis, which despite the days of boiling still had sinews attached. He lifted it out of the soup and put it in the outside basin. It steamed in little puffs.

"We'll have to do another boil," he said, "but first we need to cut as much of this stuff away as we can." He pointed to the ragged meat. Quite suddenly, my brothers lost interest in the tiger. They had better things to do on their weekend than pare flesh from a pelvis.

I changed into old clothes – paint-spattered tracksuit pants and a shirt I'd outgrown. The tub was too heavy to lift and so we emptied it with old five-litre paint tins, scoop by scoop, into the drain. First came the greasy brown foam that had risen like cream, then the grey soup. The water level dropped in strata until the jumble of bones appeared through the murk. We grabbed the big ones with our hands: femurs, ulnas, clavicles. The rest we scraped up in the kitchen sieve, a mess of vertebrae and wrist and ankle bones that we would one day have to decipher.

"Make sure the dog doesn't grab any of these," Dad said, though we both knew she wouldn't come close.

I helped to keep the bones steady as Dad carved his way around the body, dividing the soft from the hard. Everything was greasy: the bones were soap to hold. I was gripping the pelvis and Dad was manoeuvring the knife when his hand slipped and the blade sliced deep into the back of my thumb.

I had to wait for him to clean up before he could treat my wound. I sat in the passage with my head resting against the bathroom wall, holding folded toilet paper over the cut to stop the bleeding. It took fifteen minutes for him to scrub the tiger fat from his arms and hands and wrists and nails. When he returned, wet to his rolled-up shirt sleeves, he doused my wound with hydrogen peroxide. It stung and fizzed, foaming into pink bubbles that spilled over into the bath.

"That's it clearing all the germs out," he said. "It only stings if it's working."

My middle brother came to watch, leaning on the doorframe.

"You going to have tiger powers now?" he asked.

From then on I was only allowed to watch as Dad cleaned the bones. The next day, with the help of the gardener he picked up the tub and poured the rest of the water down the drain.

Dad went over the bones one by one with the blade. Then he filled the tub once more and lit the fire and returned the remains for their double-boiling. The water was much clearer the second time, and I could see down to the bubbles jostling the bones at the bottom as though they wanted to thread themselves together once more and come alive.

After work one evening, Dad fetched me and took me to the museum with him. The cut had scabbed over; in the car I played with its frayed edges. We parked under the lucky bean trees and crossed past the front entrance, past the bronze coelacanth, to a pair of tall rusted gates topped with razor wire. A man came to greet us.

"So it was you who got the tiger?"

"Most of it," Dad replied.

He showed us into his work room. It smelled of cigarettes and spray paint. A snot-coloured urethane duiker stood on a table surrounded by photostats of live antelope, running or hopping over rocks. Instead of hooves, though, this one's feet ended in wire pins. Along one wall was a huge chest freezer for keeping bits and pieces of animals in until they were ready to be reconstituted, and on a bench across from it was a deflated gymnogene, its feathered skin peeled off and then flipped the right way round like a worn sock. Over tea, he showed us how to wire bones together using a drill, copper wire and glue. It looked simple enough but he suggested we practise first rather than get it wrong on the tiger.

"Roadkill is easiest," he said. "Just keep a black bag in your cubby. Or maybe you've got an old dog?"

After he'd shown us the wirework, he and Dad got chatting about a mutual friend whose yacht had run aground and I edged away from the conversation, past the mounted hyena head and up some wooden stairs.

The attic was dark and filled with stuffed creatures, weathered and dull. There were rows of birds, each dotted with borax powder to stop the bugs, and staring blackly out of glass eyes: penguins, falcons, pigeons, loeries and vultures, set side by side, unnaturally close to one another. A nervous baboon sat in one corner holding onto its knees. Above it hung an orangutan, its hands worn down so that the white plaster cast showed through the black skin. Beside a tapir with alopecia there were glass-fronted drawers full of insects and hummingbirds and field mice and tiny dried fish, all labelled in scratchy, handwritten Latin.

And on top of the drawers, jostling for space with tiny birds on wooden perches, were skulls, lined up in a row from big to small: genet, civet, caracal, cheetah, leopard, lion and tiger.

I picked up the tiger skull to feel its weight. It was heavy with teeth. I inspected the incisors, running my fingers over them and feeling the blunt points, and I wondered whether we could ask to have it since it was just sitting here. Perhaps if I found an excuse to come back, I could stuff it in my school bag and take it home to complete the skeleton. It would be years before anyone noticed.

Dad called me down and we re-traced our steps back to the kombi, carrying a coil of copper wire and a pack of clear two-part epoxy.

"What did he say about whitening the bones?" I asked.

"Shouldn't use bleach," Dad said. "Rather paint them with peroxide."

The next weekend, I watched Dad empty the tub for the last time, five litres at a time. Then he fetched the peroxide from the bathroom cabinet and poured it into an old feta cheese tub. He put on washing-up gloves, and then he picked up each bone and painted it with the clear liquid. I expected them to fizz but they didn't.

Dad placed the bones to dry on an old dog-washing towel. They were yellow and almost transparent, saturated with the grease of zoo food, the frozen bulk braai packs of low-grade chicken pieces.

The bones sat in the sun for a week, until they were dry to touch, then Dad packed them into brown paper bags, which he labelled as meticulously as he could: *Tibia + Fibula; Left (?) Scapula + Lumbar; Misc Metatarsals L+Rmix; Tail vertebrae ad infinitum.*

He packed the brown bags on a high shelf in his study, behind some books. He put away the tub and the bricks, two by two, and the cursed knife. There was a big black burn mark on the patio and the constant dampness of an oil stain like a halo around it, where the broth had spilled from under the rim of the tub.

The dog emerged from the jungle of palms and wild banana trees beside the swimming pool and took to eating again, though she would not be bathed in that tub and she avoided the area outside the kitchen door. The next time we took her to walk on Nahoon Beach, she disappeared into the tree line above the dunes and we fetched her that evening from a woman who'd read the number on her collar.

"Probably chasing monkeys," Dad said.

*T*wo years later I was standing on Dad's wooden draughting drawers – looking for a reference book on the top shelf in his study – when I found the bones again, nestled together beside the coil of wire and the glue. I took one of the bags down. The paper was saturated with grease like a leaky Chinese take-away.

I opened it. They were still yellow and glassy, despite the peroxide. I imagined the stubborn fat that soaked up the calcium was her ghost, still haunting her bones, driving the dogs into hiding as she stalked the neighbourhood at night, unwilling to be forgotten.

And I wondered about the rest of her – her skull and her skin lying on the floor somewhere, and about her kidneys and claws and cartilage that had been sliced away before she had come to us, and also about the blanched off-cuts and the fat we'd poured down the drain. We had tried to whittle her down to her solid core, to her essence, but even that was incomplete.

There was one other bone missing apart from the skull: the very last vertebra from the tip of her tail. Dad had seen it slip through the wire mesh that he'd put over the drain. It was barely bigger, he said, than a full stop.

The Lake Retba Murder
(Le meurtre au Lac Rose)

Efemia Chela

*I*t wasn't a crime anyone had asked him to solve, but he was the person who had seen something strange in the water. To first notice the oddly shaped buoy bobbing near the edge of the lake. Roberto had turned left at a slight change in the wind when he saw it, being pushed by fate towards the shore. Towards him. He waded in. The body was painfully bloated. Even its black pores were stretched. As he turned her over, pink water pooled in the dips above her collarbones and he saw the twin bulbs of her breasts had swollen into one ugly lump. Her hair was ruined and looked like a claggy drain rag riddled with knots. Her fingertips were tightly shrivelled. Squishy nails, green and furry at the cuticles, steadily rotting up towards the tips. A helicopter filled with tourists chopped through the summer sky. From that high up, Roberto thought, he and the corpse must look like flies stranded in a strawberry milkshake.

Mireille looked down from her favourite dune and saw Roberto in the lake. She let the sand sift through her fingers as she watched the sun go down. The African sunset foreigners made so much of. Her watch seemed to tighten around her wrist when she saw him. She looked at its face. Two hours until their rendezvous. She hoped he wouldn't be late. As Mireille herself had explained, she was like a car and needed to be serviced. She'd enjoyed a certain standard and frequency of sex in the thirty-four legal years that she'd been having it.

"Thrice a week we should be having sex. Together. Obviously. My address…"

A portly fifty-year-old woman had propositioned him. Then, with her stare, she urged him to find a pen and a scrap of paper to take her address down. Had she learnt such forwardness in Iceland? he wondered. His mother, of the same age, said Mireille had left at sixteen with a policeman on holiday here. She'd upped and gone like sand on a windy day. No goodbyes, not much taken, and barely noticed. She'd returned similarly, without warning, seeking no reunions and only greeting people as she came across them. She said "Hello" and moved on with her day, as if she'd just left the house for a box of cigarettes thirty years ago.

After they had sex, he thought he could smell smoke on his own skin, as evidence of the unholy fire they'd just created. Then she'd light up. Usually saying nothing. Unless he lingered too long. In that case she winked and turned her back to him. And lay down still smoking. That back, where her underclothes had etched themselves into her body. Making lines and creases of secret hurt.

*H*e and Fatima weren't exactly friends but they had dropped out of school at the same time and that was enough. Fatima didn't feel looked at when she was with Roberto, and it was nice having a break from being a beguiling zoo animal. They saw each other by chance maybe every fortnight or so. Sometimes he saw her silhouette, sitting alone on a dune letting the world turn to black. Blotting out the natural beauty that seemed to plague her.

The last time they'd talked she'd caught him, malingering, on a break from one of his empty walks. They'd chatted, their backs being warmed by the mud wall that had soaked up the heat of the day. It had been about whether he was going to Dakar any time soon. He needed to get her a proper needle for her record player. He'd fashioned one out of a syringe he'd stolen from the clinic and it had wrecked a completely good record, *Wish You Were Here*.

"I'm not sure when," he said. "But I'll get you one. I'll fix it."

The police weren't too bothered about him working the case. To them she was just another stiff in the morgue and a case file in a corner of the office. Roberto went down there and found himself distracted by the coroner's very high-up fringe, something he'd never seen before. It showed up the bones in her forehead, two round knobs protruding rather unattractively, like an extra set of eyes.

He inspected the body, ravaged by the water, one last time. Fatima smelled salty but there was also something else. He lifted up the sheet, searching for what it was on her that was different. Something. A detail. Escaped him.

"Are you hearing me? I said strangled to death before she took in any water. She didn't drown."

Well that was obvious, Roberto thought. He looked at the burgundy bruising around her throat. Dr Diouf's observation wasn't particularly insightful. This was evident to them both in the awkward handing over of files at the end of their curt meeting. What a waste.

It was ten to sex o'clock. Mireille curled a lock of hair around her finger and smiled. Roberto fucked like a dream. She thought that, after years of harsh winds gnawing at her face, her looks were moonwalking backwards, her wrinkles blurring smooth, and the sex was what was doing it. Youth was a funny thing. Maybe it was contagious. Maybe it could be captured.

Roberto knew that he specifically had been chosen. It was him or nothing, but he didn't know why. He couldn't see the boy Mireille saw in him. What had she seen reflected in the rippling scales of fresh tilapia and mullet? That day he'd been left alone to look after the stall, his father's warning ringing in his ears. Roberto wasn't a fisherman. His father had big arms, fit for tattooing and pulling in lines weighed low by flipping fish. There were bloody grooves in his palms from earning a living on the line. He walked the same kilometre to the sea and back every day without feeling trapped. Roberto lacked heft; was lightly muscular and lean. The tides didn't interest him and neither did the heaviness of nets, so he left them all day unattended and lolling in the sea, anchored by pegs to the shore. He refused to squat near them and wait, marking time by cigarette butts, boasts and tussles with other fishermen. He left his kit behind trusting the generous sea to fill it and the other hunched fishers not to steal too much.

He walked the kilometre back, off the path, through the bush. He sat by Lake Retba knowing its every shift of colour. Mauve, lavender-pink at dusk, magenta at dawn and crayon-pink during the day. At least during dry season. When the rains came, Le Lac Rose was diluted. As boring as tap water.

He walked around the town. Up and down, through the narrow dirt streets. Chewing on a piece of briny wild samphire he'd picked up. Letting the pink juices drip off the cliff of his jaw. He walked through the world like a ghost, glancing at things and then turning away. Remembering everything but cherishing nothing. Passing through throngs of people in high season. Walking in thin air in the middle of the road in off-season. Sometimes stopping for a café crème and savouring its strength and bitterness that tasted like Mireille.

When he reached the coast, his kit was alone and pathetic. There were two common rougets du Sénégal and a small hake that would be bland in his mother's pan no matter how much she sprinkled things and tutted over it. That night he and his father would quarrel again. Threats and excuses were thrown at each other like old bent-up cards, in a game that everyone had forgotten the rules of. The night following the day he looked after the stall in town they'd quarrelled even more. Mireille had turned the day upside down. Roberto had given wrong change, slipped on guts, and filleted wonkily and shakily, leaving bones in where there shouldn't have been. Customers pursed their lips or closed their purses and moved on to rival stalls. While listening to a Miriam Makeba LP overlaid by his father's shouting, he thought about how careers couldn't be inherited like warts. He didn't know what he wanted, but it wasn't this. No. Careers, he thought, were decided in that same hellish place where the rest of the things he couldn't understand knotted over themselves – like why the lake was pink, and his love for Mireille.

He understood the physics of her. Her body and how she liked to be tossed, folded and bent on the bed. In sex he was gloriously tethered to her lurid kinetics. He loved her and how she smelt redolent of milky sleep, tobacco, juniper perfume and sweat, mingled. He knew when she crawled up him, her hip creaking over his, and pushed her face into him, she was going to whisper in his ear, "Again." And he would rise.

While dressing Mireille said, "Awful about that girl who was killed."

"Yes," Roberto said. "It hasn't even made the paper yet. We were friends."

Mireille poured herself some water from a jug and didn't offer Roberto any. He let himself out wondering where to wander next.

$\mathcal{T}$he following day Roberto set off to interview the family hoping to get some clues.

"An angry ex-boyfriend? Apart from the ones I already know about? A new one?" he asked.

"Too many to mention," her mother sobbed. "But I think they were all too still in love with her to, to-t-to…"

Fatima's three younger siblings burst into tears and it sounded like the crash of falling glasses. They knew something was wrong but they weren't sure what. All under seven, they copied their mother's emotions and didn't really know what to be sad about. Roberto wanted to warn them that that feeling would never go away. Never knowing what to be sad about.

He knew Fatima didn't keep regular hours. She was always being asked out by locals and foreigners and she led them on at different places day and night. When she was lazy she let her looks do the work: begging seated on a pavement somewhere and waiting for money to fill her lap. She lifted up her heavy skirt and went home at the end of the day, cheekily giving whoever was around a little extra to look at. The only stakes in her schedule were waitressing Mondays at La Caresse Marine and Wednesdays being a chambermaid at the hotel.

"Did she get to all her jobs last week?" he asked.

"Y-y-yes," her mother said.

Suddenly an odd thought came to Roberto. He looked down at the specks of loose-leaf tea in his cup. Had her wages drifted from her, note by note, or had they been in a bundle of bills and coins that sank to the bottom? He hadn't noticed any money nearby. Had it been taken? Robbery gone wrong? After a while all he could get out of the family was tears so he finished his tea and left. The sound of sorrow rolling away behind him.

$\mathcal{R}$oberto kicked up dust with his rubber flip flops while in a mental maze of his own making. His autopilot malfunctioned; he missed a left turn and walked crown-first into the chest of some old classmates. He butted his head again like a whirring toy car into a wall. The wall grew a hand that jerked his chin up and flipped him on to his back. Luc. Luc and his friends. They had tucked in their shirts to hide their jagged edges and rolled up the muddy parts of their trousers.

"Hey, con. Look where you're going. Wanna die like that girl?"

He didn't reply. How could he?

"Quelle nana!" one of the group said. The boys laughed at the memory of Fatima's beauty. They were passing around a red and white tub of Brylcreem and generally spiffing themselves up, which was a change from their usual endeavours. The last time Roberto had seen them they were spraying blood-like graffiti on a wall. Now they were all popped white collars.

"Where are you going?" he hadn't meant to say but did.

"L'hôtel," said another one of the boys grinning down at him still splayed on the ground.

Luc threw down a comb with some stubby broken teeth.

"We'll see you there," he said and the group erupted into laughter again.

Roberto threw the greasy comb off his stomach and thought about the gang ambling to the hotel. They moved into the early evening with their shoulders confidently squared against the unspoken rule that locals weren't let in to become familiar with the guests, lest they become familiar with the concepts of class mobility or self-improvement.

Meanwhile Mireille sat at La Caresse Marine, smoking into a gin and tonic. It was something Hans had taught her. Exhaling smoke into the drink brought out the more herbal and juniper flavours in cheaper gin. She was eavesdropping on a conversation she'd heard a hundred times. Sometimes told wrongly and half-sure. Sometimes read out loud from a guidebook with buyer's confidence.

"The lake's pink because of the algae here," a pale man said. "*Dunaliella salina*. It has a red pigment and it absorbs the light making it Le Lac Rose. Good thing we're here in dry season. It's at its best. Like some sort of sacred pool on an alien planet."

"It looks good enough to eat," said his travel mate. "Cotton candy. Or strawberry ice-cream."

They looked like the same kind of pale Hans was. Mireille and Hans loved each other. They had certainly professed it at their woodland wedding where the summer sun never set on the proceedings. They'd ignited each other when she handed him the bill at a lakeside café. She had looked into his eyes and seen no malice, just a calm sadness-tinged blue. And he saw dark honey and an inquisitiveness in hers that drove her to seek adventure away from the lake, the harsh coarse salt and the searing pink like open flesh.

Hans told her not to bother but Mireille learned Icelandic anyway to impress him and to read food labels. Then she moved on to the newspaper. What a waste. Nothing seemed to happen in Iceland. Occasionally a glacier crashed into another and a drunk froze to death on the street, the aquavit turning to ice in his veins. Problems of a different universe. Mireille was an Afronaut keeping her dictaphone up to date on her adventures. Canoeing in the fjords. Her hair breaking off because of the cold. Her boring stenographer's job at an advertising agency. She sunned herself with her happy lamp for Vitamin D and hoped that there was more to life.

It was a deafeningly quiet life they led. Their interactions with each other became ever more polite and robotic. Until they were in limbo. Neither riotously happy nor darkly sad. Too many spin cycles; their love had gone grey in the wash. Mireille blamed herself, her independence and privacy. But Hans thought stoically that it was the natural progression of love. Like flowers, it had to die. And anyway, he thought, dead flowers held some crumpled faded beauty. He couldn't recognise the girl who had chosen to marry him.

Hans suggested they go on holiday to see the steel tower in the clouds.

"You mean the Eiffel Tower, in Paris, dear. But how about further south – Cinque Terre, Italy?"

"Okay, elskan."

Mireille wondered if Hans knew this was the last hurrah, the flight to Rome and then a driving holiday where they looked out of the car windows in opposite directions, fought over how to work the Leica camera and clasped each other's hands over the shift stick some of the way. Mireille got up from her comfy spot, lying on his pot belly on the warm beach, and went to one of the many little pizzerias in Vernazza to bring back something for them to eat in the wake of the incredible marine view. She got some pizza alright, salame picante e basilico. She got in the rental car and drove away until the pizza got cold and she no longer wanted it.

Mireille stubbed her cigarette out harshly and barked for the bill. She suddenly felt sick. The waiter brought over the scribbled bill: "3 dbl G&T". As she handed him the money, she was marked by how cutting and rough his hands were. Like everyone else, he was in the salt business. People sailed out on les pirogues and gathered salt their whole lives. The salt looked like small diamonds in the sunlight, but it was much cheaper and rougher on the body. Everyone's hands looked mummified. She tipped the man and thought of how careful Roberto was. He always smelt oddly feminine from the shea butter he smothered himself in. But it kept him soft and somewhat sheltered from the world.

*A*nother day passed and Roberto was no closer to figuring out who had killed Fatima. Something small nagged at him but he just couldn't remember what it was. It was as fragile and inaccessible as a memory of an old dream. Wispy and out of grasp. He lay down at home, his parents shouting as only a fishwife and fisherman could, and cuddled a pillowcase he had stolen from Mireille's house. It smelled like everything she was made up to be. He breathed deeply. It calmed and focused him. Taking him away from the world he was born into.

Mireille tramped around town in a rage.

"Where the fuck was he? Who did he think he was?" she muttered and muttered under her breath.

CHELA

He hadn't pitched up for their rendezvous. Now what the hell was she supposed to do? She wasn't going to spend her time prowling the streets for a boy. She was in control here. She decided to sit by the lake, which was turning a dark purple because of the late hour. She sat and smoked, sulkily, angrily, needily on each drag.

Roberto crept up beside her, on the dune, the samphire and wildflowers shivering a little in the wind. He knew that smell. He'd found it. He sat by Mireille and stroked her curly bush of hair, playing at affection. But he was looking for what he already knew he would find. There it was. Round, save for some wrinkling, navy and pungent. Just like the one he'd found in Fatima's navel. A juniper berry. He picked it out of her hair and they both looked in his palm. It was so dark now they could barely see what they both knew was there and what it meant.

"You know she was never meant for this world," Mireille said. "She was too beautiful for it. It would have only scarred her and let her down. Escape would have been no escape. But staying would have eaten away and scratched at her until she was small. Disappointment would have hunted her stealthily like it did me.

"It's up to you now, Roberto. Fuck me or betray me?"

Mama Boi

Alexis Teyie

*B*arricaded behind a grille all day, Mama Boi fingered, counted, and, occasionally, sniffed money for a living. It wasn't bad, working at Afriti Bank – well, not really. They gave her a mug on the first day. And the job gave her some pocket money to supplement Baba Boi's contract with the UN. The other employees called her "Madame Import" behind her back, but she didn't mind too much. What was wrong with having good taste? After the baby, at least they stuck to "Mama Boi".

That morning, Baba Boi's words fell out of the phone, landing flat on her cramped station: "Haki sijui, it was the water! So Ghana was playing, and I looked away for just a second, I swear, but… just so much water! Please, come quickly!"

She spat out in shock, and her voice left with it. She left Baba Boi mumbling through the receiver, and hurried out with one foot already in rubber shoes, the other lagging behind, still caught in a high-heel.

"You're leaving?"

"Mama Boi?"

"And the customer?"

"Si you say something!" But Mama Boi said nothing.

Outside, the sun shone through a light drizzle. A good omen, definitely a good one, she chided herself.

"No. 39! Madame, panda twende! 39, faster-faster!"

Mama Boi had no time left to brood as the touts bundled her into a matatu blaring a bootleg Kanye West album. Her one heel remained lodged in a crack on the pavement but still she barely noticed the gravel pressing into her sole.

"*I* saw an owl this morning."

"Skiza, what we need to do now is find out who sent it."

"It's witchcraft, wallahi, you don't…"

Their rusty gate howled – why hadn't Baba Boi oiled this thing? – shattering the chatter in the compound.

The small crowd that had already gathered parted as she walked through, silent for the first and only time in the coming week.

The few who spotted her bruised foot only nudged each other and shook their heads. As she took in each face, a heaviness began to settle in her neck.

She walked through the front door – when was the last time she did that? On the left, Baba Boi sat flanked by his sisters on the couch. He hadn't cleaned up after breakfast, or lunch, and his sisters were dirtying her new carpet with their cheap shoes. He said nothing, and the women only motioned to the back of the house. She floated past the living room into the corridor. The kitchen light was on, but the dining room was dark, and the back door loomed before her. The heaviness sunk to her feet and she paused, stuck, eyes stinging, palms sweating, and a ringing in her right ear that only got louder.

"Mama Boi?"

For what seemed like an hour she simply stood there, the only movement a shaking hand reaching up, wrenching the wig from her head. And another hour, and then the next, and the people milled around her, fretting, starting a fire, fetching maize and beef, and then the sun set and she finally stepped out into the back compound, her bare foot first, the night air licking her scalp.

No one had moved the basin. Large and grey, it sat with the confidence of a monument. She had bought it on sale at Nakumatt. Water from the tank still dripped, tick-ticking. The steady stream punctured the collected water's skin into deep dimples, hissing as it hit its mark. Why hadn't anyone moved him? Her baby would get a cold, and it wasn't even time for his bath. Bubbles rose to the top, riding the ripples and popping, one by one. The heel of Boi's foot broke the surface intermittently, small and pale, like a stepping stone. Her body fell towards his. Arms stretched out, palms feeling for his sides, she lifted him out. Water clung to him, tendrils slipping back only reluctantly. Why was he wearing his favourite T-shirt? It wasn't Sunday. Ben10 was for Sunday. Today was *not* Sunday. His little fingers were still clamped around the Barbie doll, clenched into a fist. He had taught that doll everything: how to run; how to laugh; how to swim; how to eat *and* watch Dora the Explorer; how to save the world in the nick of time.

She lay back on the grass, like she used to, and raised him high, supporting his torso on her knees. Her baby's wet limbs reached for her from above, sprawled beneath an empty sky. He must be so tired, the poor thing, but it was too dark now. Why hadn't Baba Boi replaced the bulb out here? Where was the moon, round and firm? Why hadn't the heavens parted? Where was the voice that would say, *This is my son, listen to him?*

And then she saw he had no shoes on. He wasn't supposed to be outside without shoes. He knew that. Wrinkled feet. *Wrinkled baby feet.* It seemed illogical, impossible, like… like a river with legs, a river with long legs! Laughter tore out of her, and she began to shake her head, mumbling furiously to herself. *Look here, shame the devil, what legs, you, you shemeji, you think this is funny, who brought the river, aiai, whose child is this, bring my socks, I said bring the pegs, let's hang this water to dry, yaa stupid goat, did you lend someone your English, I am saying, bring Boi inside so he can eat supper, you, you there, haki wewe, kwani ni kichaa? Ni chawi? Wacha ni uchawi… Uchawi! Nasema kemea shetani shindwe pepo mbaya woiii!*

She shot up and flung the child back into the basin.

Water splashed on her suit, and hit her forehead, like the priest's blessingon a Sunday.

"*I*s she the first?"

"Who is supposed to cook for all these people?"

"Did you see what she did with the dead child?"

"She's a witch, I always said it."

Baba Boi locked the baby's room to shield Mama Boi from his sisters' heckling. He approached slowly. She lay face down on the bed, still wracked with laughter. Unsure of what to do, he paused several feet away. Sensing his presence, she turned abruptly toward him. "Did they win?"

Startled, and a little worried, he wondered whether she had fully returned to herself. He tried to be gentle. "Who, dear?"

"What do you mean *who*? Black Stars."

"Mama Boi, it might be best if you rested a little, alright?"

"Ghana. The Black Stars! *Ghana!* The World Cup?"

It was as if he had swallowed a wad of steel wool. She stared at him expectantly, and he felt the ball begin to rust, and then rise, a copper globe burning up his chest before camping behind his throat. His legs moved to the bed, and soon the rest of him obliged.

"Oh." His fingers reached for the edges of the duvet, worrying a thread loose. The other hand gripped his phone tightly; if he texted his friend for help would she notice? Eventually, he picked what seemed like the simplest option.

"Suarez is just the devil. In fact, his whole life needs a red card. And the way the supporters cheered – gosh! It's such a shame. I mean, even Boi was laughing so much at the start that…"

Mama Boi waited for him to continue, but he didn't. He shuffled out of the room, breathing through his mouth.

In a few hours, however, he returned red-eyed and determined. "Mama Boi?"

—

"Mama Boi? I Googled it, and well, can I… should I maybe read you a poem then?"

—

"So. Ehem. It's Kariara. You remember him? Remember music fest in high school? You did 'A Leopard Lives in a Muu Tree' at Nationals, right? And we split a Black Forest cake, and you said you liked my voice?"

—

"No? I… well… I'll start then. Okay. Wait, that's not part of the poem, eh. *If you should* – oh, wait. This one is called 'Grass Will Grow'. Okay, good:

> *If you should take my child Lord*
> *Give my hands strength to dig his grave*
> *Cover him with earth*
> *Lord send a little rain*
> *For grass will grow*

If my house should burn down
So that the ashes sting the nostrils
Making the eyes weep
Then Lord send a little rain
For grass will grow

"But Lord do not send me… eh, maybe that's enough for tonight."

He patted her leg awkwardly. He leaned forward for a hug but thought better of it before he could make contact with her. It was how they did it in all the movies, wasn't it? Anyhow, her friends would get here soon. They might know what to say.

That night, Mama Boi's friends cooked viciously. Plastic cups and plates flew across the living room, and the entire house echoed with clinking and clanging. The chama of eight women had tacitly agreed on shifts with Mama Boi and at 3 a.m. the kitchen company made their way up to the second floor to switch with the motivational troupe. Baba Boi still circled the bed, hoarding his own griefs to pick at later when alone. Mrs Dr Engineer from next door thrust a bowl of rice in his face without a word. It seemed she was saving up her weekly quota of humanness for her comrade, and began reciting a string of calming clichés once she neared Mama Boi. Everything happens for a reason. God gives and he takes away. He was too good, they go first, you know.

At least he had no time to commit any sins, another pitched in. Imagine he is already an angel. It will pass. Time heals all wounds. The women chanted their solace, creating a fortress of proverbs and Bible verses around their fallen friend. It went on like this until seven in the morning, and eventually Baba Boi went to seek out his own friends.

*T*he men roasted a slaughtered goat at the front of the house, and were sensitive enough to avoid the back compound. A heaviness pressed hard behind Baba Boi's eyes, and he moved closer to the fire. Two years. That's all he got. There would be no more birthdays, no circumcision, no funeral for an accomplished man in which an actual bull would be slaughtered. Just a pathetic goat hustled from the mean butcher at the estate's gate. A pathetic goat burning away in a pathetic fire, mocking him. He could hear the fire cackling, not his only child calling for him? Shouldn't he have felt something shoot through him? Isn't that the test of a father-son bond? What kind of—

"Baba Boi!"

"Tusker?"

"Mhm."

"So, the game…"

"Shh. Shut up!"

The silence was only punctuated by self-consciously noisy sips of beer, and multiple throat clearings until, "Life is hard, bwana."

"Yea."

"Ehe."

"So…"

Another brave man ventured, "The basin, I mean, shouldn't we…"

"What Franco means, is… yaani…"

"As in so… fundraising?"

"As in, maybe, you know, let's… we'll deal with it."

"Yea, yea, don't worry."

"We're brothers, hey, and when life tries one of us, you know…"

There was broad assent to this.

Baba Boi simply stared into the fire. He watched the flames lick the goat, watched fat droplets fall into the ash, sizzle and then peter out silently.

*T*he next morning, Baba Boi's sisters gathered outside Boi's door, kangas wrapped securely around their waists and heads.

"Na, yeye, PHD for what, when she has an MRS? All that working, did she expect a man to look after her child?"

"Woi shame!"

"And now. And the way it took so long to get this one…"

"A boy, imagine, how lucky!"

"So…"

"And we had closed hiyo chapter ya…"

"Second wife?"

"No!"

"This is why Africans have many children…"

"Haki!"

"Exactly!"

"Seriously, where did she get her silly ideas from? Maisha ya TV, ya nini?"

"We're not Kardashians, we're Kenyans!"

One of Mama Boi's friends broke out of their circle to wrench the separating door open. Mrs Dr Engineer growled in warning as the sisters tightened the cloth around their waists. The kitchen company joined the fray, pleading with everyone to be Christianly. No one wanted to appear less grieved than the other, and the commotion spontaneously degenerated into a wailing contest.

"Mama Boi is *sleeping*!"

Baba Boi swatted the little group away, and pushed past them into the room, locking the door behind him. Perhaps she heard the crowd mock-whispering outside her door. Perhaps she was tired of Baba Boi's pacing, or her thoughts had finally pushed out the ringing in her ear. Whatever the reason, Mama Boi rose from her son's bed two days later. She seemed to vibrate to a secret frequency, like a taut string that had been struck, and made a peculiar music.

She demanded to see the water.

*O*n the day before she is let go from work, Mama Boi calls a plumber. She would have asked Baba Boi to fix the pipes, but she's worried about him. He showers four to five times a day, and insists that she do the same. He barely speaks, and last week he kicked in their TV screen. It wouldn't be so bad, but he wouldn't feed Boi, let alone play with him. She might have to talk to the pastor about it.

"Madame, what's the problem?"

Mama Boi points to the guest bathroom, "The taps aren't working. I paid the bill, but I don't know."

"Okay."

"Look, I'm going to buy Boi some milk so you anza job let me rush to the kiosk."

The plumber glances at the Boi in question as he and Mama pass him. But he can barely see his face through the shawls he is secured in. It seems odd considering how hot this town is. But his job is to fix the pipes not stick his nose in others' business. He knows how touchy people are about their children. He has no intentions of getting any of the little things himself. But he has heard stories of women who lure drunken men in bars and sleep with them without protection. Sometimes they just want to get pregnant; others are malicious and want to spread HIV. He is too careful to be trapped though. He shakes his head to chase away such terrifying thoughts, and takes out his equipment.

Mama Boi hurries to the shop, already regretting her decision to leave a strange man alone in the house. Having to carry Boi slowed her down. For some reason he had refused to walk these past three weeks. She had decided not to worry. The doctor had been coming to the house frequently, yet had not mentioned anything about Boi's little phase. However, he did seem to have a lot of questions for her. She found it frustrating but she knew any detail might help him fix whatever was eating at Baba Boi. Maybe it was Ghana losing the World Cup. He did take football seriously, but that couldn't be it. Was he seeing another woman? No. He wasn't the sort of man to do that. It would take too much energy on his part even if—

Yesu! Her left foot dipped into a pothole. Stupid estate council.

Finally at the kiosk, she steels herself to deal with Mama Duka. Lately, the woman had been staring at her strangely, and Mama Boi could swear she'd been gossiping about her. That is all people who don't have real jobs know to do. It's fine. She had made sure she wouldn't need any change, and if they were lucky, Boi and she would be done in two minutes, tops. But of course, she had not factored in Mama Duka's incessant babbling.

"Did you hear the radio? It's another referendum."

"Oh?"

"Ehe, but you know that MP is sleeping with that shameless girl, what's her name?"

"Oh. Brookside mbili."

"Just milk? No bread? Who drinks tea without bread?"

"Two loaves, then."

"And Blue Band for the bread, right? Kwanza since you've reminded me, the advert is so funny si ndio?"

"I haven't seen it."

"Oh, don't you watch TV? Anyway, you should come to our church. The new pastor is full of the Spirit. It's like AfroCinema during service. Nollywood, I tell you!"

"Thank you, Mama Duka, but can you just give me a lollipop for Boi. He has been asking you for one but you're ignoring him."

"Oh? What? Ah. Boi. Of course. I just… I must not have been listening!"

Mama Boi grabs the cherry lollipop and scurries away with her bags and Boi bouncing about in her arms.

*B*ack at the house, Mama Boi leaves the milk and bread in the kitchen, sets Boi down with his lollipop in the living room and heads upstairs to check on the plumber guy. Her ankle is already throbbing from earlier, and she ascends slowly. The house is quiet now since Baba Boi attacked the TV, and she can hear water falling from the pair of taps in the bathroom sink, quietly at first, its pitter-patter hesitant, like small feet on cold tiles, but it soon becomes more vigorous, even forcing its way from the shower head. Her body feels unnaturally heavy, and a palm reaches for the wall. She sinks to the floor as a yellowing leaf does: in spite of itself. The plumber's tinkering and triumphal cries come to her as if from a deep well. She begins to crawl forward on all fours, releasing small spurts of hot air through her mouth.

The plumber steps out to check if the Madame has returned. He nearly walks into her crouching close to the floor.

"Madame?"

He is worried. This is stranger than any of his previous experiences. She rises to her knees and unbuttons her jeans. She reaches for her blouse, and the plumber jumps backward, raising his arms to shield his eyes.

"No. No no no. I'm not that kind of fundi, no. If you want another baby, no, call your husband!"

Her head hangs limply, and she falls back down completely.

"It's just so hot. So hot."

The plumber holds out his large hands in front of him, uncertain. He finally resorts to fanning the air between them and making cooing noises, as if coaxing a rabid dog into its kennel.

Water, he thinks. Water! He scrambles downstairs and returns wheezing. He finds the fluid from the bathroom pooling round Mama Boi's thighs. Her shattered breathing echoes in the corridor, and the sound, trapped, settles over them.

At the shop, Mama Duka continued to look out at the road long after Mama Boi had left. Shaking her head, she turned to her niece unpacking supplies at the back.

"It's so sad about her, hey?"

"What? Why? This estate is not that bad."

"Oh no, not that. Didn't you see the thing she was carrying?"

"Why are you calling someone's baby a thing, surely?"

"No. No, it's a Quencher bottle!"

"That makes no sense. Don't lie now."

"Wallahi! Baba Boi went round the estate two weeks ago, telling everyone to be patient. Not to say anything. That they had called a doctor. And it was only temporary."

"What do you mean?"

"She's the woman, you remember! The one whose baby died!"

"Kwani? How many children did she have?"

"Just the one. Our neighbour's brother's cousin says that bottle she's carrying has the same water the baby drowned in. The same water!"

"Gosh. Yuck."

"We should pray for her on Sunday."

"Mm. But what mzungu problems are these? Can't she just cry like everyone else?"

"Ai. Me, I don't know."

Oasis

Louis Greenberg

"*D*eclare your liquids. It is an offence under the Water Control Act to conceal…"

Even the recorded voice sounded bored. The announcement played every three minutes and twenty seconds, looped in a regular series between "Thank you for choosing Pure Geneva Airport" and "Report all suspicious articles". Normally I'd have ignored it and let the voice blend into the thrum and bustle of the departures terminal, but it was oddly provocative that morning. I felt an angry blush burning my cheeks.

"You okay?" Jame asked, hitching eir backpack further onto eir shoulder, and I knew that if even e'd picked up on my irritation, I'd better get myself in check. I took a deep breath, forcing back a cough that raked its way up my throat. I scanned the passport control hall with bulging eyes for any switch in attention, the slightest twitch of a head, a movement of a hand beneath a jacket.

"I'm fine," I said, but had to clear my throat again.

"Do you need some water?" e asked.

My gut lurched. "Jesus, Jame," I whispered. "Not here."

E looked up at me with such a perfect pre-teen do-you-really-think-I'm-that-stupid sneer that I had to laugh. "I meant Pure," e said, pointing out the bank of Pure Water dispensers with their ubiquitous sky-blue and leaf-green yin-yang logos.

It was a tempting offer. I was thirsty; I hadn't had anything to drink since the night before. Ally's fever had nudged up to forty despite the medication, and I'd had to use Lib's tag to fill up my smartbottle and douse eir face cloth in Premium to cool eir forehead. I hadn't wanted to take any chances on Standard, especially after that graze on eir knee had got re-infected. I knew that Lib's charity was soon going to wear thin, but I still didn't know when I'd next get paid. So the sight of those green and blue curling fish, those water-drop lovers, made my tongue tacky. But of course I couldn't accept Jame's offer. I'd have some Standard when I got thirsty enough. "Thanks," I said, "but I'm fine."

"Sure? I've got Premium credits. I won't need them where I… I suppose."

"Of course you're going to need them. You'll be back soon. You'll use them then." I put all my energy into convincing myself so that I could sound convincing to ir. I think it worked, because e shrugged, hitched eir backpack and flipped eir headphones back on, staring ahead with a twelve-year-old's trainee nonchalance as the queue shuffled forward. I expected that we'd be stopped at one of many hurdles between the train to the airport and the boarding gate, and my strategy was to nurture a sense of resignation. I didn't know Jame, I owed ir nothing; I was doing ir a favour – ir and eir parent, and the science teacher who'd identified that e was a Maker in the first place. Either way it was nothing really to do with me, just a couple of days' work escorting ir out of Switzerland, out of Europe, into the uncontrolled zone. I'd heard of the Oasis group in the course of my work, knew that Makers had been smuggled out to the noncompliant zone to join them in their resistance against the Pure Water monopoly, but to be honest, I hadn't seen the effects of any resistance. I don't know if it was because the net of propaganda was so tight here, but Oasis was a non-entity in the general Swiss or European consciousness. Resistance didn't exist; Pure Water wanted us all to believe there was nothing to resist.

"I don't even work there anymore," I'd told the teacher when e called. "Liquid Advocacy International has been defunded. It's been shut down for eight months already.'

"So why did you answer the phone?" e said.

"I have my own child; I don't need to put ir at risk," I complained. We both knew I'd help, though I had no idea why.

I'd been surprised when we made it past the check-in counter, the operative there barely glancing at us as e scanned our passports and registered that we only carried two small backpacks between us. I was sure they were onto us. I fully expected someone to emerge out of the crowd, discreetly clamp our arms behind us, and take Jame off wherever the government takes Makers. Letting us through check-in was probably just a step in their plan: to make us complacent, put us off our guard; allow us to incriminate ourselves.

Now our treason would be recorded on their computer system before they arrested us at the passport check.

I'd escorted people out of the country before. But never a child; never a Maker. To be honest, I wasn't entirely sure I believed that Makers existed before I met Jame, and I still hadn't seen ir Making. It's not my business, I reminded myself; it hasn't been my business for eight months.

That's what I tried to tell myself, but I failed.

Of course I knew why I was doing it. For Ally. For Ally's future, and for every child who hopes to live a life of choice.

I try not to think what things were like when I was a kid, but lately I find myself going back there, taking long, deep baths in the memories. I remember my parents sending me out to play and we'd come back muddy-kneed and shredded up and they'd open up the tap and let Premium pour as they splashed it all over us. Safety, home, loving smiles, like an advertisement.

Happily, I get snapped out of my self-indulgent reverie by the waft — it's their smell that confronts me first: cheap deodorant, Exelia softener on their uniform, leather polish, gun oil and sweat; one of them has halitosis — of three black-clad Special Security soldiers pushing up the line behind us.

This is it, I thought. I'm sorry I failed you so soon, Jame.

They were nudging up behind me, the queue rippling with stifled sighs and reluctant shuffles, eyes microscopically rolled, the most profound protest we good citizens could muster against tyranny.

Tyranny. What sort of old-fashioned, radical language was that? This is why I'm in this position, now, I thought; and exactly why I shouldn't be. It's not safe to play at politics anymore. I drew closer to Jame, shielding ir. They'll sniff ir out, surely. I put my hand on eir shoulder, pretending to be just a parent with eir child, warding ir out of harm's way. Jame had eir earphones on, staring vacantly up at the advertising screens, nodding eir head to the rhythm, tapping eir foot. E so successfully made irself invisible, just another inconsequential kid, that as the soldiers shoved by, I knew that Jame was smarter than e let on.

"You do that on purpose, don't you?" I said to ir once they'd gone, leaning close in to eir face.

"Do what?" e said, with a small twist of self-satisfaction. Of course there was no music playing in the headphones.

The Special Security trio had stationed themselves against a pillar, watching the passport queues. As subtly as I could, I glanced at them as we proceeded, but I had the sense they were looking for somebody else right then – their gazes seemed trained half a metre above Jame's head – or maybe they just wanted me to believe that. They're going to stop us, I told myself again, to try to control my breathing. It's inevitable. It won't be my fault. Jame will be all right. I tried not to think of Ally. E loves Lib; they'd be alright on their own.

Then we were ushered up to a free window. I handed over our passports.

"Where are you travelling?" the officer asked me, but e was looking at Jame.

"Mindelo, Cape Verde. Vacation with relatives."

"What's your relationship to the child?"

"I'm eir guardian. I am escorting ir on eir parent's behalf."

The officer scrutinised me, knowing that nobody would try to get away with a lie like that, especially travelling so close to the noncompliant nations. "You have the parent's authorisation?"

I removed the sheaf of documents from my backpack, concentrating on keeping my face relaxed.

The officer scanned carefully through the forms, correctly filed and notarised, with the necessary affidavits and certified copies of all the relevant identity cards and passports. Finding nothing out of order, e turned to Jame, who was picking an invisible something out of eir teeth. "Are you looking forward to your vacation?"

"Yes, M." I worried that Jame was laying the politeness on a little thick, but the officer seemed charmed, smiling back.

"How long will you stay?"

"Two weeks."

"And where are you staying? On Sal?" A test. There's nothing much for tourists to do on Sal, apart from hang out at the transit airport or work in the salt mines. If Jame had said e was holidaying on Sal, it would have been as good as an admission that e was simply using it as a waystation to be smuggled by boat into Mauritania and through to the Oasis enclave in Mali.

"Oh, no." Jame smiled. "My cousin Ariel has a house on Santo Antão and all my relatives are getting together. We're just going to chill, hike, swim. I love to swim."

The officer shrugged – e'd tried, but there was no real reason to stop us. "Enjoy yourself," e said to Jame as e stamped and returned our documents. E waved us through. I glanced behind me, but the Special Security soldiers had disappeared.

"Good work," I said, as we found a couple of seats in the waiting area. "But that swimming quip. Are you trying to get caught?"

"But that was a passport person," e said, "not police or Security or anyone from Pure Water. Why would e care what I say about swimming?"

"They're all connected," I said, my voice too loud, then I sat down next to ir, levelling my tone. "The government agencies work hand-in-glove with the corporations. You don't think that…" But I stopped. I realised I sounded like a paranoid delusional. Let Jame keep eir innocence for a moment longer.

E shrugged and pouted, and started fiddling with eir phone. I stared at ir, really taking ir in for the first time since I'd collected ir that morning. Loose black hair, grown devil-may-care; jeans, sneakers, Manor T-shirt, casual hooded jacket – any twelve-year-old, anywhere. Except that face, streaked with intelligence beyond eir years, confidence burning out of those honey-brown eyes. When e smiled, it was almost a snarl. There was a power there, behind eir generic disguise, something I knew would be hard to control.

And those fingers, stained grey on the forefinger and middle finger of each hand; the Maker's brand, I suspected. I'd heard about it, seen it happen on poor-quality video, but never in real life. I'm not sure I fully understood it.

E noticed me staring at eir hands and folded them over eir lap.

"So how do you do it?"

E shot me a side-eye. "I thought you said I shouldn't do it here."

"Of course you shouldn't," I said. "I'm just asking how it works."

"I don't know. It's just… there's an agent and a re-agent and a catalyst. The agent and the re-agent aren't particularly uncommon. What's really surprising is that it's so rare – we're all made of water, after all. The difference is," – and here e betrays enough self-aware-ness to glance behind ir and lower eir voice – "that we, Makers, can spontaneously produce the catalyst in the right form. That's how my parent explained it to me anyway. It's in our genes… and in our hormones. That's why only a few of us can do it, and only at a certain age." This was the first time Jame had mentioned eir parent the whole morning. I hadn't expected ir to confide – which youngster would tell a stranger that e was missing eir parent? – but still eir peculiar calmness was unsettling to me. It was as if e was just going off to school or the shops. As if this were an every-day outing.

"I've seen it on a video. It looks like magic."

E straightened eir back. "It's not magic," e snapped. "It's science."

"You wish you weren't a Maker, don't you? It bothers you, doesn't it? That you have the…" – *power* would sound too comic-book – "the skill?"

E locked eir eyes on the advertising screens in front of us. A Pure Water ad was playing: glistening waterfalls, forests, bright-coloured birds.

"I can understand," I said. "It must be difficult. Why does it have to be you?" My thoughts turned to Ally. If e were a Maker, if I had to send ir away from me, I'd… well, I didn't know what I'd do.

For a long moment, Jame said nothing. I thought e was done with the conversation, so I leant across to pick up a magazine someone had discarded two seats over from me. But then e said, "It's not the worst thing in the world to be able to do this." The words sounded rehearsed, as if they were something eir parent had told ir. I nodded. "But I don't know what it's for," e added, eir voice at last crackling minutely around the edges. "I want it to mean something, you know."

I didn't want to lie, so I said nothing. Even though I wasn't sure that it was the right thing to do, I reached out and squeezed ir on the leg. This reassurance would probably mean nothing after all. I mean, we weren't going to get on this plane. Jame would get caught and Pure Water's stock would continue on its never-ending ascent. Nothing would change. After twenty years of working in polite social activism and advocacy, constantly eroded away until there was nothing left of us, the only certainty that I retained was that individuals were powerless.

There was a café opposite us with a scarlet rope barrier across its entranceway and a hefty waiter apportioning welcomes. Beyond ir, in plain sight, rich businesspeople and trust-fund babies sat drinking sparkling Premium-based drinks in Premium-ice-filled glasses. The café was decorated in sky blue and leaf green, the brand colours of a luxurious slake. The needle inside my throat turned to a rusty nail and the more I tried to suppress the cough, the more it burnt, until I had to hack it out in a gasping choke.

"Come on," Jame said. "Let me get you some water."

"No, thanks."

"I'm thirsty. I'm going to get some anyway."

I watched ir walk across to the nearest dispenser, fit eir smartbottle to the nozzle and swipe eir tag. The dispenser spat out no more than two hundred mils.

"You're out of credits, aren't you?" I said when e came back.

E sighed in a way that sounds wrong from a twelve-year-old. "Have this, please. You know I don't need it.'

"Actually, no, I don't know that. I only have an e-mail your school teacher sent to the organisation and a second-hand report from your parent."

E jutted eir hip. "So you think I'm a con artist scamming my way into a free trip to Mali so—"

"Ssh! For God's sake, Jame!"

E was embarrassed. That was a slip e shouldn't have made. "Sorry." E dumped the bottle down next to ir.

"No, I'm sorry." I said. "You're just being kind and I'm being rude." But e hadn't heard me because eir headphones were back on. This time there was a beat hissing out of them.

The screens were now playing the airport's redacted version of the news, with anything potentially panic-inducing edited out. They wanted to keep the passengers in here bored, compliant, half-asleep, before they herded us onto our planes.

I gathered the magazine – a copy of *Proud*, one of those glossy advertorials masquerading as a lifestyle magazine – and started flipping through it. I wasn't especially surprised to see the pinched, tanned face of Frances Brabeck fronting a feature. As if in duty to my past life, I dipped into the article, trying to block out the noise of competing soundtracks and announcements and shrieking kids and rattling trolleys around me.

"As we've stated repeatedly before, we offer fully subsidised Standard Water to non-subscribers, even among non-compliant nations."

It was a blatant PR exercise between the magazine – loyally funded by Pure Water advertising – and Brabeck. E'd said more regrettable things in the wake of the latest round of protests from the uncontrolled zone. Protests that had achieved nothing.

I could almost hear the interviewer's breathlessness in the questions. "And what would you say to protesters and civil organisations who allege that increases in cholera and gastrointestinal diseases stem from failings in Pure Water's treatment of their Standard Water offerings to those countries?"

"We say that the complaints are unfounded." Brabeck trotted out the lines e'd spun so often before. "As you know, the United Nations, in their wisdom, has declared water a right. And although it is not our job as Pure Water to supply free water to the world's exploding population, yet we work hard to subsidise the requirements of as many citizens as possible. This is our philanthropic offering to the global community. We are grateful to live and operate in a free market, and India is free to follow the example of other third-world regimes to try to source and purify their own water. Unfortunately, they may well find that their own efforts will fall short of their frankly unreasonable expectations. Pure Water offers the people of the world acceptably clean water at below cost; we invite all nations to benefit from our centuries of experience and our world-leading infrastructure."

On the next page, another shot of Brabeck, doing eir best to soften those narrow eyes at the camera, like one of those smug old people on an ancient cigarette advertisement, the Pure Water logo boldly over eir left shoulder. I flipped the magazine aside and watched the Premium-drinkers in their café. Acceptably clean. Sure, if you find the taste of shit and bleach acceptable.

Maybe my memories are gilded, but I'm sure everyone had Premium in those days, for free, piped in from underground, dams and reservoirs. We'd take baths in Premium, and I swear I can remember that some normal citizens even had holes in their gardens filled up with Premium. No, that can't be. It must be a story I heard when I was small. Holes in private gardens, full of Premium. I don't think so.

"*J*ust boarded, love," I texted to Ally. "Be good for Lib." I started typing "See you in a week", but I was cut short by a pain in my eyes which made them sting and run. It was only when my chest tried to implode, when I struggled to catch my breath, that I realised my body was remembering what it was like to cry. That, or having a panic attack. Or both.

I'd convinced myself that we wouldn't get on this plane, that I would be back home with Ally by the evening, but now I was strapped into a narrow seat next to Jame, who I was vaguely aware was trying to talk to me, but it was all I could do to keep curled into myself, my head down, my hands clasping my phone on my lap; all I could do not to jump and scream and run.

When the phone vibrated, I thought it was because I'd broken it, but I managed to force open an eyelid and squint at the screen.

Ally: "I will. Lib's going to take me to the pet expo when I'm better. Have fun! xx"

My sweet Ally. E'd be all right. Ally'd always been fine when

I'd travelled before, looking forward to the presents I'd bring back. But I'd never escorted a Maker.

"You get better soon, love. Make sure Lib takes you somewhere fun EVERY day. Message any time. I'll call back ASAP. I love you."

Now, at least, I could look up and around me. The stewards were already doing the safety demonstration and the plane was being tugged back. I glanced across at Jame, who was staring out of the window. I wondered if e'd ever been on a plane before. I wanted to ask, but I didn't want to disturb ir, and my throat felt like a load of concrete had dried in it. As soon as we were flying, they'd bring around drinks – just Standard-based in economy, but that would be fine; I'd mix in a whiskey to kill most of the bugs. Meanwhile, I tried to clear the itch with a series of soft panting coughs, then breathed heavily in my throat, hoping my inhalations might condense a little moisture in there.

As we ascended, I got my throat under control and settled into a type of calm. Jame stared out of the window until we levelled off in the centre of a cloud bank, and as e started fiddling with the entertainment screen in front of ir, the steward started eir announcement:

"We have now exited Swiss airspace and are authorised to serve beverages to our customers. We regret to inform you that our Standard beverage suppliers were late with their delivery and the stock could not be uploaded before departure. We regret any inconvenience, but as always we can offer you our full range of Premium-based beverages. Check the back of your in-flight magazine for the prices."

Next to me, Jame was staring at the flight map on the screen. I tapped ir on the leg and e turned to me.

"I'm sorry," I said, "but I'm going to have to ask you for a sip of that water after all."

"Sure," e said, and went under the seat in front to get eir backpack, but when e rifled through the bag, e couldn't find eir smartbottle. "Shit. I must have left it behind. What can I—"

"It's all right. I'll be able to wait 'til we land." But I wasn't sure if I would. I was feeling too dizzy and my tongue felt too large for my mouth.

"It's not all right," e said. "I'm sorry."

But there was nothing either of us could do. I watched as the steward poured sparkling drinks in little plastic cups for every passenger ahead of us, swiping their Premium tags as e went. "Anything to drink?" the steward asked, parking the trolley in our row.

I shook my head and a brief look of pity, or perhaps disgust, crossed the steward's face before e asked. "You're certain? Nothing for your child?'"

"No."

E shrugged microscopically, the fake smile still pasted over eir painted features, and turned to the passenger across the aisle.

I thought about how we used to go to Lake Geneva on summer weekends, when the Jet d'Eau still ran, forcing its one-megawatt spray a hundred and forty metres into the air. The wind would always be blowing off the Lake's surface and we'd run through the mist-drift in the sun along the promenade, freezing and burning at the same time, shrieking to be free. If I just imagined it, the spray would salve my throat for a few more hours.

When I looked at ir a few minutes later, Jame was still doggedly staring at the flight map on the screen.

"What are you doing?" I asked.

"Nothing." But eir leg was jiggling manically.

"Is anything wrong?"

"No."

But now e unclipped eir seatbelt, stood up and leaned over the seat behind ir. "You mind?" e asked the passenger behind us. "Can I…?" Now holding an empty plastic cup, e settled back down into eir seat and folded open the tray table.

E pointed at the map on the screen. The cartoon aeroplane was halfway across the Mediterranean. "We're out of Europe now."

We're on a European airline, spending Swiss money, carrying European identity chips, I wanted to say. I knew that there were

Security marshals dotted throughout every flight; I knew who the stewards reported to.

We are never out of Europe, I wanted to say.

But I said nothing, transfixed as e put eir hands into the pockets of eir jeans. E drew out two grey blobs, one darker, one lighter. Stones maybe, or something like hard putty because they seemed to give a little as e rubbed them between eir thumbs and fingertips. When e put the knobs back in eir pockets, I could smell a faint odour of metallic singe, like the trailings of a welding rod far away. Now e closed eir eyes, turned eir hands, slightly curled, palms up like a benediction, over the empty plastic cup. E smiled, an inward smile of the purest satisfaction, and pressed eir fingertips together.

I was there; I saw it. It mystified me as much as the video, because water materialised out of the air in front of eir fingers and filled the cup. Then, like turning off a tap, e disconnected eir fingers and the water stopped.

E passed me the cup, a voluntary act of mercy.

The first gulp washed through me like a flood over parched earth; I barely noticed it apart from a slight swelling inside. I swirled the second in my mouth. It tasted of peat, of earth, of air, of blood red; it filled me. The third sip – a blue fish of love and a green fish of hope.

And Then We Disappeared into Some Guy's Car

Siyanda Mohutsiwa

I

I have a test on Monday. I have a test on Monday, I have to keep reminding myself. Sometimes I forget. I have a test on Monday. But I keep checking my phone. The money is supposed to be in now. I'm supposed to get a little beep-beep and a message from the bank. He said he would send it today. He said so last week and I don't want to have to call to remind him. I said I wanted it for shoes. I think I meant it at the time. I was even thinking of shoes as I asked for the money in the first place. Purple shoes in the window display at Options. Pink laces and good for running. My friend Sarah said I should get heels, but I need shoes for running. They aren't actual running shoes, of course. Not Nikes or anything like that. They look nice, and so in addition to doing some running in them I can pair them with jeans and a tight t-shirt and look fresh.

I'm supposed to get a notification. It's supposed to be six hundred pula, seven hundred rand, sixty dollars. I always do conversions in my head so I know how much it will be if I have to withdraw it in another country. But don't think I have some sort of plan, because I don't.

I have a test on Monday. PHY312: Fundamentals of Hydro-physics. A class with lectures I don't attend. The professor is an asshole. Once, he called me a liar in front of the whole class. All I said to him was that you promised you'd give us our assignments today. He called me a liar in front of everyone. And they all looked at me, bright white eyes in deep brown faces, wondering why I was stupid enough to open my mouth. So I stood up and flipped the desk over. I remember that part because I didn't plan it. I just saw the table bounce on the floor and the girls in front cover their mouths and stare. The professor stuttered and I walked out.

So that's why I don't go. I don't need to attend anyway, water isn't that hard. It's the same thing over and over again.

The many unique properties of water are due to the hydrogen bonds (read: water does some cool shit because hydrogen is so fucking special).

Ice floats because hydrogen bonds hold water molecules further apart in a solid than in a liquid, where there is one less hydrogen bond per molecule.

Water has a high vaporization temperature, strong surface tension, high specific heat, and nearly universal solvent properties, blah blah blah. What more do you expect from a course advertised as "marketable in the developing world"?

It's all so meaningless. So what? I once wrote that in a test when I forgot I had a test and showed up twenty minutes late in socks that didn't match. I wrote, "So what?" After that, someone said the professor was looking for me but I don't remember whether I went to see him later or not.

So what?

The money should be in by now. It's been an hour. It's only six hundred pula. It doesn't take that long to send it. You just press *123*9# and that's all. He can do that in the toilet. I don't even really care where or how he does it. I just need to know I have it. I haven't eaten in a while. I was supposed to use my allowance to open an account at the cafeteria. Don't remember why I didn't. Maybe it didn't seem like a good deal at the time. The food is shit and everybody looks at you while you eat. I don't know why Batswana are always doing that. Just eat your fucking food, I want to say, but never do.

I have a test on Monday. That's what I should be saying to myself as I get into the car with my friend and her boyfriend. We're going to his house to drink cider and smoke cigarettes. We'll sit outside on beanbags and his old duvet will be on the ground, picking up dust, and ants will crawl all over it.

I will keep checking my phone. My friend will ask me if I'm okay and I'll say yes. Or maybe I'll say something else and look away when she asks for more. I'll tell her she looks good. Has she lost weight? You're losing too much, I'll say. Then I will smile. Then I will forget what I am supposed to remember.

I have a test on Monday. And now it's Monday. I don't remember where the test is. I should have written it down. It's somewhere in the social sciences building – was it upstairs or downstairs? I walk around the building. Or at least I think I do. Maybe I'm sitting on the bench and nothing is happening. I feel tired. Maybe I was walking around. I know it's half-done now. My phone is almost empty, but I know I can't phone anyone anyway. The time says 9:30. There's no point in trying to find the venue anymore: I know they won't let me in, even if it's just to fail.

*I*t's Tuesday when the money comes in. I'm standing in line at Liquorama. There's a special on box wine. I get two boxes and hug them close to my chest, as I walk fast as I can out of the store. I forgot all about the shoes. Papa didn't ask. He just sent the money and an SMS: A tsene, Lovie?

Thank you papa love you! I replied. I will avoid his calls for the rest of the week.

I sit in the courtyard outside my hostel, the box wine on the cement-paved ground in front of my crossed legs. The wine tastes too sweet and burns my chest, but I feel like smiling and joking now. I pour and drink two full cups of the wine, sipping it quickly from my dirty coffee mug. The girl from 209 comes outside, power-walking across the courtyard. "Why are you rushing?" I shout at her. "Is your boyfriend that hot, you can't leave him alone?" She laughs because that's what she is supposed to do.

I think the girl from 209 wants to feel sorry for me. Nobody in this place drinks. They're so boring. All church this, church that. But it's all an act. They walk into parked BMWs like the rest of us. Some of their boyfriends have gold teeth. And at 2 a.m., when I'm smoking outside near the laundry lines, they come to me and ask for cigarettes. Then they try to tell me about God.

I wake up in the hot afternoon. My roommate has gone to class, or whatever. I miss her when she's gone. Not that she does anything entertaining – all she does is study – but at least she reminds me to eat. Sometimes when she can't sleep she squeezes into my small bed, which is identical to hers except for the bed covers – mine are dark brown with beige flowers, hers have Hannah Montana – and she tells me about her family in the village. They're all teachers. They love her a lot. She says it repeatedly. They love me a lot. I ask her to tell me funny stories about her mum and her big sisters. She does. She loves them a lot. Then she falls asleep. When I wake up she is gone.

It's so hot. I can hear the girl from 201 howling in the bathroom. She loves to sing. I don't know why her friends encourage her. Good friends tell you that you suck when you suck. Better friends hug you while you cry over your dead dreams. My friends have always been better friends. You can tell by the number of crushed dreams I have.

My head is heavy. My stomach hurts. Box wine. I always promise myself I'll stick to the stuff I drink when I'm out: dry Merlot, oaked Chardonnay, Bells, Glenfiddich. But you know how it is: you get to the bottle store and you don't want the store clerks and everyone else seeing you buy two-hundred pula wine in flip-flops with ashy hands. You don't need an education to recognise someone pathetic.

With every move I make, I can actually *feel* my potential leak out of me. When I finally check the time. When my eyes grow wide and I throw the sheet off of me. When I uncurl myself and slip into my shower shoes. When I hover my ass over the toilet seat and pass my eyes mindlessly over the graffiti on the walls. When I stand under the water and feel my head throb. I can feel it all drip out of me, into the drains and under the busted cubicle door, into the sinks where it will clog and stink.

This isn't the first time I've thought about killing myself. There was a phase I had last year where I wrote it down everyday at the end of the day. A plan for death. I'd sit in bed and tearfully map out every second of my last day, whenever I would decide that would be, from what I would wear to what I would eat. Exactly how many teaspoons of which food. Usually I'd fall asleep in the middle of writing it all down, and then I would wake up, realising I had forgotten to add the part about killing myself. My last day on earth would end without explanation at 8 p.m., after a dinner of two teaspoons of beef stew with four teaspoons of rice. And then I would promise myself to Google actual methods of suicide. But before I knew it I would be drunk at lunchtime again and forget all about it.

Nothing came of these plans. Obviously. I don't remember why I stopped fantasising about it. Maybe it's because I lost the green little notebook I used to write in. I only know I lost it because some weeks later, when I'd forgotten all about it, my friend CJ found it when she was spending the night in my room. She mumbled something about therapy. I mumbled back. We were drunk or something. I said something about not having parents with PhDs and grandparents who played golf with the first Khama. And then we disappeared into some guy's car and re-appeared on a dancefloor in an abandoned bar outside town.

II

I'm thinking of eating something, I don't know what. I look at the time now, and I wonder if I really did sleep for twelve hours. I went to bed at 9 p.m. I have some messages on my phone from the guy who sent the money, saying why don't I answer the phone. Saying I should call him when I'm out of the library, saying I should send a call-me-back, saying his family is going to the village over the weekend. Punctuating with a smiley face. I want to reply, Look at your birth certificate, old man. But I don't do that because I get a text from CJ that's far more interesting.

She's smoking weed at another hostel. She says I should come.

I don't like weed so much. It makes me nauseous. Nevertheless I'm rummaging through the heap of clothes on my study table, smelling for something clean. Shorts and a T-shirt. I walk quickly past the mirror. Good enough. There's no reason to stop.

CJ is sitting on a green bench behind the hostels that were christened Vegas by the Class of 2007. (There was a reason for this that I've forgotten.) The wind is whipping her braids around.

She's talking to some guy she once told me is from the swim team. He doesn't look like a swimmer, but then again no one does in Gaborone. He's short and light-skinned and smiling too much. I stand in front of CJ for a long time before she sees I'm there. "My friend!" she finally shouts. I smile. I'm dizzy. I squeeze myself between her and the short swimmer.

They go on talking. I stare straight ahead. The weed smoke slithers into one of my nostrils and out the other. They don't offer me a puff, and I don't ask. They pass it over my face and laugh and laugh and laugh. I'm looking at the students walking out of the refec, carrying polystyrene plates and chatting. A group comes out wearing lab-coats and eating a small, shared bag of chips. On first sight they could be anything: chemistry students, biology students, engineering students. But I tell myself they are medical students. I tell myself they are heavy under the weight of being this university's first batch of medical students. I watch one of them take a clipboard from beneath their armpit and point at something. The others laugh and shake their heads.

CJ is talking to me. Her fingers are pinching my elbow. She's saying something about something. A name I haven't heard before. Tuelo? "She's pregnant," CJ says, and takes a deep drag of the blunt. "Okay," I say. My mind is blank. The swim team guy says he wishes he could have a kid. Says he's planning it actually, to have a baby by next year. He thinks now is the best time because "your parents can take care of the child while you hustle". CJ brings up some guy from her neighbourhood who has two kids and is failing just as bad as he was before he had them. Smoking weed all day and spending the night at some girl's house in Braudhurst. Swim team guy says that's a bad example. "A kid can really motivate you," he says. He's absolutely sure his will.

CJ says we should all chip in five pula and buy a meal at the refec. My stomach rumbles on cue. I shove my hand into my pocket and pull out a twenty and say we can pay for two meals and get three plates. One with chicken and one with beef. They like that idea more.

We march in and we get in the line leading to the counter. The woman at the till is short and sweaty, her head topped with a mass of hairnet struggling to cover an elaborate hairstyle. People are handing her money and orders and she offers back a blank face. She doesn't lift her eyes to meet mine when she takes our cash. She mumbles something at us and the swim team guy mumbles something back.

CJ has gone quiet. Maybe the joint has kicked in. We stand in another line to get the food. It's not moving at all because the chicken has run out and everybody prefers the chicken. The kitchen staff avoid eye contact with the students as they talk softly amongst themselves.

A pink hand rests on my shoulder. Ross is standing behind me with that American grin on his face. I suppose he thinks it's non-threatening. It's not. He says my name and I smile back. The people behind me in the line stop their conversations to stare at us. Or at least that's what it feels like. He's only a bit taller than me but he seems to tower over everyone else.

"How are you?"

"Fine."

"You?"

"I'm great."

"It's a bit hot, but what's new?"

I nod.

"Are you sure you're okay?"

I blink hard a few times. I think the weed must have gotten in somehow.

"I'm fine," I say after too many seconds.

He continues to smile at me and then his smile expands to include my friends who I have not introduced and who do not look like they've noticed Ross's presence. They are both staring blurrily at the trays of food behind the glass.

"Call me later, a bunch of us are going to Jesse's room to watch Kindergarten Cop." He winks and disappears.

I turn back to CJ and the swim team guy. "This chicken is taking way too long," CJ says, to no one in particular. Swim team guy is overcome with laughter, but quietly, in that way that weed takes you.

I turn away from them and stare at the door Ross walked out of.

T hat night I find myself wandering around the library. I had woken up after dark and went out looking to buy cigarettes before going to find someplace to read. But the ladies who sell stuff by the university gate are gone, their tables packed up and chained to something heavy.

I have a book under my arm and a bunch of coins weighing down my pocket. It isn't even my book. I must have taken my roommate's by mistake. Or maybe it's CJ's. All I know is I'm almost completely sure that I study Physics, not Finance.

A security guard by the entrance is staring too much at me. He looks like he might come by and chat. Talking to security guards is the worst. They spend too much time alone, and as such have all these half-baked philosophical questions they think they've invented. Even worse when they're at a university, because they're always trying to impress. Once I found myself smoking where I wasn't supposed to be, near the post office boxes at the campus bus stop, and one guard came up to me and stared thoughtfully into the distance.

"Why are you smoking?"

I threw my cigarette down unfinished and stepped on it.

"No, don't worry," he said, apologetic. "I just want to know."

I tried to look uncomfortable. He continued to stare at nothing. He said that he had always wondered why women smoke, because they don't have any real problems. I remember I laughed at him, despite myself.

So I walk away from the library, and somehow I end up in the area Ross's hostel is in. For the first time since this morning, I look at my phone, which I'm glad I remembered. There's a message from his number, I think. I haven't saved it. It's a reminder about going to Jesse's room and watching ironic movies.

I check the time. It's 11 p.m. I call him anyway. It rings for a while, but he answers before it goes to his voice mailbox. His voice is groggy, even more American than I'm used to.

"I'm outside your building," I whisper.

"What?" He sounds like he is propping himself up. I can hear the ruffle of his blankets in the background.

"Do you have cigarettes?" I ask. He repeats his drawling "What?" once more. I repeat myself, this time trying to sound nicer and add an explanation about the ladies being gone.

In a few minutes I'm outside his room and I suddenly realise I'm cold. My T-shirt is damp with the sweat of a hot afternoon spent napping. When he opens the door he is in shorts and my eyes follow the hair that grows from his chest to his stomach.

"Hi." He crouches to meet my eyes and I laugh.

I say hi and suddenly I feel like being shy, the way girls are supposed to be.

Ross is a very American name. Like Jesse and Hannah and Emma-Lee, which are actual names exchange students have here. Names that are almost too American. I've found myself in their company only once before. I felt like an audience at a pantomime, listening to them miss McDonald's and convenience stores and speak almost entirely in TV show quotes. Or at least I assume they were TV show quotes, otherwise I'd have to assume exchanging unrelated one-liners is how American English works.

Ross is a very American guy. He says he is from the Midwest, whatever that means. He is very average, but kind, and easy to understand.

We are sitting on the steps of his hostel's fire escape. His room is on the top floor, so we have a clear view of the medicine faculty, all new and shiny, half made of glass and half made of the hopes of my ancestors. I am wearing one of his jerseys, big, red, and not particularly fashionable. We're smoking cigarettes and drinking gin. I remembered he had a stash of spirits in his closet next to his MacBook, so when he invited me into his room I first asked casually for a drink. He didn't respond, becoming suddenly fixated with the search for his box of cigarettes.

Then I polished and pushed forward the desperation that lies behind almost all of my requests. Quickly he made some excuse to himself about not having classes the next day.

Soon we had two dirty glasses between us and we made our way to the stairs. We had to be quiet: neither alcohol nor alcoholic girls are allowed in the boys' hostels, and I didn't have the charm to promise a security guard a bribe right then.

Now that we're here, I'm drinking fast but at the same time trying not to look like I'm drinking fast. Whenever I take a sip of my gin, I wait until he isn't looking and take a sip of his, too. This way he will think we're drinking at the same pace.

*W*hen I wake up it is raining. There is a small roaring sound coming from someplace that is far away and also near. I realise it's inside my own head.

I open my eyes and run them drearily around the contents of an unfamiliar room. They land on a sleeping body, naked and pale on top of bunched up sheets on a bed on the other side of the room.

I'm watching its back move up and down as the body breathes in air. A mop of dark, straight hair hangs over an unshaven face screwed tight in a fitful rest.

His room is identical to mine. I am sleeping in his roommate's bed and smelling the boyish sweat of a stranger in the pillow. Normally this would make me nauseous, but now I'm just glad for the darkness and the sound of rain, interrupted infrequently by boys shouting in the corridors. I stare up at the ceiling. There are cracks in the paint and a small stream of grey light dancing from the gap left in the window by too short university-standard curtains.

I start humming to myself a song that isn't a song at first. I lie on my back and my hands sit on my belly and then the song becomes a memory of a song, a song someone sang to me when I was a small girl, or maybe something I heard in a kombi on a hot Sunday, and then it feels like my eyes close and I melt back to sleep. And this time the darkness doesn't follow me.

III

*I*t's Thursday afternoon and I'm sitting on a golf cart in Mafikeng. Eddy – some guy I met a month ago who decided to invite me along to one of his club's outings – is shouting at his friend in the cart ahead. Middle-aged men in expensive golf shirts with bargain-price clubs race each other, like boys pushing old tires with sticks. I'm wearing short-shorts and smiling through a whiskey daze.

The sun is on us like an excited commentator, loud and cheerful. Eddy leans in and whispers into my ear about the guy ahead. He is the CEO of something somewhere. I laugh and nod and think of other things, like where the next stop for whiskey will be. Or where my lighter is.

Then I am sitting at The Mistress Table with four other bored girls. They speak in quick sentences and shut me out of the conversation. But I don't care. I brought a book with me, an autobiography of some Australian actress I found in the ladies' room at the border. I'm not really reading it, just skimming through the pages for something. I don't know what exactly – maybe something life-changing. But it's all about auditions and diets and names I don't recognise.

Then, in walks a small group of men in golf shirts and Jordans, led by a similarly dressed obese man, trailing with him a tall gorgeous woman with pinewood skin. Even with my unfocused eyes, I can see she's dressed expensively. Her face is perfectly made up and her designer sunglasses sit proudly on her cheekbones, propped up by a wide, permanent smile. She doesn't come and sit with us. Instead she saunters over to a chair beside her fat, dark man. Her arms relax around his shoulders and she laughs beautifully at most of what he says, making her own jokes to his friends when the mood goes quiet.

I've forgotten about the Australian actress and her dull life. My eyes and ears are on the pretty girl and those guys. I like to look at her. Her hair – its price I won't dare guess – dances calmly in the draught. Even her crooked teeth are endearing.

A few months later, I will meet her in a bathroom of a mid-level Italian place in town and she will say that she remembers my face from somewhere. My heart will flutter and we will both be drunk enough to talk freely. She'll tell me the fat guy and her broke up not long after their trip to Mafikeng. He will have taken back her black Range Rover and kicked her out of their Phakalane house. She'll say these things in passing, as if she thinks I won't believe her if she doesn't mention things and just tells me the truth: that she loved him more than anything and eventually he grew tired of her. I will believe her because I like how she smells when she hugs me goodbye and tells me to call her whenever I'm around.

The whiskey at the golf course tastes cheap. We're back to riding carts in an old golf course that looks like nobody's given a fuck about it since apartheid ended. Eddy's finished playing his turn. He's sunk a ball in three turns. That's good, apparently, and he's happy. His hand slides up my thigh and my mind returns to the location of my lighter. I'd bought it at the airport two months ago, when I dropped off my little sister to go to the States, somewhere in New England, wherever that is, on a scholarship.

I'm thinking of the blue and white design on the lighter's sides. I couldn't tell what it had looked like through my tears at the time. But when I used it to light a cigarette in the parking lot, my tears dried up: I thought I could see in it the outline of a frowning woman.

That night, after more whiskey, I leave Eddy on the bed while he texts his wife, the base of his phone resting on his bulging stomach. I say something about needing the bathroom, but instead I climb out of the window onto the balcony of our hotel room. I wait until I can hear his snores reverberate through the sliding door. The whiskey burns in my belly, and then it doesn't, and then I'm awake again, shivering. Small raindrops are being blown into my face. I don't bother to move, to climb back through the bathroom window, so I drift back to sleep.

I wake up, or at least I think I wake up, to a grey day. He is gone. Everybody is gone. I knock on the bathroom window. I knock on the sliding door. Not even the maid who comes in at eleven hears me. I am sure this time I have disappeared.

I do not blame him for leaving. The layer of resentment between us was clear even to the waiter at the restaurant we met at a week ago. Though we were strangers to one another, and it appears still are, we fell into our roles with familiar ease. The over-confident old man with pants that are too short, speaking in outdated American slang – "Yeah, baby-girl", "Oh yeah, daddio" – slurred to me over local beer and over-fried chips. His friend looking up occasionally from his cell to wink at me. My cold eyes set in an over-animated face. Laughing a little off-key, my hand too rough on his thigh. A wink to the waiter that said "Keep them coming!" And now sneaking out before he could reap the reward for bearing my I'm-better-than-this attitude to the sugar-daddy-poor-student dynamic.

I do not blame him for leaving.

And then the sky opens up. The rain is no longer soft. An ocean falls upon me in angry bullets. I lie down and spread my arms and legs wide on the balcony floor, praying for the sky to shoot off every last piece of my skin.

I lift my top over my stomach so that the old scars from the donkey-whip show, my beer-belly free from the hold of its role in crop-tops and high-waisted skirts. I reveal myself to the sky in all my glory. The rain streams off me, and it feels like ice.

I close my eyes and the song that is not quite a song roars in me, like a mother's at the funeral of a relative's small child. Singing to a god who hovers just above the casket, eyes still with pain. Mouths ashamed by their talent to serenade a god who hears no serenading.

I lie still. The water slows down and I hope and hope. I pray and hum. My song mingles with their song. It mingles and multiplies and maginifies until it is a serenade for all the gods who have ever lived, blind and unknowing. Maybe, I think, if the rain dissolves into me, I will dissolve into it. Maybe one day I too might evaporate and shoot down from thankless clouds, the clouds that have absorbed the gazes – the spirits – of millions of hopeful ancestors before me.

And maybe then I will become something.

Water No Get Enemy

Fred Khumalo

1

*E*khaya Jazz Restaurant recommends itself to clients (both existing and potential) through one thing and one thing only: consistency. Take their steaks, for example. They are always huge and rubbery, and unfailingly, excessively salty. Customer service here is a persistent rumour. You have to shout, threaten the beginning of jihad, intifada, chimurenga, toyi-toyi – all rolled in one – before Gift, the alleged waiter, lifts his head from the lotto tickets that he is forever filling out. Then he will shoot you a malevolent look that says: Why are you driving a wedge between me and my lotto millions? On the wine list there are some mouth-watering goody-goodies, but when you order any of the listed items, they are "unavailable from supplier". Now, that's consistency.

Yet the place attracts some of the city's top actors and lawyers; some would-be musicians and writers; journalists and conmen (if there's any difference between the two). What's the attraction, then? The answer: location, location, location. You see Ekhaya is the only remaining South African-owned business in the legendary Rockey Street strip in Yeoville. As a result, when you sit on the verandah at Ekhaya you get blessed with a kaleidoscope of human movement and a babel of languages. Next door is Kin Malebo Restaurant, where you can see the Congolese in colourful clothes, doing their kwasa-kwasa. Cast your eyes across the road, you will be rewarded with the sight and noise of Nigerian brothers arguing at the top of their voices from the entrance to the Rotisserie. Next to this hangout, Zimbabweans are quaffing quart after quart of beer at The Londoner, or Time Square next to it. On the pavements, chaps from Mozambique are roasting chicken gizzards and peddling boiled eggs. Their women are selling mealies, chocolate eclairs and cigarettes; an Ethiopian chap is doing roaring business from his telephone booth where people pay to make and receive calls. All these things combined are a boon to the armchair traveller who, without having left South Africa, can have a peek into the lives of "others".

The parade of humanity on the road never fails to trigger a

comment among us as we sit on the verandah. Or a memory, which will in turn give birth to a story. Ekhaya is about stories. Hence the place's appeal to artistic types, who come here for inspiration – a euphemism for stealing other people's ideas.

Now, there are storytellers, and there are Storytellers. One who fits in the latter category is Guz-Magesh, a regular at Ekhaya.

Let's watch our hero now as he settles down on his chair and takes a sip from his whiskey. He pushes his chair as far back as possible, the better to give room to his generous abdominal protuberance.

"You know," says Guz-Magesh, "I've just been to the toilet. That it does not smell very well is an established fact. What has always worried me, but something I have never vocalised, is that the urinal has a perpetual stream of water coming out of it. And then the faucet at the hand basin does not close properly. The toilet is forever leaking."

Clearly not captivated by Guz-Magesh, some of the customers start shouting abuse at Gift, the alleged waiter.

"You know, just like all of you darkies around this table, I used to be careless and presumptuous about water – until one day at our Liberation camp in Angola. And my awareness of the importance of water was occasioned by an encounter with a baboon." He surveys his audience, realises that they are leaning forward now. He smiles, checks his watch, and says, "What time does the game start on TV?"

"Three-thirty," somebody says, "But what about the baboon and water?"

"Oh, I thought you were not listening."

"Do tell us about the baboon," says the one they call The Snatcher.

"You people do not understand the importance of water. We've had the land wars, the gold wars, the diamond wars, the oil wars and all that. What do you think the next war is going to be about? I know you're going to say: food. Yes it will be about food, but there can't be no food without water. The next war will be about water. It has already started. Look at those water boys in Nigeria. They can wash your car right there in the street, at the height of a water rationing period. Where do you think they get their water from?"

He pauses.

"These boys steal the water, that's what."

"Ag," says The Snatcher, "Water is boring. Tell us about the baboon. Eintlik, eintlik what story are you telling, kanti wena?"

"Listening is a skill you can acquire for free, comrade. It doesn't require of you to be educated to be able to listen. Nor do you have to be as rich as Motsepe in order to be able to acquire the ability to listen. So, sit back, comrade, and listen."

II

*G*uz-Magesh was still relatively new at the military camp in Angola when they put him on guard duty. All rookies had to start there. When you were on guard duty, they gave you an AK-47 and a ration of ammunition. Those on guard duty patrolled the perimeters of the camp, on the lookout for suspicious movement. Liberation Army camps were forever falling under bombardment from members of the apartheid government's Defence Force. In hunting down members of the Liberation Army, the apartheid forces worked in collaboration with Jonas Savimbi's Unita. The apartheid defence force, in turn, helped Unita insurgents in their long-drawn war against the armed forces of the Angolan communist government.

Guard duty was not popular among members of the Liberation Army as it brought them in close proximity to the enemy. But someone had to do it. The patrols were carried out day and night. Those on duty always worked in teams of two. When the team got off duty, the camp commander would count the bullets. If there was a bullet missing, the soldier had to explain. However, if there was a bullet missing, and the member was carrying an antelope on his person, not much needed to be said. In fact, the soldier in question became something of the man of the moment, a hero, among his comrades at base camp. For meat was scarce. Even then, the top brass officially did not share in the enthusiasm of the utilisation of ammunition to kill antelope. "We're not on a hunting expedition here. We're engaged in combat against the enemy. The bullets are reserved for the enemy."

The firing of arms was also discouraged because every time a member shot his gun, he was bound to alert the enemy of his team's whereabouts. Because those Unita bastards were good trackers who knew the bush intimately, they could hear the sound of gunfire from miles off, and then track the source of that gunfire quickly. And before you knew it, the guards would have been cornered and overpowered, their weapons stolen from them. Sometimes they would be killed or, worse, abducted.

"You shoot your gun only under extreme circumstances. When your life is under threat. When you encounter a lion or some other extremely dangerous animal."

That was the mantra from the top brass.

III

*G*uz-Magesh takes a sip from his drink, and continues, "So, on this particular day I am with a comrade from the Eastern Cape. We called him Cofimvaba, on account of the village of his origin. That's another thing they did, the commanders. They always paired a township clever like me with a moegoe from some rural backwater. They would never pair two city clevers, never. They said we city clevers always got up to shit. Said we treated this war as just another game being played in a township street. They said the moegoes from the sticks were responsible and disciplined. But what the commanders did not realise was that, rural as he was, Cofimvaba was clever. Clever in the bookish kind of way, if you get my drift. His head was bursting with information. Now that I think about it, I think it was exactly for that reason that they put Cofimvaba on night duty. He used to say things that confused and embarrassed even the commanders who paraded themselves as know-it-all figures. Cofimvaba knew about Martin Luther, the

King. He spoke about Malcolm X. He also knew MacGyver. Not the TV MacGyver, mind you. The MacGyver from Jamaica. The guy with the big ship who wanted to bring all the black people from America and Jamaica, bring them back to Africa where they came from. A crazy idea, if you ask me. Black people are having it nice in America and you want to ship them back to Africa where we are struggling to survive! Anyway, Cofimvaba used to get so inspired when he spoke of MacGyver he would start singing a song. Said the song was by someone called Burning Spear. Went something like No one remembers Old MacGyver, no one remembers…"

Some of the chaps are chuckling, until one of them bursts out and says, "Guzzie, it's not MacGyver, it's Marcus Garvey…"

"You bloody agent, that's what I said. Marcus Garvey. You must learn not to disturb me. Don't jump onto my moustache, do you hear!" He bangs the table so hard the interlocutor jerks his head to the side as if he had been punched.

Guz-Magesh sighs, and speaks in a controlled voice again: "Anyway, Cofimvaba knew many other interesting cats, apart from the MacGyver character. He mentioned another cat called Amir Cabral. Another one called Fanon something or the other. I remember it was Fanon 'cause someone decided to call him the Funny One, on account of the funny stories Cofimvaba and the other educated ones used to tell about this character.

"Anyway, many of us never paid attention to all that name dropping that was done by the likes of Cofimvaba. You see, we went into exile not to learn about some deluded MacGyver who wanted to take black Americans from their country back to Africa. We went into exile to learn how to handle guns and how to plant bombs. Yes, so we could liberate this country from the oppressor. The Cofimvabas of this world spent too much time talking about dialectical something, something. The Cofimvabas felt very important because they knew all those things. Where were they when the Boers were shooting us in Soweto in 1976? The Boers did not care if someone knew MacGyver and Cabral. They just saw a kaffir child and they shot. So we had left the country in order to learn how to fight back. No manga-manga business; no Fanon this, Fanon that. You see, Cofimvaba could even tell you where and when these characters of his were born. As if it mattered. But what must have pissed the commanders off was when Cofimvaba, during one political education class, started talking about a place called Diaspora. He said the Movement was an inspiration to the other people in this place called Diaspora. So, the commanders started looking for this place called Diaspora on the map. They looked and looked, couldn't find it. It did not help that Cofimvaba started laughing out loud.

"*You are making fun of us! they said. This Diaspora is not on the map. Don't you know we are the leadership?*

"*But, my leadership, of course Diaspora does not appear on the map.*

"*Then you are making fools of us, sending us on a wild goose chase!*

"*But my leadership, Diaspora simply means the dispersion of people from their homeland.*

"*Okay, clever Xhosa boy, you are going to be on permanent guard duty. Permanent until we get reunited with those friends of yours in your Diaspora.*

"And so, there I was with Cofimvaba on the shift. Deep into it, after telling me about this Fanon character – who it turns out is actually not even an African yet teaches Africans how to liberate themselves – and getting me confused by it all, Cofimvaba suddenly starts taking off his pants. He squats on the ground, intent on taking a dump right there in front of me! I shout at him to go and shit over there in the bush. I tell him I don't want to step on his shit.

"*What if there's a dangerous animal over there?*

"*Go over, man, a man who knows about Fanon and the Diaspora can't be scared of anything. People in the Diaspora do not sound like people who scare easily,* I say.

"He won't budge. So I playfully point my gun at him and say, *Okay, go over there, I'll cover you.* I also tell him that the comrades who will come on the next shift won't appreciate stepping into his poo. *Go over there,* I say pointing at a clump of trees. *The comrades who will come on the next shift would be grateful if you dumped your stuff where they can't see or smell it...* Only then does he move."

"But where is this story going?" the Misunderstood Genius grumbles. He is one of those chaps who analyse everything. He will analyse each strand of hair on your head if you let him. He is already in his cups, hence the impatience.

We all glower at him. Guz–Magesh continues: "Come to think of it, had I allowed Cofimvaba to shit right there, in front of me, I wouldn't be sitting here, telling this story. Cofi's shit changed my destiny. So, anyway, Comrade Cofimvaba reluctantly walks over to the clump of trees that I've just pointed out. I turn my back on him. With nothing else to do, I light a cigarette. It's against regulations while on duty, as the smell can betray your position to the enemy. But we do it anyway, as long as we believe we won't be caught. But I have to smoke to take my mind away from Cofi. Why did he wait until now before emptying his bowels? He should have relieved himself back at the camp, for crying out loud!

"I am exhaling slowly, enjoying my cigarette when suddenly I hear a ruckus coming from the clump of trees where Cofimvaba is taking a dump. Before I could say *Viva the National Democratic Revolution*, I see the comrade running towards me, his pants in his hands. He is screaming his lungs out: *Heeelp! Heeelp!* So I say: *What the fuck is wrong with you, Diaspora! Where's your weapon?*

"Indeed, the comrade is running naked, pants in his one hand, but no weapon. *The baboon! The baboon! The baboon!* he is crying like a motherless child, the fucker. So I say, *What baboon?*

"He finally reaches me, and clings to me like he has seen a ghost. The bugger hasn't even washed his hands, and he's touching me. I push him away angrily, but his fear is so intense he clings to me body and soul. *Comrade, I am dead*, he says, *The commander is going to murder me. Help me, comrade! The baboon stole my weapon. It stole my weapon!*

"I'm thinking: *What is this fucker on about? Is he drunk or what?* And right then, a baboon comes barrelling out of the bushes. Instinctively, I let out a volley of bullets. The wily baboon ducks behind a tree. Now, Cofi's words begin to make sense. The hairy fucker has my comrade's AK-47. Which can only mean I'm also in trouble. Back at camp they will ask: *Where were you when he lost his weapon? How did you help him?*

"I do not have enough time to dwell on that thought, for the bloody baboon is aiming at us! Can you believe the pluck! I know you don't believe me. And if you don't believe me, how much less would a battle-hardened man in charge of ill-equipped soldiers in the middle of fucking Angola? But there. A bloody baboon messing around with the property of the Liberation Movement!

"I try to take aim at it. Listen to this: the bloody baboon fires first! It squeezes a round. And it pauses. It knows how to handle an AK. That's when we run towards camp. No, this can't be a real baboon. These people, the Unita people, have got bad medicine. Why, just not so long ago we'd heard that Savimbi could change himself into a hyena. Yes, you are sitting in the bush, dreaming. And you hear the howl of a hyena in the distance. Then the next thing you know the hyena is right underneath you, trying to reach for your balls. No ordinary hyena can do that. It's Savimbi under muti disguise! But, until I encountered that baboon, I hadn't really believed the stories about Savimbi, the Hyena. I used to listen, just like everyone else, and then laugh dismissively. A man who can turn himself into a hyena! Come on, give me a break. I am from the township, not some backward village where they believe all that nonsense.

"Anyway, by the time we get to camp, the other comrades are outdoors, craning their necks, scouring the horizon. They had surely heard the unmistakable report of the AK-47. They are all armed, ready to repulse an enemy attack. They chorus in excitement: *Comrades, what's happening? What's happening! What was that shooting all about?*

"*A baboon! A baboon!* I shout. *What?* Commander Zwai shouts. *Two trained fighters of the Liberation Movement are running away from a baboon! In the name of Moses Mabhida and Nelson Mandela, what is this world coming to?*

"*No, Comrade Commander, the baboon's got Comrade Cofimvaba's weapon!* I explain.

"By now, the comrades who have gathered around us are laughing: *Disarmed by a baboon!*

"Commander Zwai orders the comrades to shut up and go back to their posts. We are marched to Commander Zwai's office. This is where we are going to be interrogated. The interrogation lasts about five hours, during which time we are stripped naked. One of the commander's sidekicks squeezes our balls with a pair of pliers. Commander Zwai and his two sidekicks, who are always suspicious, think we have sold Comrade Cofimvaba's weapon to some passing villager. They try their damnedest to squeeze a confession out of us.

"Then they decide to get us to perform water-fetching duties, a task that had broken many spies who had been planted among our ranks. When I say water fetching duties it sounds simple. It's not like you get up, go to the kitchen, fill a glass with water. No. You are given a huge drum, a fifty-litre drum. You roll it down the steep slope, because the reservoir is located down there in the valley. Going down there is easy. You just roll the drum down the slope, and you run after it. At the reservoir, you fill it up. Then begins the tough part. You must carry the fifty-litre drum up the slope. Under normal circumstances, these huge water drums would be drawn by heavy military trucks. From the reservoir up to camp is a distance of about three to four kilometres. So, like cattle we would struggle up the slope, with the commanders wielding sticks, whipping our backs. Wincing from the pain, you lose control of the drum. It rolls back down the slope. You run after it, catch up with it. The pushing, shoving process starts all over again. It takes hours. The commanders are kicking you, beating you with sticks and whips. Sometimes even shooting rounds at your feet, which is a contradiction if you consider what I've just said about the scarcity of ammunition.

"Anyway, this is a water drum, my brothers. It is heavy. As I am pushing, blinded by my own tears, I find myself thinking of the water games we used to play at home. In the summer, if it got too hot, and the children were restless, someone would attach a hose to the tap and let them play in the water the whole afternoon. Now, I am thinking of that wastefulness, thinking how those children must laugh to see me pushing a water-filled drum up the slope. I am thinking of guys in the township, attaching a hose to a tap and washing their cars at a leisurely pace, listening to jazz music, pausing every now and then to take a sip from a beer. Or share a story with a passing friend. All the while, the hose is running. This is your tap, this is your hose, this is your car. Who can tell you? After washing your car, you have to water your lawn. This invention called a hosepipe comes in handy. If you are advanced, you attach a sprinkler to your hose, and you leave it running while you go and see your friends in another part of the township.

"I am thinking of my mother's white employers who had a water feature in the garden, a huge feature in the form of a dolphin spouting water. I picture that dolphin laughing at me as I push the water drum up the slope. Water, brothers, something I'd taken for granted. The commander's whip cracks. I am crying, cursing. I am thinking of guys from our neighbourhood in the township, those lucky enough to have bakkies. They would load a bakkie with water-filled drums which they would then ferry to their friends and relatives who lived in one of the outlying villages, where the people were stupid enough not to have taps. Yes, that was the attitude among those of us in the townships: you don't have a tap, you don't have a flushable toilet, you must be stupid. Now, I am feeling stupid. For two weeks, I do the water duty.

"The commanders are still convinced that we haven't told the whole truth, by the way. So, I get thrown into solitary confinement. Once a day, they bring me a cup of water to drink. Just one cup. I treasure every drop of it, this precious thing, this liquid gold I've always taken for granted. Every time I take a sip, I hum my jumbled version of Fela Kuti's song, 'Water No Get Enemy'. I hum, *If you wan to go wash, na water you go use. If your child de grow, na water he go use. If water kill your child, na water you go use. Nothing without water. Water 'im no get enemy.*

"Comrade Cofimvaba, I later hear, got stripped naked. Then they buried him up to his neck in a hole that he had been ordered to dig. I later hear that he had been left there for two full days, without water or food. Every now and then, a bored commander would walk up to him, pee in his face, saying, *Have a drink of water, Comrade Sell-out*, to the uproarious laughter of other comrades.

"A week after my release from solitary confinement I am working in the garden when all of a sudden I hear screams. I look up. There're commander Zwai and his two sidekicks running for their lives, towards camp. I dropped my spade, picked up my weapon and followed them, ready to offer assistance.

"When they finally regained their breath, one of the sidekicks said, *Shit, mfondini, so this gun-toting baboon actually exists!*"

The Misunderstood Genius is hopping up and down the verandah, in paroxysms of laughter, spilling his drinks all over the place. The Snatcher is furiously typing away on his expensive smartphone. We know what he is doing: he is writing a Facebook post, telling Guz-Magesh's story as if it were his own creation. That's why we call him The Snatcher: he steals people's stories, dresses them up in new clothes, and parades them as his own creations.

But it doesn't bother Guz-Magesh. His well of tales is bottomless. Guz-Magesh takes a swig from his glass. He smiles contentedly. I can sense words gathering inside his mouth, dancing on the tip of his tongue, jostling with each other, trying to stand in proper formation, so they can come out of his mouth in the form of yet another tale. But instead, he simply winks at The Snatcher, and starts singing, *Water, 'im no get enemy. Nothing without water. Water 'im no get enemy.*

Ink

Mark Winkler

Card 1

I thought you were only supposed to see one thing, but apparently you're allowed to find more. You should see a bat or a butterfly or a moth, and also the figure of a woman in the centre, if you're "normal". If you're not, you might see breasts, vaginas, perhaps a penis. I cannot see any of those things. I suppose it's mostly the men that do.

How can identifying the figure of a woman be "normal"? When I find her, I see she has no head, and her hands are aloft as though searching for it. Or else they're expressing pain, or despair. The bat or butterfly image is hardly innocent – its wings are shredded, torn, holed. It seems a sad thing to find.

Me, I see the face of a beast. A hellish wild pig, with angry mad eyes and tusks. Apparently that makes me a little paranoid. Tell me something I don't know. Am I the only one who feels this city shift as if it were floating on water? I feel it shiver in its changes, a tectonic island nudged here and there by what lies beneath, and it feels like the slipping of a carpet on a tiled floor. What could it be other than water? And if it is, why do we have so little, eking out our rations between sunset and sunrise, if and when the Council of Ten allows it, filling pots and jugs so that we may make tea or wash our armpits?

S ome nights I dream of walking in the rain I've never seen. It falls warm on my bare skin, and when I awake my pillow is soaked with perspiration.

T here comes Douglas, scooping his fingers through his long hair. Dashing Douglas, Sindi calls him. I find his teeth rather long and his breath often reminds of yesterday's garlic. I hide the browser before he gets to my desk, and the pig is gone.

"You'd have much more space in here if you put your desk against the wall," Douglas says. Again.

But then my back would be to the room, I don't say, and people like Douglas would see whatever I'm busy with. Maps unfinished, dead-end research paths, the black blots of wild pigs.

"How is Jeezette today, anyway?" Jeezette is Douglas's phonetic version of the female form of Jesus, and when he's in a flippant mood, it's what he calls me instead of Angela. A few years ago, I'd had a bit too much to drink at our little Christmas party, and had let on that my mother is a nun. You can imagine the mirth, the virgin birth jokes, the requests that I walk across the empty swimming pool outside the restaurant. They have long forgotten Douglas's karaoke, and Sindi's dancing, but they've never forgotten that one little comment of mine.

"I'm fine," I say, like a teenager. Douglas comes around and leans over my desk. He peers at the map on my screen, breathing on me.

"And where are we now?"

"Early 1700s."

"Okay, good," Douglas says, as he always does. "You have fun now." And off he goes, scooping at his hair and making sure to show off his broad shoulders and his slim dancer's hips.

Card 2

*T*he second card surprises me. I'd thought they all consisted of a watery wash of black ink. Like the others, this is symmetrical, and black, but there are smears of red top and bottom.

I see human forms, clowns or children, each one's hands up against the other's as if they were playing a clapping game. *Three-six-nine, the goose drank wine.* Somehow the song they were singing had stopped mid-phrase, freezing them forever on the page just as their hands touched.

I'm relieved that what I see is regarded as normal. It means I relate to people. The implication is that if you don't see the blot this way, you're a sociopath, or worse.

At least I am spared that.

I am a cartographer. Or more accurately, a geography honours graduate who fell into making maps. What else would you do with a geography degree? And now I work for Douglas, who works for the Bond Foundation, as does Sindi, and as James used to before his body was found washed up in the desert against the dry wave of a dune. That his lungs were full of water left no doubt that he had drowned, although nobody could say how, or why.

It was after James's death that I began to feel our city shift under me. Sometimes at night the slightest wave will lift my bed before putting it gently down again. A sudden subtle movement might cause a stumble on the stairs. Just a few days ago when crossing the Square during my lunch break I saw perhaps two dozen people waver, just once, like reeds in a gust, as the world undulated beneath us.

"Did you feel that?" I said to an old man near me as the lunch crowd carried on about its business.

He held his bottle of water closer to his chest and his eyes narrowed. "Feel what?" he growled, and scuttled off.

Card 3

I cannot see anything but two figures beating on a shared drum. There is something ancient about them. They remind me of the whispers I've heard of the Primitives who – according to City legend – once lived off the land before it turned to dust, and fished in the sea before it withdrew its waves and allowed the desert to claim its sandy underbelly as its own. When we arrived – depending on who you're listening to – we either chased them into the hinterland with our machines, or killed them off with our other machines.

Most apparent are the breasts on the figures. But above their knees is a protrusion, a broken femur perhaps, or the representation of a penis as painted by someone who has never seen one.

The notes are vexing. To see the figures as female, as I have, is to be homosexual. To see them as male is to be heterosexual. Does this apply to men and women alike? I cannot tell. And the notes say nothing about the foetuses I see dangling in the void behind each figure.

Card 4

A great beast or man, feet made enormous by the low perspective, threatens from the card, ready to attack.

This, say the notes, is a "bad" answer. You should simply see a standing figure, or a bear, or a gorilla. I learn that it's called the "father card", and the way you see it equates to your perception of male authority figures, or of your father.

No surprises there, then.

"*W*hat's it like having a nun for a mother?" Douglas asks one Saturdaymorning as he rolls off me.

He probes the issue often, from different angles. I wonder how much time he spends thinking up new ways to ask the old question, while Sindi and I compare centuries-old maps with the way our city is laid out today. Even Douglas must know by now that I will not speak about it.

I get out of the bed. I have nothing on, except too much flesh for a young woman. But I have little – in this sense – to hide from Douglas.He has no interest in the skinny women who wander the City with their crotch-gaps and their tiny tits and their blued cheeks and their hair piled high in stiff sculptures on their heads. He has said as much, often, nuzzling into my softness. This is why I overlook his long teeth and garlic-tainted kisses, and why I forgive him his constant hair-tossing.

From the dresser I take a sheet of paper and hold it up to him. On it is a map I have drawn – in the old style, with ink and water and brushes with points no thicker than a pencil's – of a place that exists only in my head. There are forests, which I have drawn by clumping together what I recall of images of trees. They are a patchwork of greens, some dark where I've allowed the ink to run thick, and some pale where I've thinned it with water. Running from the hills are streams and rivers that I've rendered in cool blues, and they fill irregular lakes among the forests. I cannot think of a way to indicate the glacial depths of the lakes, and hope that their purple-inked surfaces might be enough.

There are two towns with names I've made up to sound like the Old Language, and I have marked them on the paper with a calligraphy pen in stiff serif lettering.

"What do you think?" I ask Douglas. I suddenly feel shy, as if the map has made me more naked than I am.

He sits up in the bed and leans forward, squinting at the paper. I know what he's going to say, because he always says it.

"Where's that?"

Usually I tell him it doesn't matter. This time I say, "Nowhere. Everywhere. It's how I think the world once used to be."

"It's beautiful, Angela." He holds his hand out for it and places it across his knees and for long moments examines my work while I imagine walking in the shade of the forests and wading through the coolness of the streams in the way our people must once have done. He looks up at me to tease. "Don't you get enough of maps at work?"

Card 5

I do better with the fifth card, and see a bat as I'm supposed to. To me, he – I can't say why it's a he – has his back to me, and what should be seen as antennae I see as long fluffy ears. I'm hardly the girlie type, but I do find the little soft-edged creature inexplicably cute.

T hey say that there used to be millions of bats in the caves and crevasses of the mountains behind the City. Silent and invisible during the day, they would mass at night and float shrieking over the streets in great dark clouds as they cleaned the air of the mosquitoes and midges that used to breed in the swamps. There are scratchings on the walls of a few caves that some believe show a close relationship between the bats and the Primitives, although the nature of the relationship is yet to be defined. Sometimes schoolboys will bring home frail matchstick bones or eggshell skulls from their adventures, giving credence to the old stories.

After the swamps dried up, the elders say, the insects died out and the bats starved. In the caves that once dripped with water only stalagmites and stalactites bear witness to that faraway past, even as they crumble to dust.

*I*t's our job – mine and Sindi's and Douglas's – to rediscover the old watercourses that once sustained the mosquitos and the bats and the City itself. Sindi trawls through the City Archives and the only museum that is still functional, and she scans the ancient charts she finds on the machine seconded to us by the Bond Foundation.

The three of us will pore over the scans and, based on the indications of old ponds and wells and streams, will try to determine where the water once came from, using logic and deduction rather than fact to pinpoint the mountain aquifers, old sewers, market gardens, remnants of dams and ponds that may once have held ground water, or reservoirs that once drew the living water from the veins and arteries of the mountain streams to slake the numerous thirsts of the City.

Then I take Sindi's scans and overlay them on our modern maps, and I mark up our most likely leads. In the four years we've been doing this, our recommendations to the Bond Foundation have led to the digging up of disused parking lots, the excavation of the basement of the City Hall – rendering the old building unsafe and forcing the Council of Ten to take up residence in the Old Library – and in one sad case, the relocation of an entire community. The results have been interesting only archaeologically, when old walls that bore the marks of water erosion were turned up, or canals filled with sand uncovered, or the bones of a mother and child buried in a bag found – all of them stained black or purple or deep ochres by the soil.

Not once has water, or damp evidence of it, been discovered as a consequence of our work. And yet when least expected, the city shudders with the power of it.

Card 6

*I*t's too easy. After the cotton crops failed and the sheep all died in the sun, the people of the City turned to their dogs for food and clothing. Often in my childhood I would see their hides salted white and pegged out in the sun to dry, later to be turned into coats or bedcovers. The sixth image shows such a pelt, stretched taut across the card. I do not see the mushroom cloud or the men with goatees who may or may not be there. The card has to do with one's attitude to sexuality, but the notes do not elaborate.

*D*ouglas comes over to my desk and once more I hide what I am looking at. He asks where Sindi is and I tell him she is out scouring the City for maps, even though her pickings are becoming thinner with every passing day. He looks around to make sure of her absence, and then he pulls her chair towards my desk and sits down.

"I have heard that the Bond Foundation is considering closing us down," he says. "Apparently our inability to deliver water has frustrated them."

I am not sure what he wants me to say.

"There isn't much work for us map-makers in the City. I can't see what we will do to make a living." He sounds close to tears. I try to recall a moment when Douglas has allowed his confidence to flag like this, slipping like a bathrobe from his shoulders, and I cannot.

"Perhaps we should move away from this dry place," I say. "There must be a need for our skills somewhere else."

Douglas snorts. "And how are we going to do that without dying in the desert?" he says. "Sail?"

Card 7

*T*wo little girls, rendered in soft greys, face each other with their ponytails flying in the air. That's what I'm supposed to see, and it's what I do see. What the notes don't mention are their little thalidomide arms or their jointed crustacean bodies. These aspects give the girls a certain vulnerability, and if their ponytails are flying, they must be jumping, which makes me wonder what will happen when they land.

*T*he City is a dangerous place. People are sometimes killed for a bottle of water and a few coins. Thirst-crazed bands have been known to invade family homes for their last drops of water, and if they are caught they try to deflect blame to the Primitives.

The Bond Foundation has for some years deployed a private security force to protect citizens buying water from its stores. You get inked on a thumbnail every time you buy a bottle, and the ink fades in the time the Bond people have decided it takes to consume the contents. Being discovered with a bottle of water in your hand and no ink on your thumb could see you arrested, so it's best to drink up before the ink fades and to buy another bottle. At the office we have to display a current certificate, known as a "Bond", on the front door. The Bond is replaced, newly stamped and sealed, along with our weekly container of water to confirm our compliance.

*I*t is illegal to investigate, or even to ask questions about, the source of the Bond Foundation's water. I suppose they have yet to find a way to make it illegal to think about it.

*T*hey say that beyond the walls of the City other dangers lurk. The gates are closed and barred at sunset, and male citizens between the ages of twenty and forty stand guard through the night as the annual roster decrees. In all my life, there has never been an attack, but the old people say that there are still Primitives in the desert, that they are gathering their strength and their resources, and that it is only a matter of time before they bring their spears and their anger to the City gates.

*I*n the heat of the day the children are called inside to play in the shade and the adults take to their beds to prevent precious sweat escaping their pores. Crying, even in the face of bereavement or pain, is frowned upon for the water it wastes.

*D*ouglas is twitchy today. His fingers scrape through his hair more frequently than ever. I wonder whether the rumours of our disbanding are weighing on his mind, but when I ask him he retires to his little office in the corner and closes the door.

It has an internal window, so it's not much of a hiding place, but I suppose it's all he has.

Card 8

*T*he colours are at once jarring and soft. I've seen black cards and grey cards and cards with splashes of red, so the vividness of the eighth is a surprise. To my eye, the oranges and pinks and blues show damp lungs, wet innards, the hint of a spine capped by the grey skull of some animal. A vivid and semi-living thing with no skin and the head of a dead creature. Climbing up its sides, and using the horns of the skull for purchase, are two pink beasts. I cannot decide whether they are hostile or benign, whether they seek the succour of the skinless being, or are bent on assaulting it.

This is what you're supposed to see, but the notes do not mention a skull.

*W*e have been irresponsible with our water this working week, and on this last day we share the dribbles left in the container among the three of us. My urine is a dark amber and has a bitter smell. I remember reading somewhere that we are three-quarters water, and as the last sour drops fall from me I wonder how this can be, when we have so little, and whether it might be illegal to ask the question aloud.

Card 9

I don't know what to make of these oranges, pinks and greens. I wait until Douglas and Sindi are occupied with other things before I print out a copy so that I can view it from other angles. Ninety degrees this way, ninety that, and still I see nothing but blots of watery colour. I turn it upside down, cock my head and give up.

The notes say that most people struggle to find anything in it.

Sometimes my normality amazes me. But I do find this trickery annoying.

*D*ouglas has retreated into his office, and again he has closed the door. I see him through the window, though, hunched and anxious as he talks on the phone. I wouldn't be surprised if he tells us it's all over when he emerges. But instead he leaves without a word, screwing his hat onto his head as he goes, and then slamming the door behind him.

I glance at Sindi, but she is bent over an image and hasn't noticed Douglas leaving. I look at the door. I wonder why fate would set two random vectors – call one *a* and the other *d* – on their individual arcs to intersect at precisely the same place and time on the infinite map of the universe.

Card 10

I am surprised that there are only ten cards, and also that they are so specific. I'd always imagined them as a random infinity of black patterns, put together with a bottle of ink and some blotting paper between consultations in the back office of psychologists' rooms; each counsellor's interpretation no more objective, nor more accurate, than the patient's.

I am irritated, too, that the last card is once again a trick card.

No matter how I cock my head or narrow my eyes I see nothing in its symmetry of colour. But the notes say that seeing sea-creatures is the most common, and most acceptable, response.

How could I see sea-creatures if I've never seen one before?

I cannot imagine these spiny, many-legged things alive. How big were they? Microscopic, or as substantial as a wild City cat? Did they smell? Could they bite? Did they cause disease? Make a nun pregnant? And what was their concentration in the sea, say, in parts-per-million?

Perhaps they have by now evolved to live beneath the sand, sculling their way through the endless grains, somehow sucking oxygen and sustenance from the lifelessness around them.

I close the image of the last card. I have learnt that I am no more normal or abnormal than the dull median. I close the other maps – the inaccurate old doodlings that Sindi has dug up and scanned, the precision of the modern ones supplied by the Foundation. It is early to go in search for lunch, but I need the air.

Instead of food, I find Douglas at a table in the shade across the Square. With him is an emaciation of a woman, her cheeks sunken and her cheekbones protruding, burnished with the fashionable blue. Douglas has before him a bottle of cactus liquor, and he pours generously into two glasses and dilutes the stuff with precious splashes from his bottle of water. I step behind a pillar and watch them toast, glasses held high above their heads. Then they drink and the woman leans in and says something. Douglas laughs long and hard and so does she.

Sindi sometimes brings back images that have nothing to do with the Bond project. The three of us huddle around them like children over a storybook even though there is always work to be done. Sindi selects these superfluous pictures for their curiosity value, and they invariably feature long-ago scenes of life with water.

She has shown us City streets glistening wet, and through them people running with umbrellas, or their coats over their heads. A

94

man in the sun with no shirt, pushing a handle to propel a small machine across an expanse of the richest green. A lithe woman who has stretched herself into the shape of an exclamation mark, hanging suspended in the air above a pool of pale blue. Toddlers in a bright yellow tub in the sun, splashing water into the air, and you could all but hear their shrieks of joy.

One of Sindi's images comes back to me as I watch Douglas from behind my pillar. It shows people wearing the smallest items of clothing. Adults are lying on the sand of a beach while children play. A brief – and surely dangerous – distance away, rolling white waves crash in the shallows while people cavort among them with their hands in the air. Across a bay of an impossible blue stand the mountains behind the City. It's disconcerting, in the least, to see your hometown in this way, at a time when it was almost subsumed by sea, when today the half-basin of the bay is no more than a repository of sand and rock and dust and household garbage dumped by City workers. Stranger even than this is the thought that the people in the image would have ventured smiling and laughing into a sea full of the beasts shown on the last card. But the ink and the water say it was so.

Perhaps the City floats on ink rather than water. Perhaps it is not water but ink that has written its story, in blacks and blues and fathomless deep purples. Perhaps without the ink there would be no City, and without the City there would be only water.

Douglas is laughing again, and I see that the woman has moved around the table to be closer to him. She rests her elbow and she holds her glass aloft between thumb and forefinger.

I lean against the pillar and through my shoulder I feel the world quiver as another slow wave disturbs the City beneath my feet.

Love Like Blue

Wairimu Muriithi

I did not even know Ma had tinnitus until I found her trying to fit inside the freezer. Our favourite movie when I was six used to be The Prince of Egypt. I watch it once in a while now as an adult, and every time I do I wonder if the inside of Moses' basket smelled like God.

She only ever sent me one letter, when I was in my first year of university in Cape Town. She tried to explain: *The voices lived in my ears. They used to be made of ocean.* After reading it, I let the paper disintegrate in a puddle outside the chemistry department, like the poetic genius I thought I was at nineteen. At my father's behest, I wrote back. She didn't reply.

And then, as if all of a sudden, I am thirty-two, and sometimes I live with stray cats. They seem to know how to find me when they are at their weakest and leave when they feel better. People call me an artist now. My name is semi-important in certain academic and literary circles because – I am told – the stories I write, the music I make and the pictures I paint are "pertinent to the condition of the postcolony." People ask me about my *inspiration*, and I give them the complex answers they want because I enjoy living in a decent apartment. I do not tell them that everything is produced by a tiny memory of a little girl surrounded by the gleaming-white inside of a freezer gifted to her parents on their wedding day.

"She says she wants to see you," says the voice on my answering machine. "*I* think she should see you." At this point I haven't been able to work for almost two months. My fingers, with all this free time, keep picking my belly button raw of their own accord. I have made two hospital visits for the infections I create, and had one session with a therapist with thick hair growing out of his ears. I itched to braid it. Most days my body floats between errands, and then it floats to places in the city I have never been before. I take up baking because it is cheaper than the ER.

So I figure I might as well book some plane tickets.

"I'm going on holiday," I say to my landlord, and to my part-time girlfriend. "I'm going home," I say to the mirror, but just saying those words makes my mouth taste like groundnuts, which I am allergic to, so I empty my bottle of mouthwash and make a mental note to buy another when I get to the airport. I forget the mouthwash. It is so dark outside the plane's window we could easily be flying underground. *What if my teeth aren't as white as hers always have been? What if I get there and find she's changed her mind about me, again?* I am wearing thick gloves to keep from excavating in my belly, even though my palms are sweaty. *What if I still cannot work, even after this?*

"*I* have a plan. Who is that on the radio?" She has not looked up at me once.

"Laura Mvula." I do not wonder about her plan. I am, for now, categorically anti-plan.

"She has a lovely voice. I am tired. Can you come back tomorrow?" I have painted three nails on her right hand blue. She has not looked up at me once.

"Yes."

*I*n my father's living room, there is a framed photo of my stepmother and me on a crowded beach in Dar es Salaam. It is the only holiday I took with her and my father before she died. The scar on my left tricep, which faded when I gained weight in my first year of university, was still visible then.

I pretend I am here to see him. When I arrive he says he has been meaning to ask me to take a break and visit. I say nothing about the freezer he probably got rid of as soon as I left home. He pretends not to hear me talking to myself in the mornings. He still plays the piano. I lie about what I get up to in the daytime. In the evenings, he tells me the different versions of the same story.

"Only people who live in a house like this would let their daughter become a carpenter." My grandparents bought the place when my mother had just started school. She remembered helping them fix it up, as much as a five-year-old can help with beams and wires and rotting floorboards. Later, she made many of the things inside the house; pieces of furniture created when she was much older, after she got married. Most of them have survived my father's silence. It is still a beautiful, peculiar house. It traps the wind in its foundations; it dances when no one is inside.

"When she was sure she would marry me, she brought me here and tried to introduce me to her dead father. She said he was waiting for his wife to die. The story is that she burned in a fire when your mother was in high school, and she was declared dead even though her body was never found. He had looked for her wherever it is one looks for souls, but had not found her. So he came back to haunt the house. Your mother said he would help her make furniture while he waited."

"Did you believe her?"

"Yes. I couldn't see or hear him, but that did not mean anything. I never knew the man. I didn't need to, because I knew your mother."

The freezer had been a wedding gift from one of her clients.

"Your grandmother must have really died when you were a little girl, but we never found out how. Your grandfather left a goodbye inscribed onto a small bookcase I found chopped to pieces in the garden."

This is how he explains my mother to me. Even though I already know all this, I let him do it over and over again because this seems to be the only memory he has left of her.

In a short story by Dorothy Tse, "Woman Fish", a man's wife can no longer tell lies because she turns into a fish with legs. He feeds her in a fish tank and makes love to her with his eyes closed and goes with her to their usual Japanese restaurant. Nothing quite so dramatic happened to Ma, but things might have been better if it had. When the ocean waves became ocean-voices, she initially thought they were speaking fish. And then she decided they were water spirits, and she was not lonely anymore.

"They kept her company, they made her laugh. They tormented her."

*I*t is a Saturday when I find bricks of meat and ice cream on the kitchen floor, and Ma trying to get inside the freezer. When she sees she cannot fit, she claws at her ears, trying to pull them off. When she cannot do that either, she goes to bed, walking past me without seeing me. The next day, my father feels like roast chicken for lunch and finds me suffocated nearly to death inside the freezer, between the frozen peas and a tub of strawberry sundae. I would not have told on her if he had asked, but she figures out I must have seen her and tells him herself. I am in the hospital when they take her away. I return home to the quietest place on earth.

*E*very night, after he has gone to bed, I bake for her. He is a heavy sleeper and I leave the kitchen as clean as he likes when I am done, and I hide the muffins or cookies in my bedroom to sneak them out in the morning. They never survive the drive to the hospital. In the heat of the traffic jam on Langata Road, there is a woman who sells bottles of cold water to sweaty drivers and matatu passengers. She wears a large, heavy sweater and a wool cap. The first time I give her the cookies becomes the second and the third, and every day after that. She gives me a bottle of water a day in return. We exchange pleasantries, growing into something of a tacit friendship, even though we never learn each other's names.

*T*he orderlies and nurses all have "smpcf" stitched onto their left breast pockets in stiff black letters. They shuffle papers in a thick file and then make vague sounds about how much she has improved. I do not believe them because I do not recognise them from her earlier days. They must not know how bad things were when she first got here. I do not know how bad they are now.

"She does not want to see you today," one of the orderlies says to me, a young man with a beautiful nose, but I insist until I am near tears. My mother's face breaks into a smile when I walk in, as if she expected me to fight my way in anyway, but I am in no mood for tests.

"You have a child." She is looking my body over, still avoiding my face.

"Had." I correct her as if she should have known.

"Okay," she says. She takes my hand and leads me to the window, where a bottle of nail polish, green this time, and small balls of cotton wool have been laid out for me to finish what I had started. Outside, a brightly painted sign smiles up at us mockingly: SUNSHINE MEMORIES PSYCHIATRIC CARE FACILITY. The steel legs of the sign are wrapped in barbed wire.

"They have had to buy a new sign six times this year. Last year, it was eight. Nobody here likes it, so finding new ways to destroy it keeps us clever."

"Have you ever tried?" I ask her, unscrewing the top of the nail polish.

The muscles in her neck betray how much she is struggling to look at me. "Before I made you stop visiting, my doctor tried to fix me using you. He told me that you qualified as a 'sunshine memory', so that focusing on earlier times with you would drown out the voices. It was so fucking painful. My head hurt all the time." She coughs a soft cough. "And then you were gone and there was only that useless signboard left, and the dust would get washed off it when it rained and it just would not stop laughing at me. So I found where they had hidden the big flowerpots, and I rolled one over there and threw it at the sign. It stood at about your height then. I managed to create a dent the size of my head, and destroy half the paint job. I haven't gone near it since."

I hold her gaze until I cannot anymore, then I drop the bottle on purpose. It shatters on the concrete floor and the glass glistens in beautiful puddles of green. My first instinct is to wipe the floor clean with my tongue, but I reach for the cotton balls instead. I wonder why lying does not come to her as easily as it does to me.

She gets up and walks to the other end of the room, making sure I know from the heaviness of her footsteps that she expects me to join her when I am finished. I throw the green wads away and leave, not even breaking my step when she says, "Baby, I have a plan for us." To hell with her plan.

I visit her two days a week after she is admitted, even though she cannot hear me anymore. I never go with my father; he picks me up an hour after he leaves me with her.

"Has she gone deaf?" I ask him more than once.

"No, love. She just needs time," he says, and I do not push because he has come to hate the sound of his own voice. I try to take her my bedroom clock, which I cannot read yet, but the orderlies check the big bag I try to smuggle inside and return it to my father.

I take to watching her face and making up the conversations she is having with the ocean-voices. Over time, I speak these made-up conversations out loud, pretending I am in sync with the voices so that occasionally, she may catch mine. And she does, on the afternoon we are lying on the trampoline in the garden with my ear resting on her stomach. Her hunger from a skipped meal interrupts the jokes I am exchanging with myself. So I say, "There's a helicopter in your tummy, mummy," for my own entertainment, and then I am flying and she is clawing at her stomach the way I had seen her go at her ears. "How? How did it get in there, you bitch?!" she screams in the direction she threw me. The orderlies came running out for her, and she spends the next five weeks plugging her belly button with her finger in case something else tries to find its way in.

"Perhaps it would be a good idea to stop visiting for a while," one doctor tells my father. "Your daughter's imagination is detrimental to your wife's health." If my father says yes then, it will destroy me. Ma, even in her silence, is a loudness I miss sorely.

"No," he says, offering no further explanation, and for the first time, I forgive his brevity.

After that, I try to stop imagining dialogues out loud when I am with her. Whenever I find myself itching to, I remember the inside of the freezer, and write about the things I think I saw. Sometimes, I make up songs about them. This is how, on another afternoon, I am too pre-occupied to notice her lifting a flowerpot half my size and hurling it at me until it knocks me off the bench I am sitting on. I scrape my arm on the bench's sharp edge on the way down, but all I can do is sing louder and louder. She probably does not say, "You stupid child, I never want to hear you again!", maybe it is just my singing that takes her words and strangles them into what I hear. My father is called. "We cannot come back for a while," he tells me as we drive past the Sunshine Memories sign. I nod. A while becomes never.

"*D*o you know what blue sounds like?" This time, the nail polish is a garish orange, but the blue on the first three remains.

"Water. Sadness. Peace. Stillness?"

"I love you," she says, her words mingling with a beautiful laugh that makes me warm behind my eyes and in my ears. "Blue only sometimes sounds like water, but if it sounds like stillness, it cannot sound like water. It's not often you find perfectly still waters," she says. She sounds old and sagely, which I suppose she must be, and I resent that I could not watch age come to her.

"And sometimes blue *does* sound like sadness, but I have never had a sadness that is peaceful. Have you?"

I do not answer, and the question mark sits between us until I have painted her toenails, too. Her feet, unlike mine, are still smooth. They feel like butter. Yellow must sound like her feet.

She tries something else. "You know, I used to think I was a mermaid when I was a child. That is how I would explain the sound of waves in my ears. When the ocean-voices came, it felt like other mermaids were finally speaking back to me."

"What would they say?" I asked, not really wanting to know but knowing she wants me to wonder.

"They would remind me to do the things I used to do before my baba left, learning from my body's muscle memory. But things work differently in the water than they do here, and when I found I could not move the way they wanted me to, or breathe the way they told me to, all I wanted to do was to get them out." She clenches her toes together – I get some orange on the skin of her tiniest one. "Eventually my doctor gave up on sunshine memories.

Instead, he tried to teach me to make them say what I needed them to say to make me better."

"Did it work?" I ask, stupidly, because this is how the conversation is supposed to go.

She smiles curiously. "I'm still here, aren't I?"

"Are they here now? Can they hear me?"

"They have become me. And I, them. Who do you think is talking to you right now?"

I have so many questions, but the time to learn my mother well enough to ask them is long gone. Suddenly, I want to know what they – Ma, the ocean-voices – think of my baking. I promise myself to make two of anything, or maybe even three, so I can leave one at home for later.

*M*y father has guessed by now that I spend my days with her. He seems hurt by this – not that I see her, but that I came back to see her – but like always, he says nothing. I know he knows because my pancakes are smaller, and he waits until I have left the house to play the piano. The photo of my stepmother and me has quietly disappeared.

*M*a tries other ways to stop the ocean-voices long before she tries to freeze them. Sometimes, she suddenly ends her day in the middle of it and closes her bedroom door behind her. After I have waited long enough to be prudent, I find her in bed, her face contorted in pain from fierce migraines. Later, she undresses and inspects herself all over, then asks me to check if her back is leaking. "You'll know if it is different from sweat," she insists. But sweat is all I see. I even taste it to make sure.

*I*t takes a fractured father, a flowerpot, a dead stepmother, a college degree (almost), several border crossings, a permanent residence application and a short stint with a married man for me to realise what she had been doing. When my baby is stillborn, I spend a week in bed before I discover it is physically possible, through an excruciatingly painful *process, to purge memory forever. One has to accumulate memories of every size from every reachable time, and stockpile them so that the brain bulges and tires. Once saturated with them, the brain contracts like a muscle and the unwanted memory seeps out every which way it can. Ma was right: you would know if it is different from sweat, or tears, or piss. But Ma was wrong, too: this only works for memories, not for voices that do not require memories to sustain them. I never forget I had a baby, but I do not remember what I named it, or if I named it at all. I do not even remember its father's face. The art project and the accompanying story that pays the first and last month's rent for my apartment is a brain, shrivelled and painted grey from exhaustion, and a puddle of memories beneath it. The puddle is blue. I now wish I had left it colourless.*

She asks me to tell her about my life between the letter she sent me at nineteen and my appearance in front of her at thirty-two. At least she can look at me now. She is even doing my nails.

I tell her about my music, which I inherited from my father, and about my migraines, which I inherited from her. I take off my hat and show her the strands of hair on my head that are already greying. I show her that my drawing has become my living but I do not tell her why. In the privacy of her room, I show her that my pubic hair has all turned white already. I tell her that Meela loves it. While she examines it in awe – hers is still a dark, dark black – I tell her that Meela says she loves me. I read the short passage cut and pasted neatly on the wall above her bed:

> *But water always goes where it wants to go,*
> *and nothing in the end can stand against it.*
> *Water is patient.*
> *– Margaret Atwood,* The Penelopiad

She sees where I am looking and tries to glue my attention to it – "That's my plan" – but I keep talking, telling her my father is lonely and old. I do not mention my dead stepmother, but I show her where the scar used to be and after she asks and after I acquiesce, she licks its ghost. I tell her I have not been able to work in a long while, and that I am not sure I can go back to the things that have made my life. I do not tell her about the hours I spend shining a light into my belly button so I can find the dead skin to pick out. She asks me about my college years in South Africa, my growing years in Senegal and my now-years in Canada: *What did you get your degree in?* (I didn't graduate); *What is your furniture like?* (mismatched and functional); *What colour is your car?* (I sold it, I was broke, it was green, I cycle now); *What colour is your bike?* (also green); *Have you always lived alone?* (I briefly lived with a lover in Senegal, he worked for the WHO); *Do you have friends?* (sometimes).

By this time there are tears in my voice, and I am sitting on the floor between her legs while she braids my hair. As gently as she touches my head, she says, "I need to get out of here." At first I think she means her bedroom, and then I realise she means she needs out of Sunshine Memories. Perhaps this means I can never go back to Canada, but she hasn't stopped talking. She is saying something about furniture.

"The house needs new furniture." She has not seen the house in over twenty years. "The old furniture used to have fragments of my father and me living in its crevices, but he left mine in there. I want to get the rest of me back; I need to burn the furniture and let me out. And then the house will need new furniture, and we're going to China to get it."

I knew I had not wanted to hear her plan, but now it is sitting on my lap as if it were waiting for a hug and a kiss on its cheek. Already, I am tripping over the logistical hurdles in my head so I can rationalise out loud my inevitable rejection. She does not have a passport. She cannot apply for one as long as she is committed. I cannot get one for her because she is still legally under the charge of a man she has not seen or heard from in over a decade. Everything will need money – I have money, but barely enough for import charges and plane tickets and this is all impossible,

I don't even know why I am giving it this much thought like I am trying to convince myself, I just need to tell her no.

"How do you plan to get to China?" I hear myself asking, although I can guess at the answer already.

In my first year in South Africa, I had travelled to Grahamstown for an arts festival, where I watched a play about Makhanda, the Xhosa prophet. In the midst of their struggles against the British in the early 19th century, Makhanda believed that the god of the black people – Mdalidiphu, the god of the Deep – would finally help the Xhosa overcome the white people's conquest. The white people, he said, were held in disfavour by their own god, Thixo, who had banished them from their homeland across the waters for murdering his son. At the height of the war in 1819, Makhanda led the Xhosa in an attack against the British at their garrison in Grahamstown. They were defeated, and three months after the siege, Makhanda surrendered himself and was imprisoned on Robben Island. But like many in that fated prison, he didn't stop struggling. On Christmas Day of that year, Makhanda and thirty other men escaped the island by boat. But somewhere along the nine-kilometre stretch between the island and the mainland, the boat capsized, and Makhanda drowned. Many of the amaXhosa refused to believe he was dead: his funeral rites were only observed fifty years later, because his people still thought he would return.

Maybe he did, I thought, after I had watched the play.

When I eventually got back to Cape Town from that trip, Ma's letter for me was waiting. I filled my reply with stories I thought would not matter to her. I told her about the drowned prophet. She never forgot about him.

"The distance between the ports of Djibouti and Mawei is 6305 nautical miles. The voices know the way, they will take me." She says this with such conviction that I am finally forced to tell her that she is being ridiculous. "I do not want to die here, love," she says as stoically as she can, which is not at all, and I tell her she does not have to, but also that she is not going to China. I promise to speak to my father about getting her out, but we both see the problem: the only place she would have to go is the house with the chairs and beds and cupboards she refuses to return to if she cannot destroy them. I promise to look into getting new furniture, even though I know that is not the point.

Perhaps it is because her eyes harden that I miss the desperation. My father comes into the kitchen two nights later, as I pull three loaves of banana bread out of the oven.

"She finally found her way out."

I age quickly. Now it is six years since she set her own bed on fire and disappeared, and every day, I want to look for her. That same night, over slices of banana bread, my father and I sat at the dining table, that she had made, and decided against it. I told him she was going to China. He told me – I had never known this – about her hydrophobia, which I still think is a little silly. Who has ever heard of a mermaid afraid of water? I told him she was as much water now as the voices in her ears were. We told the police so that we could look concerned, but we knew they would never even try to find her. "There is too much crazy out there already for us to do anything about it," the inspector's eyes said, while his mouth promised she would not get past the border, even if she made it that far. It was late, so we did not contradict him.

We got rid of the furniture, and then the house. He and I parted ways for good. I now have a copy of *The Penelopiad* and an online subscription to every newspaper and magazine from Eritrea, Djibouti and Ethiopia I can find, but I have never actively sought her out. I convince myself that if she emerges somewhere, the people of that place cannot miss her and they will be unable to resist her, even though it is unreasonable to think so. In the years between the flowerpot and Laura Mvula on the radio, she had become less and less extraordinary.

Hans Christian Andersen once wrote about a beautiful, young woman on a ship, who is instructed to kill the man she loves when he marries another woman so that she may live. She cannot bring herself to do it, though, so at sunrise she throws the knife out to sea, kisses the man's forehead and flings herself overboard. She expects to turn into foam, perhaps the way the woman in Tse's story turns into a fish, or the way the waves in Ma's ears turned into voices.

Instead, the young woman becomes the wind, a daughter of the air. If Ma and her voices do not make it to China, I hope they at least find their way under the gaze of a sun hot enough to make them evaporate.

Native Mayonnaise

Thabo Jijana

*J*osiah, my brother, the first thing you can do to help your case is to admit that it was all your fault, that you should not have gone to your neighbour's house, that you danced too much at Polina's party, that you sat down on the sofa and thought it was your own bed, and that you woke up far too late to do anything about the warm puddle under you.

You might want to tell the policewoman at the reception area, "I mean every word, my sister." Don't forget to say "my sister" each time you say something, even if the officer is as young as your own last-born. Even when you're giving an answer, say, "That's right, my sister," or, "No, no, that is not how it happened, my sister," or, "My sister, give me a moment to explain."

It helps if it's not five in the morning, if your outfit does not leave something to be desired, and a pint of iqhilika is not among the things you desperately need at that moment. I know, the gatas will be here any moment, I know. What do you do? I will tell you what you do. Just listen to me.

Here, have this skyf first. I'll roll another one for myself.

We'll see their glowing lights when they come down the street, don't worry. They will stop at Polina's house first, anyway, and she'll point them to your dwelling, and when she does, that's that. We're going nowhere; even when they come, we'll sit here like there's no problem. We'll wait until we hear the plank gate groan open and we can see they have entered the yard. They have to act nice, otherwise they'll be in trouble with Sporty.

One of them will say, "Molweni ekhaya."

We will let a moment of silence pass and then you say, confidently, "Greetings to you too, young man."

"We're looking for Josiah Mtati," he says.

No introductions, no names, absolutely nothing for you to use if you want to get friendly with him. That's fine, we've met his type before.

You stand up and say, "Yes my dear officers, you have found the man you are looking for."

You walk with them to the khwela-khwela, all the while saying nice things to them, trying to speak like you have met them somewhere before. When you get off at the police station, do not pretend like maybe you are wondering where the policeman got his driving licence, even if you suspect one of your kidneys might not be functioning properly due to the amount of painful banging your ribs and back endured against the canopy. Be a happy chap, alright?

At this time you are brought to the reception area. Take off your newsboy cap when you walk through the door and smile kindly when you come before the policewoman: she must see your gold tooth, she must see how your hair is as white as snow. (And you better hope it's a woman, otherwise you're in big trouble, Josiah, my brother. These boys don't laugh, they don't make it easy on you when you want to make a case disappear.) She will probably have a youthful face, black like me, with relaxed hair that stops at the neck. She will say, probably, "Start from the beginning, meneer. Tell me what happened."

You smile – smile, Josiah. Smile every moment you can my brother: talk, pause and smile; smile, pause and be sad; smile, my brother, smile.

"You see my sister," you say, "Polina was having a party and she sent word around to her neighbours – I am one of her neighbours, you see; I live seven houses down from hers; on that street of ours, Yohane Street – and Polina says, my sister, Polina says that we must come tonight. She's having a big party, a party to celebrate her boy finishing university. So of course, my sister, we are happy for young Thando. We are happy to have a teacher in our street. So I take out my Sunday best, I take out my suit and I iron my tie and I polish my shoes until they shine like a car that is returning from the car wash."

You don't rush the telling of your story in the beginning, Josiah, my brother. You must make sure the policewoman is interested and that she wants to hear everything.

Maybe she will say, "Do you live here in Msobomvu?" You say yes, of course.

She wants to know what your section of the township is called. What is your house number?

You tell her all those things. And then she says, "You may continue."

Begin by how you left for the party, dressed in that brown checked blazer of yours, with a green shirt and red tie underneath, and those matching trousers that have to be folded twice at the hem otherwise they drag on the ground. Tell the policewoman you were looking like a younger Walter Sisulu with your light complexion and your eyeglasses and your hair combed and your mouth full of all its teeth.

You say, "Yes, my sister, so at six I hear the music already playing at loud volume and I decide the boring speeches must be over by now and maybe it's about time the plates are being handed out and the booze allocated, and maybe Polina is not worrying too much about who is attending and whether they brought a gift for young Thando or not."

You smile a little here. The policewoman doesn't, but there is no harm in that.

You say, "I get there and immediately young Thando comes to shake hands with his uncles and of course I call him over and I say hello. I tell him, 'You've gotten quite chubby, my boy! What were they feeding you at school?' He laughs with me. The boy is happy. And that is when I ask to see the insides of his pockets. He grimaces and says a bucket of traditional brew will be out shortly, but no, I tell him, I'm looking for the good stuff. I say, 'You came out of these hands my boy', and as I say this I'm holding my hands before my chest so that young Thando can see my palms. I say to him, 'Are you going to turn around and be ungrateful?' He's still a laaitie this boy – you know, meek as a sheep, my sister – and I figure I can get one beer, maybe two, out of him before the party really gets noisy."

Pause and smile here, Josiah my brother. Pause and smile.

You say, "He tells me he will see what he can do, that he will be back in a moment. A while later he returns with a jug of Paarl Perle and I don't complain. I'm excited as a mosquito. Young Thando has served his purpose, and I pat him on the back and never see him again in all of last night."

You must be sure not to be too slow with your storytelling Josiah my brother, otherwise you will tire the policewoman too much too early. Say something now to show that you are going somewhere with your story. Say something like, "Or so I thought." Or, "That was not the last time I saw young Thando, not after what happened last night."

"What happened later last night?" she will say.

You will say, "Polina. Polina happened."

"What do you mean 'Polina happened'?" she will ask.

"I tell you, sister, that woman has wanted to see my bedroom since I arrived here and she won't give up until I do as she wants me," you will say.

If she asks "What do you mean she wants to see your bedroom?", you must pause for a moment and stare mischievously into her eyes, so that she knows exactly what you mean. Be clear that where you come from for a woman to want to see your bedroom, there is only one way to see your bedroom, and that is if you, the man, take her to see your bedroom. Say this with only your eyes as much as possible, Josiah, my brother. Play with your cap if you must, but smile – don't forget to smile.

"The thing is, my sister," you will say, "I arrived here from Rooikoppies and Polina was—"

The policewoman will likely interrupt you. "Where is that?" she will say.

"Where is what?" you will say.

"The place you just mentioned now."

"You mean Rooikoppies?"

"Yes," she will say, "that place."

"You have not heard of Marikana before?" you will say with surprise in your voice.

"Oh," she will say, "you meant that?"

"Yes, yes," you will say. "Forgive me. I call Marikana by the old name, Rooikoppies. It means 'red hills', my sister. Not because of the miners' blood, no, no – it's the minerals in the soil, is why."

If she is the curious type, and you better hope she is, now she might say to you, "What was your occupation? What did you do there?"

"Ndandiligoduka," you will say. A migrant labourer. There is nothing wrong with telling her about your life back in Marikana, Josiah, or to be nostalgic. Maybe you can tell her, "You know, my sister, when I started as a rock driller, our supervisor, a white man named Marius, would tell us that when his own father had his job in the mines he would go down into the tunnels with a canary bird, and when it died they knew there was very little oxygen down there and so it was unsafe to work there. But Marius lied sometimes and so I didn't trust that story." Smile, Josiah, and say, "Mining is like separating peanuts from raisins, really – if you know what I mean."

If you're lucky she'll smile back and say, "Continue your story." And you will.

"Polina was the first woman to come and shake my hand," you'll say. "It had been many years since her husband died. She told me herself. She said she had come to welcome me as her new neighbour."

Possibly the policewoman will then ask you, "How did you come to live here?"

If there is a time to be dejected, Josiah, my brother, it is now. Be gloomy, yes. A look of deep reflection in your eyes.

"Ah, my sister, it is a long story that one." You should pause a moment here. "The short answer is that I was out of work. The strike, the killings, and all that. But the long answer is that I had been coughing for months long before the strike and the cough would not disappear. None of the herbal medicines I used had worked. So I thought it best to go to the clinic there in Rooikoppies, and they told me I had the illness of the lungs. By then I had worked in the mines since I was a young man and saw it proper to retire from work when that strike happened."

She will probably nod, with a shadow of pity on her face, and you take this to mean you should carry on.

"That house is my sister's house, but she has always been a village girl. She had come here to work in the kitchens, for the madams, and when she grew tired of the city, she left. By the time I arrived, she had been living back home in Tsomo, in the Transkei – you know the Transkei, mos? but of course you do, my sister, what I am asking – she had lived there in Tsomo for two years."

You don't need to tell her that your sister is the only sibling you have still alive, your three brothers all dead; that you are the youngest at home; that you are sixty-one now; that your wife Notiliti died young; that you have a yard full of brick houses back in Tsomo, houses that are now occupied by your sister and one of the children Notiliti begat you. You only have to focus on the story about Polina. So now you say, "Yes, my sister, that is how I came to live here."

"You were telling me about this lady," she will say. "You were telling me about this Polina." But do not jump straight into the incident at Polina's house, no. Go back to when you arrived here from the mines. Go back to those years when Polina befriended you.

You say, "I wanted to beat the illness of the lungs, of course. I wanted not to cough anymore. At the clinic here, they told me about the pills and a lady came to my house every week to put a thing here on my chest and listen to my lungs, or else she would put a thing in my mouth and tell me to breathe hard, and after that she would speak to me like she was speaking to a child, telling me she was not satisfied that I was not doing well, that I was not honest with her and taking my pills like she told me to, and that I would not be free of the cough if I continued to behave like that. It took me a long time before I began to take my pills faithfully, and finally I was in the pink of health."

Pause.

You should keep the rest of your story brief. You do not need to tell her, for example, how you met me at the vegetable garden at Sebenzani Primary, and that we were the most senior of the garden's members. The policewoman will probably not want to know about the visit Minister Moshoeshoe made last August to donate a water tank and wheelbarrows and pipes and all sorts of tools to our group.

You do not need to tell the policewoman that a young woman from the newspaper called you aside and asked you what challenges we had faced in our agricultural endeavours at Sebenzani. "Water," you said, "that is the biggest problem in Msobomvu my child. We have a great shortage of it."

The young woman from the newspaper wanted to know how we managed.

"We have to fill containers at the communal tap outside the school each day," you said, "and then transport them in wheelbarrows to water our plots."

"This must be hard work for you," she said.

"Yes, yes, that is true," you said. "You see my child, the communal taps are never without long queues of people, and everyday women are doing their clothes-washing there or filling their own containers for daily use. You get there at noon maybe and often you do not return to the garden until after the children have left school and gone home.

"Just because of the long lines of people?" she asked.

"Well, yes my child," you said, "but also because the water comes out so slowly, so slowly that an earthworm slithers faster out of its burrowing hole – if you hear me clearly; the water does not gush out of the taps fast enough, is what I'm trying to say. An hour goes by and your container is only half-filled. So the water tank the minister has gifted us with today will be a big help. We are thankful to the government."

The policewoman will not care to know that, inside a marquee that had been erected on the school sports ground, Minister Moshoeshoe addressed us at lunchtime. She will not care to know how his words inspired mixed reactions in us when he concluded his speech by saying, "God helps those who help themselves, and so does your government. The youth of today loaf on street corners and then they complain about lack of jobs. You have shown them that there is always work to be found, if they have the energy and motivation to look for it. It is their loss if they do not look at you and follow your example."

The policewoman will not want to hear about the picture that young woman from the newspaper took of you and me while a grinning Minister Moshoeshoe pressed into the ground a fork spade, our names mentioned in full alongside the minister's the next day: *Senior members of the garden group, Mr Xabiso Mtati (in blazer) and Mr Vulisango Jela (in cardigan), are seen here with Ernest Moshoeshoe, the Minister of Health, at yesterday's hand-over ceremony. Minister Moshoeshoe praised the group's members and encouraged other residents of Msobomvu Township to grow their own vegetables as this would go a long way in helping them lead a healthy lifestyle.* Instead, maybe you can say something about Polina. You must know her real name is Pauline Plaatjie, and that every person here calls her Polina because it was what her own mother, a black woman who had been fathered by a Griqua chief with that surname, called her when she was still alive. You have to mention that Polina has skin the colour of coffee when mixed with Cremora; that she always wears pants, never a skirt, and a smart afro wig, and regularly paints her nails a pinkish red. Say she looks the part of an old dignified church woman, the kind you could have made your wife in another lifetime. Do not say anything about Polina's brother and sister and how they rarely visit her, even though Polina is older than all of them. You may want to say a word or two about Polina's late husband, a municipal worker who died of diabetes in 1998, leaving Polina with Emihle, a divorcee who runs a day-care centre out of a plank shack behind Polina's house, and of course young Thando, the pride of Yohane Street.

It may be wise to not discuss your own children: the eldest Lizeka, married to a man in Uitenhage and with her own troubles; Zonwabele, a bus driver back in Tsomo; and Khangelani, your last-born and the apple of your eye.

Say nothing of how overjoyed you were when Khangelani

arrived here in Msobomvu in the year you slayed a bull in your yard and made room for your ancestors in your house. You will not discuss how prosperous you were then, when your son had just become a delivery driver for a bread company and took a beautiful city girl for a wife, and your moolah from the mines arrived and so you bought a van and sent two Jerseys back to Tsomo, where you had added another rondavel to your yard.

You will not discuss your blossoming friendship with Polina. You will not discuss how in the early days the whole of Yohane Street was abuzz with the news of your romance after your van was seen in her yard on many a night, or how it was Polina who made you join the vegetable garden in the first place and fetched you from your house each morning and afternoon when she was coming to water her seedlings and you yours.

At that time, Khangelani and his wife were living with you in a back room you had built for them behind your own house. That was when it happened, the thing that set you down this path. You will not touch the incident from before, when you were not so fond of the drink as you are now.

You were a good man Josiah, my brother – you are still a good man. A good man who knew how to look after himself and his house, a good man who went to church and became a good friend to all his neighbours, a good man better than me in so many ways. That is the Josiah I know. That is the Josiah we still see in you.

How could you have known his wife would leave him one night, breaking his heart and sending him to the bottle, and that a month later he would be lying in the mortuary, dead from a knife wound – all because of an argument with a friend of his over soccer? That was when you became a friend of the bottle yourself, Josiah, my brother. We have watched you lose yourself, little by little, over the years: first the car, then some furniture of your house, and now yourself. It was you who chose to stay away from Polina's bed. Yohane Street cries with you. Polina cries with you. I cry with you.

You could not have helped it, Josiah my brother. Your son's

death as much as tonight's incident. Tell this to the policewoman, at least. Tell her you could not have helped it.

*O*h, yes, the policewoman... well, she should be thoroughly weary of standing on the same spot and listening to your story by now, anyhow.

If the police picked you up at this hour, which is what we expect if we should believe that Polina has already called them – if they come at the time we expect them to come, which means you could be at the police station just before midnight – then the policewoman will not want you to make the first hours of her Saturday morning too busy. It's weekend. There is too much trouble in the streets for her to waste an hour on you and your trivial matter, I am sure of that. So it's best, Josiah, my brother, that you do not make things difficult for her. Be the exception. Make her feel like she was lucky to get a visit from you, and use whatever time you stand before him to tell your story and to tell it successfully.

It should not surprise you at all if at this point the policewoman wants you to get to the end of your story. In fact, you ought to expect that at this point that is what she will say.

"The party meneer," perhaps she will say. "Make your statement. What happened at the party?"

"The party, yes, my sister," you'll say. "It is eight or maybe nine last night and the yard is swarming with people, young people mostly who are making a lot of noise, and the few old men yet to leave for their homes are getting quite concerned at how the young people are behaving, so one by one we get up from our stools and we search for the gate. I had only wanted to go and say goodbye to Polina. I don't remember clearly how it happened. I must have met Emihle. That is Polina's daughter. She is a cheeky one, my sister. We're at the dining room. There are a lot of people and loud music is playing. Here she comes; she holds my hand as if in greeting. She says, 'I know you are a good dancer.' And that is when the problem starts."

I doubt the policewoman will care to hear if you are a good dancer or not, so what is wise at this point, Josiah, my brother, is to run through the dancing part. You asked Emihle to back off, and as you stood there before all of them in the dining room, you danced as in the old ways of our bare-chested ancestors in the villages, with strings of beads draped over their bodies down to the waist, the tops of their doeks spiky like the peaks of Mount Tsatsana. Tell the policewoman everyone cheered you on. Tell her you bopped and hopped and swayed joyously for a very long time. Tell her you had fun. Tell her by the time you finished your dance, you had either forgotten about Polina or had been quite taken by the contents of the glass Emihle had thrust into your hand the moment you sat down on the sofa. Tell her this is when your recollection of tonight's events becomes cloudy.

You had closed your eyes and a short while later you opened them and there was young Thando standing over you, shouting and laughing too. Your mind had cleared and you could see that the party was long over, the dining room emptied of all its lively occupants a moment before. You rose from the sofa, and that's when young Thando said something to his mother.

You repent to the policewoman at this point. The dance wore you out. The stained sofa. Such shame in your heart.

You'll say, "I did wrong my sister. I knew I was reeling drunk. I should have just gone home, but I didn't and that was the problem."

Tell her about how young Thando called me at home five houses down and I came to fetch you.

Tell her, "I had been together with Jela – Jela is my friend, my sister, we know each other from back home in the villages. He has a thick moustache and likes to wear a balaclava folded in half so that it is no different to a knitted cap, even on days when it's very hot outside. Jela was the one who was with me when your people came to fetch me at my house; everyone calls him by his surname, Jela." Pause. Do not get too sidetracked, Josiah, my brother. Continue: "I was saying I had been together with Jela at the party. Jela had left Polina's party early, intoxicated too, but probably not as much as I was."

It is probably best that you not tell her that Polina addressed us as we walked out of the door, my right arm kneaded under your left armpit so as to offer you support until we got to the gate and, after that, to the stoep of your house, exactly where we are sitting at this moment, right after you went into the house and changed into a pair of clean overalls, and then you joined me outside and we rolled our cigarettes and waited for the gatas to arrive.

Don't tell the policewoman that Polina said, "I don't know why Jela is taking you home since the police are on the way. I have already called them. He should just let you stay here so they may find you easily."

Don't tell the policewoman that you told Polina, "Woman, I know what you want. You'll get it, don't worry. You're going to get it."

Don't repeat for the policewoman how insulted Polina was at your words, raising her voice when she told you, "You have to pay Josiah. You damaged my property. I called the police just now. They will be here any moment."

Don't tell her Polina was a little drunk too. Don't tell her we didn't believe she had ever called the police to begin with.

If you are lucky, Josiah, my brother, your statement will now be noted down in full, and you shall have to wait only a moment before you are told to find a chair in the waiting area and sit there until you can be taken home, or until it is light enough outside that you can go home on your own. Only then can you be truly out of trouble, Josiah, my brother, much as the policewoman might say there is still a possibility that another call could be made to your house in the week that follows.

If you leave at daybreak, which is what you should expect, you are likely to see the young policeman who came to fetch you at your own house as he enters the police station at the same time that you are leaving.

Maybe he will say in jest, "I see you are lucky, old man. You will not be staying over at our hotel for the weekend."

Smile at him, like I have been telling you, Josiah, my brother. Smile at him and go about your way.

Should you see Polina after you get off the taxi and are walking down Yohane Street towards your own house, it will be a blessing in disguise for you, Josiah, my brother. Probably she will already be awake and out in the front yard, gathering into black rubbish bags the bottles and the paper plates and broken bones from the night before. As you walk past her gate, Josiah, my brother, I suggest you slow down your stride, that you raise your head and greet Polina a cheery good morning.

Call her by name and then – waving lovingly – say, "Ah, my dear friend." And smile, Josiah, my brother. Smile.

Urgency

Mark Mngomezulu

*A*ll I want to do is piss, but I can't because the kombi is in full speed towards Johannesburg. On the last piss station, at Middelburg, I went to the toilet and pushed out every drop of water that was in me. After washing my hands, when I was about to leave, I felt that unmistakable tingling sensation: a few droplets left in my shaft. I returned to the urinal stall again. The gigantic Afrikaner man in the stall next to mine, who'd seen me practising the absurdity of washing my hands before urinating, looked at me quizzically and asked, "Is jy okay?" I don't speak Afrikaans, but I at least knew what he'd asked. I was fine, I said, zipping up my jeans and going to wash my hands again. He just smiled at me, for some reason.

I am afraid to ask the driver to stop at a filling station, or just on the side of the road so that I can piss. You see, everyone who's travelled to Jo'burg from Mbabane on a kombi knows that there are two pissing points: one at the Ngwenya Border Gate and one at the Middelburg Ultra City. Then you just have to keep it in until you get to Johannesburg, the city of more than one kind of gold. Those are the rules. Every traveller knows them. I know them. Besides, the other passengers would eat me alive if I asked the driver to stop. There is a man who asked the driver to step on it just after we left the border post. He needs to get to Jozi on time for a connection to Mahikeng. "I am on the morning shift tomorrow!" he announced loudly. Judging by his s-curled hair, gold bracelet and matching necklace dangling around his neck, he is a miner. They all look the same, these miners, with a penchant for gold accessories and extra-gelled hair. Each profession has a kind of uniform, you see. Lawyers with their dull-coloured suits and their briefcases, and their noses facing upwards as if to breathe a different kind of air. Or professors with their old jerseys and unkemptness. Or primary school teachers with their cheap formal shirts.

But, man, do I need to piss all of a sudden. When we left Middelburg I was fine. I was enjoying the conversations in the kombi. Sometimes when I go to Jozi I bring a book, thinking that it will come in handy during the long journey, but the passengers never allow me to read. Not physically, of course, but because they render even the best detective novel dull in comparison. But today I'd do anything for a book. Anything to distract myself. You see, I have always had a weak bladder and, recognising my weakness, I never drink more than one bottle of water before a journey such as this. Usually I turn out okay. But today, no, I am just like a leaking bucket. You can cover the crack with Bostik and duct-tape, but the water will still seep out somehow.

My concentration has broken down completely. I can feel the piss pushing and pushing inside my belly. I take a deep breath and hold it in, while simultaneously closing my thighs and tensing up my muscles. The pressure is relieved for five seconds or so, but when I breathe out the sting returns. I turn my ear to the other passengers, and I hope to catch an interesting conversation to take my mind off things. Anything to stop wondering what it would be like to become the first person in the world to die from holding in their pee.

There is a man with seven large dreadlocks on his head, each like the frond of an aloe, but light brown and streaked with grey. He has been speaking to the driver loudly ever since we left Mbabane: "Yes," he says, "Haile Selassie is the Lion of Judah – an incarnation, *mahn!* No man nah got to shave his head. Remember the story of Samson in Judges?" The driver has not said much in return, only laughing at the Rasta every now and again. But now the Rasta is annoyed by the conversation of two young boys sitting just behind him. He keeps turning towards them and giving them the eye. But the two lads are not paying him any attention.

"No, no, *skeem,*" the smaller one says, "a Maserati can accelerate to 120 in less than six seconds! Now that is a car and a half! Driving around Sandton in that one – bra wami, what can I say? – panties drop." The other laughs deeply, like he has an amplifier in his throat. For a few seconds all the other conversations in the taxi die out in deference to it.

"Whatever," he says once he's done laughing. "That car has no class, and you know it. Now, the Merc AMG. *Wuu*! Now, *that* is a car. It has everything: horse-power, turbos, space inside to host more than one girl. It's a hotel on wheels. The leather seats! Think of the possibilities!"

I can see the Rasta from the rear-view mirror, his face like a stepped-on Coca-Cola can on the side of the street. His dreads sway left and right, in unhidden contempt at every sentence coming out of the boy's mouth. The large boy laughs again and the Rasta turns to him.

"*Shaarraap*!" he roars, his eyes like a headmaster's in front of a skiver. "Stop this silliness! Talking about cars like you own them. Ee! Can you bhantintis even drive in the first place?" Silence envelops the kombi.

"Ja," the Rasta says after a moment. "That's what I thought. You are in this khohloliya kombi with us, but you are too busy *pra-pra-pra*, Maserati this, AMG that, Porsche that, *nyef-nyef-nyef*! I am sick of it. Gatvol!" He smacks his chin with the back of his hand. "That is why you will end up stealing cars and becoming gangsters. 26s and 28s, and all of that shit." The boys are sitting back in their seats, eyes wide open. "So," the Rasta continues, "if you dare open your stupid little mouths again, I want to hear only three things from you: Mickey-Mouse, Smoothies and Fizz-Pops!" The Rasta faces the front again, and reclines back on his seat. He closes his eyes, as if meditating on the silence that lingers after the echoes of his voice disappear.

But the silence doesn't last long: all the passengers explode into laughter, much to the embarrassment of the boys. I also want to laugh, but I understand the danger that might come with it in my present situation. We are in Daveyton now, just the beginning of Jozi, about thirty minutes until we get to the Wanderers taxi rank, where I'll get off.

You can only hold it for twenty minutes, says the voice in my head. *Twenty-five, tops*. I lean on the seat in front of me and keep my hands firmly on my stomach, fighting against the rumble of the suspension. I see an empty 500ml spring water bottle rolling on the floor. For a moment I consider it. I guess I could just take that bottle and… urinate in it? But there are fifteen other people in this kombi. And I'm sitting next to a woman. Mxm, you still have time for manners when you are dying.

The woman next to me puts her hand on my back. "Are you okay, my son?"

I plaster a smile on my face. "I'm okay, *make.*" She nods and smiles. I turn to face her properly. There's a feast on her lap: a KFC pack rests on her handbag next to her belly, with a two-litre Coca-Cola held between her considerable thighs. She takes big gulps from the bottle in between bites of the chicken. The kombi judders over a rough bit of the highway. I watch the bubbles rise and the brown-black liquid slosh and foam in the bottle. The inside of me feels like it's about to explode, about to shoot out of me like a bottle that's been shaken up. I need to piss, I need to piss. I close my eyes. I avert my gaze. I can't piss now.

I can't piss, I can't piss.

I had trouble with wetting the bed until I was in Grade 6. When I was smaller I wet my sheets almost every night, until my mother resorted to making me wear a waterproof diaper to bed. As I grew older I refused to wear these things: they were more embarrassing than wetting the bed. On one of her visits – I must have been ten, then – my aunt made me eat a wasps' nest before I went to bed. It was the only cure, she said. She'd gotten rid of all the wasps, of course, but there were dozens of little larvae still inside. They popped under my teeth. I wanted to throw up, but my aunt sat in front of me, making sure I ate everything. I went to bed picking out pieces of pasty wood from my teeth.

The morning after, I woke up dry. My aunt celebrated, told me that she told me so. It had worked.

And then the next day I was wet again.

"He is just a lazy child," my aunt concluded. Everyone agreed. What was so difficult about waking up in the middle of the night and going to the toilet, just like everyone else did? "Yes," she argued, "we all like the warmth of the blankets, but we go to the bathroom in the right place because that is the way it is."

But I don't think I was lazy. In my dreams, I was pissing in the right place. In this one dream I remember vividly, I was with friends playing at the Coronation Park. We had played ourselves dog-tired, our sweat-soaked T-shirts clinging to our bodies like paint. We then sat staring at the blue sky, our little bodies satisfied by the pleasure of the swings, the roundabouts, the see-saws. After a drink of water out of a tap, I asked my friends if they needed to pee, too. So we went to the edge of the park, pulled down our shorts, and let go.

When I woke up, I realised I'd have to wash my sheets. Again.

*S*uddenly we all jerk forward. The young boys curse. Others call their dead ancestors. Nginginini! Bhodloza! The woman next to me with the KFC calls on Jesus. The driver swiftly apologises: "Argh, man, that truck driver didn't indicate!"

We have just passed East Gate Mall. We are at the heart of Jozi now. City of Gold. Gauteng. Maboneng. The place that Swazis go to and come back home trying to impress us with their broken Zulu and mumbo-jumbo Sotho-Tswana. Fifteen minutes to Park Station without traffic. Or roadblocks. Lord, no – please, no road blocks today.

*T*here was this other time that someone tried to fix my bed-wetting problem. I was sleeping over at Mluga's house with his younger brother Sabza. They were the only friends of mine who knew about my leaking problem, and that night they had devised a way to stop it – at least for that night.

When I heard the plan, however, I thought I'd rather wear a diaper. "Come on man," Mluga said. "It's not a big deal. It's going to work perfectly, you'll see." Sabza just stared at me with his warm, big eyes; and foolishly enough I agreed to their plan.

Before we went to bed, sometime just before midnight, Sabza went to the kitchen cupboard and came back with a short length of cotton thread, the kind you would use to sew together a hole in a sock. I took off my pants and Mluga instructed Sabza to then tie the string around the end of my foreskin. One time, two times, three times the string went around, before he tied the knot. One time, two times, three times he knotted it over, to make sure it would hold under pressure. Both Mluga and Sabza inspected the knot, before declaring that it would do.

"Now you won't wet our sheets," Mluga said. "You'll feel the water, but then you'll be able to go to the bathroom and just untie the string. Easy-peasy." He sounded like a salesman reading out a TV manual.

"This will train you to keep it in," Sabza reassured me. "It totally works. I have seen it work before, on Mjava."

"Who?" I asked, looking at my foreskin and the tiny end of the knot I'd have to untangle when the water woke me up.

"A cousin of a cousin," Sabza said, turning to his brother. Mluga nodded. Something told me they were lying, but their faces looked so sincere. In the worst case, they were just trying to help me. We'd been friends for a long time, after all, and they'd never told anyone else about my problem. I could trust them.

A few hours later, I woke up. The cotton string was cutting through my foreskin, which had bulged like a balloon with pee that couldn't escape. It felt unreal: as a child I was such a deep sleeper that it took a few moments for the pain to finally come through to me. But when it did, I squealed like a pig, holding my engorged penis under the blanket in shock.

I threw off the blanket to inspect it, being careful not to move too much. The lights were already on because Mluga was afraid of sleeping in the dark, and when I pulled down my shorts the sight of it almost gave me a stroke. It looked like a taunted bullfrog, throbbing like a heart, waiting to explode in anger.

I called to the double bed across the room. "Sabza! Mluga!" Tears welled in my eyes. They didn't respond. One of them was snoring.

"Guys!" I called again, this time shouting in half-panic.

"What?" croaked Mluga, irritated.

"My thing," I said. "It's sick." My eyes bounced back and forth between it and Mluga's face, which was peeking out, half-exposed, from under a blanket.

"Of course it's sick," he said. "It passes water without a push." Sabza had also woken up, and was resting the side of his head on his arm, looking towards me. He and Mluga were suddenly convulsing with a hissing laughter, the kind that bored teenagers do in church when they hear the pastor make a double-entendre, or mispronounce a word. I was astonished. I felt like I was dying, and now my friends found it funny? Was I dreaming?

"You are not going to die," said Sabza, coolly, like a doctor speaking to a patient. "Look, we found a way to help you, and it has worked!" He chuckled. "Now you just need to go to the bathroom and untie the knot. We will tie another one after you are done."

At that point I burst into tears. Not the loud bawls that old women do at funerals, but just a normal kind of crying, with tears flowing down my cheeks silently like small waterfalls. I couldn't look at my penis anymore, its veins now all popped-up and green, twisting and turning like contour lines. It was only then that my friends took me seriously, scrambling towards me like they were on a race for the last plates of pudding.

Mluga was frowning. "It's your fault, Sabza," he said. "You said we must do this." I folded up my legs like an okapi knife. It felt like the cotton knot had been swallowed by the bulge. When Mluga tried to pull on it, I cried out loud.

At that moment there was a voice at the door. "What is happening here, now?" Mluga and Sabza's mother asked. "Eh?" The doek on her head covered her eyebrows. She pushed it up with one hand. "This noise in the middle of the night! Are you boys crazy?" There was a silence in the room like the moments before a judge delivers their verdict to a courthouse.

"Mlungisi! Sabelo! Answer me, mani!" Their full names. No matter how badly this turned out for me, I knew it was also going to be bad for them. So I raised my voice like a drunk disturbing the speeches at a wake. "They tied my gwayi-gwayi with a string!" I screamed. "They said it would help me not to wet myself!"

"*What?*" Mrs Mvubu glared at her sons as if she was already imagining a punishment for them. Maybe the belt. Maybe making them start a fire with green grass and wet branches. She moved towards me and inspected my injury. If she was scared, she didn't show it. She picked me up in her powerful arms and hauled me to the bathroom. The sudden movement made me go faint, so much so that I couldn't stand in front of the toilet when she put me down. So she moved me to the bathtub. She undressed me and made me sit with my legs crossed, my gwayi-gwayi resting like a water balloon on the cold ceramic. She turned to the cupboard and came back holding a blade from Mr Mvubu's razor.

It was as if she had done this before. In one palm she delicately held my gwayi-gwayi, and with the other hand expertly ran the sharp edge of the blade against the cotton thread until suddenly it snapped. Piss, yellow from the Coca-Cola we'd been drinking all day, shot out of me like water from a hosepipe.

People like to say "What a relief!" for even the most banal happenings. Like catching the right taxi, or finding one more egg in the cupboard. But I can tell you, from that day, I have known exactly what a relief really felt like.

*T*he driver manoeuvres the vehicle under the Park Station concourse, between columns of human beings and buses and cars, all hauling or packed with luggage. Every time I come to Jozi, I think of Noah and all the animals in the Ark. That must have been some noise pollution, something like the cacophony of this city.

Finally the kombi stops, and the man sitting next to the door slides it open with a heavy click. A group of men rush forward, and offer to carry my fellow passengers' goods for them, to wherever their transfer is. They negotiate a price. They coax. Some try to carry people's stuff by force. The driver gets out his door, his fist raised above his head, telling them to bugger off before he calls the police. I stay in my seat, letting everyone go out before me. I need a straight line. I can't afford any delays.

Slowly I rise from my seat, careful not to make any sudden movements. A man appears in front of me, offering to carry my gym bag. I raise my face into the worst scowl I can possibly make. In the mood I'm in, it's not difficult. "Ke sharp, my outjie," I say. It works. He buggers off.

I turn and go down a flight of concrete steps just behind where the kombi is parked. There are men and women hawking all sorts of stuff here. I pick my way through them carefully, avoiding their wares and eyes, lest they think I am interested. At the bottom of the stairs, to the left, I see the sign – two yellow stick-men, one naked, and one wearing a triangle in the middle of its body. It's not a relief yet. A stench of filth rises to greet me – dirt and chlorine and shit – but right now I really don't care. I walk towards the signs, counting my steps.

Finding Mermaids

Chido Muchemwa

"*M*ermaids? Who the fuck still believes in mermaids?" I said it under my breath, but still glanced at my mother in the passenger's seat. I shouldn't have been concerned. She had fallen asleep again. Since the funeral she had mostly slept, snatched into long deep slumbers whenever there was silence. I remember reading once that when small children are worried, they sleep because it's the only way that they can deal with their lack of control over the situation. Maybe that's what Mum was doing.

Thirty-eight days before, my father, Baba, had died. Thirty-nine days before, I had left America with an expired visa knowing that I wouldn't be going back. And now here I was headed to Manicaland with the mother who had never supported this "journalism nonsense" of mine, in search of mermaids for a story. There had been a series of mysterious drownings in one of the small villages. The villagers thought mermaids were responsible. I was to interview one of the residents who had apparently been returned by the mermaids thirty years before. They weren't mermaids really, at least not like friendly Ariel and her singing crab. These were Shona mermaids; njuzu, vicious, powerful, half-human, half-fish creatures who lived in the deep waters, communing with the spirit world and waiting to capture unwary humans who ventured near. I doubted their existence, but I had accepted the assignment when an old friend offered me a chance to write for his fledgling magazine.

When we reached Chemvura village, all the small children ran up to the car smiling. They rushed to my door and squealed when I gave them the sweets that I had brought for them. I picked one up, a small pretty girl, but placed her back on the ground immediately when I encountered a wet bottom. When Mum opened her door, the kids ran to welcome her too. Women emerged from the huts and slowly walked towards us, more wary than their children.

"I'm looking for Lovemore," I said.

"Rudo," Mum hissed. "Greet them properly."

I rolled my eyes, but then extended my hands to shake with each of the women, curtseying slightly.

"How are you?"

"We are fine if you are fine too?"

"We are fine."

"Then we are fine too."

After what felt like ten minutes of enquiring how they were and how we were and how the children were and how the crops and goats were, I finally said what I wanted to say: "I've come from Harare and I am looking for Lovemore."

Lovemore was my contact in Chemvura. I had spoken to him on the phone a couple of times over the last week. The self-appointed village elder, all twenty-six years of him, had told me that he would be my guide during my two days in the village – but the stream of messages sitting unreplied-to on my phone suggested he hoped for more than just guiding. Eventually he came bounding up to me like an overeager puppy. He was vaguely attractive in that rural, sweaty kind of way: tall and muscular like a man who spent a lot of time in the field.

"My sister, you've come," he said, shaking my hand vigorously. "Mother! How are you?" Mum looked bemused as Lovemore shook her hand, smiling like he had known her all his life. "Come now. I'll introduce you to everyone!"

As he shepherded us around, I couldn't help feeling appropriated. By the second house, we had become "my visitors" and by the fifth "my relatives". I found it irritating that he did all the talking with my mother and I barely got out a hello before he whisked us off to the next home. When we got to his mother's house, he took me by the hand and said to his mother, "Ndauya nemuroora wenyu. Here is your daughter-in-law." It was said in a joking manner but it was obvious that Lovemore wouldn't mind if this was true. But I said nothing. Mum had chuckled at this introduction.

Lovemore tried to convince me that there was nothing that I could learn from the villagers that I couldn't learn from him, but I insisted on meeting the men. So as the sun set, Lovemore accompanied me to the centre of the village where the men were gathered around a fire. Lovemore took a seat on one of the free stools, but I sat on the ground. Even this returning diaspora knew better than to challenge rural sensibilities by sitting on the stool like I was equal to the men, at least not when I wanted something from them. I could see the disapproving looks directed towards my skinny jeans and sleeveless top. Lovemore began another round of extended greeting formalities. I felt like I had been through this routine a million times since I got back. A month after my father's death, visitors were still streaming in to pay their respects. They expressed their condolences only to my mother, always asking her first how she was. But with me, they sat back. I had to ask them how they were. I had to say how sorry I was for their loss even though I was the one who had lost a father. It was silly, but I did it because mother expected it. Since Baba's death, she had become more thoughtful about cultural practices and making sure that I conducted myself like a properly behaved Shona daughter.

When Lovemore finally finished his introduction, I asked my questions. "What do you think happened to the girls?" I said.

"They were taken," said one of the men.

"They drowned," said Lovemore. I ignored him.

"Taken by what?" No one responded. "Do you think something pulled them into the river?" Still nothing. "Do you believe in njuzu?" The crowd became restless.

"Fairy tales," Lovemore mumbled.

"Fairy tales?" said one of the older men. "Njuzu are not fairy tales!"

"Who are you?" I said. The man looked sharply at me. I guess I could have been more respectful.

"Munemo. I've lived here for twenty years."

"And what do you think happened to the girls?"

Munemo looked around nervously at the other men. "Mermaids."

There was grumbling amongst the men and some head-shaking. "I know to an Americano like you it might seem improbable. Even here in the village, the youngsters think that those of us who believe are ridiculous." A smattering of sniggers. From the corner of my eye, I saw Lovemore smirking. "But it's mermaids I tell you. People won't say it out loud, as if the njuzu might hear us calling their names and emerge out of the water to take more girls – but it's happening anyway. We should be grateful that the mermaids have chosen our village." At this last bit, the grumbling devolved into shouting.

"Grateful, Munemo?" said Lovemore. "You want us to be grateful? This here is the epitome of rural passivity. You never want to change your lives. Always ready to accept whatever lot you receive even when you could change it. Kuda kwashe, right?"

"Yes Lovemore, kuda kwashe. We should be grateful."

"Grateful?" I said, finally managing to get myself heard over the crowd.

"Yes. That they've chosen our village as the place to find the next generation of witchdoctors."

I was still confused.

"They say that mermaids take the girls underwater to teach them about the spirit world and the magic they need to be a witchdoctor," Lovemore said. I should have been grateful but a part of me was tired of having my culture explained to me.

"Yes," Munemo said. "It's for our own benefit. I think the mermaids are just looking out for us, you know. They can't just show up and say, 'Can we have your daughter for a month or two?' Some people would kill them or at the very least trap them given half a chance. Anyway, who would agree to that? We all want our daughters to get married so that our kraals fill up with cows and our yards with grandchildren. Witchdoctors don't get married. But we need them and the mermaids make sure we always have them."

"And how many of your daughters would you volunteer?" Lovemore asked, "Which one of those six would you give to the mermaids? None! So shut your mouth about things you do not understand."

"Things I don't understand? What do I not understand? Everyone in this village knows that you only need to talk to Zvichadzokera and she'll tell you. Mermaids are real whether you like it or not. You only need to look at Zvichadzokera's power to see that."

"Hai suka wena! Rudo, let's go." Lovemore thundered away and I had to run to catch up. "Villagers! They'll always look for the impossible before they accept the obvious. Mermaids? Honestly. This is why Chemvura is so backwards. Five girls who can't swim turn up dead by the river. Do the villagers think it's crocodiles? Do they think the girls might have drowned? No. The only possible explanation is bloody mermaids."

"Who is Zvichadzokera?" I said.

"Zvichadzokera means 'it will return'. Zvichadzokera is the name the village gave to the woman you're here to interview. She sits there in her hut by the river and apparently she's evidence of the power of mermaids. She conjures minor tricks, but she's a fraud."

The look on his face discouraged further questioning, but I couldn't help myself. "Fraud?"

He stopped as we reached his mother's gate. "She killed my father."

I said nothing.

"I was still working in Mutare back then," he continued. "I rushed home in response to a frantic call from my mother saying my father was dying. I wanted to take him to the hospital but mother insisted on going to Zvichadzokera instead. The woman filled the room with smoke and chanted as she sprinkled water over my father's prone body. My father coughed violently for a while, but then fell silent and I knew he was gone. We still took him to the hospital where he didn't last the hour. The doctors said it was emphysema."

"I'm sorry."

"For what? The ignorance of villagers? None of it matters anyway. She'd probably still be sprinkling water over his dead body as if it could bring him back if I hadn't dragged the man out."

I wanted to say I understood. I wanted to tell him that I too had arrived home too late to be of any use to my dying father. That I'd spent the last three months of his life refusing to talk to him, fearing that he would try to say goodbye, but insisting I would soon be on my way home. That finally, Mother had said, "If you want to see him alive, get on the plane now." That even then, I had dallied for another couple of days before finally departing. And that when I was somewhere over the Atlantic, my father had died. I wanted to tell him, but instead I slipped my hand into his and repeated the words that I'd heard so many times these last thirty-eight days.

"I'm sorry."

We stood there in silence for a few minutes before he let go of my hand and we finally went into the kitchen. Mai Lovemore had already made dinner. Apparently she was taking this whole muroora business seriously because she had killed a rooster, and it looked like half the bird was on my plate. It was delicious, but I struggled with the sadza. It felt like there was grit in it, but every time I was ready to give up, Mum glared at me and I continued to force the sadza down my throat until my plate was clear. Lovemore smiled at the plate as if there was meaning in it.

Mum and I were given a small hut to sleep in. We laid out our blankets and pillows on the floor on opposite sides of the hut. Twice I blew out the candle by mistake as I aired out my blankets. Mother was amused but said nothing. Then suddenly she was singing a song that my dead grandmother used to sing before she went to bed. It wasn't just that Mum was singing, but that she was singing "The Lord Is My Shepherd". Mum had never been religious. She would drop us off at Sunday school on her way to work and return to pick us up when she knew that Mass was well and truly over and the judgmental nuns had gone to lunch. And here she was singing the favourite hymn of the mother-in-law she had never liked. For a second, I thought I might join in, but then decided that singing hymns by candlelight at night felt a little too much like calling death into your home.

I slipped into my blankets and turned away from Mum. After a few minutes, she was silent and I thought she had fallen asleep. I could not sleep. I kept trying to find a comfortable position but that was impossible on a cold cement floor. While I was all smiles when we were shown to our very own pole and dagga hut, once we were inside, I bristled at the inconvenience. This was exactly the type of thing I did not miss in America. Eventually I lay on my back planning the next day's interview as I listened to the rain being swallowed by the thatched roof. I wondered what the witchdoctor – the n'anga – would say about mermaids. I couldn't help but think of the last n'anga I had seen.

The day after Baba's funeral, I had been dragged to see a different n'anga, back in Masvingo where Baba had grown up. We had gone to the spiritual healer to perform Gata, a ceremony when the n'anga consults the spirits to find out what killed your loved one. When I'd questioned the point of this trip, seeing as we knew it was prostate cancer that killed Baba, I had been told our culture says munhu haangofe. There is always someone responsible. It was just a matter of finding out who the killer was.

We had gathered in the hut: my mother, my father's three brothers and I. The n'anga picked up the goat bones that he would throw to see what the spirits said and he blew on them like they were dice. He shook them in his hands and he too began to shake. His eyes lost focus as he entered a trance. He began to make strange noises like he was dry heaving as the bones started to shake faster. Suddenly he stopped, he opened his eyes. But there was no recognition there. It was like something else had taken his place. He turned to me and offered the bones to me. We were all taken aback.

"You mean to give them to me, right? They belong to me," said Baba's eldest brother. He reached over as if to grab the bones, but the n'anga growled like a rabid beast. Once again, he proffered them to me. I looked over to my mother but even then she had fallen asleep. I turned back to the healer and held out my hands. He dropped the bones into them.

"Chukucha." I shook the bones. "Kanda." I dropped them in front of me on the grass mat. The healer moved the bones around with his stick as he read them, moaning as he deciphered meaning.

There was no good news in those bones. But who ever found good news on a witch-hunt? The healer sat back, wailed like a wounded dog and fell silent. He shut his eyes. When he reopened them, he was back. He pushed forward his small wooden plate and waited. I didn't know what the gesture meant.

"Money," my uncle said. I hastily pulled out a $20 note from the small wad in my bra and put it in the plate. From the n'anga's gleeful look, I knew it was too much. He began to speak and he appeared to be addressing me alone.

"I spoke to the spirits. Your ancestors are not happy. You broke your father's heart." The man pulled out a pouch of snuff from somewhere in his many animal hides and took a big sniff before replacing the pouch. "What kind of child leaves and never comes back? You children, we send you to these foreign lands to work so that you can take care of us mochonyerako. The white man calls it cancer, but its real name is grief."

Grief. I wondered if Zvichadzokera would make the same abstract claims, if she would so pointedly ask for money.

"You know, I never learnt how to swim." My mother's voice startled me.

"You didn't?" I said as if I didn't already know.

"I used to watch your aunts and uncles happily splashing around in the river on the farm, but I never joined in."

"Why not?"

"I was scared of the mermaids." In the distance thunder rumbled. "When I was seven or so, your Uncle Simba told me that mermaids live in the lakes but sometimes swim up to the river in search of girls. They grab unsuspecting girls and drag them down to their caves near the bottom of the lake to teach them about the spiritual world so that they could become witchdoctors. That was only if no one cried. But if they cried about your loss, the mermaids would kill you. I didn't want to be a witchdoctor. Anyway, you know your grandmother: at the first hint that I was missing, she would have been wailing at the top of a hill. So I figured it was best to stay out of water altogether."

We laughed.

"It's strange, isn't it," I said, "how grandma can be so generous with her tears when the two of us never cry in public?"

"And the way she insists that there's something wrong with you if you don't cry the way she does. Remember at your father's funeral, the way she kept imploring me to wail. 'Wakaita sei mwana waRichard? Why can't you weep for your own husband?'"

"Imagine. Your own mother accusing you of witchcraft at your husband's funeral."

"She was one step away from saying I killed him, I tell you."

"All because you couldn't shed a tear."

"*I couldn't shed a tear...* Maybe I was hoping they would send him back."

Zvichadzokera turned out to be an anti-climax. When I entered her hut, it took a few seconds for my eyes to adjust to the darkness of the room and the smoke. Across from the door, Zvichadzokera sat on a grass mat. She wore a head band made from goat skin and had a cow hide pinned around her shoulder, but under the hide was a black System of a Down T-shirt with the sleeves ripped off. I knelt on the cement floor, clapping my cupped hands slowly, eyes cast down. Zvichadzokera shook the stick in her right hand.

"Mwanangu, chii chanetsa?" *What's wrong?*

"Zvichadzokera, I'm a journalist and I'm investigating the drownings. I wondered what you might know about them."

"What have they told you?"

"The villagers? They said it might be mermaids."

"Is that all they said?"

"They said you disappeared too." Her eyes lit up. "They said the mermaids took you and that's how you became Zvichadzokera."

"Do you believe?"

"In the mermaids?"

"In the spirits."

I felt tired. So very tired and weary. Tired of missing America.

Tired of these villagers and their bloody mermaids. Tired of having to relearn how to be a "good" woman in Zimbabwe. But mostly tired of this burden of grief. Tired of missing and tired of trying to understand this person my mother had become.

"Rudo, do you believe in spirits?" How did Zvichadzokera know my name?

"I think grief drives people crazy, a madness so foreign that they can't see how ordinary life could explain it. So they look to the spirits." The words felt empty but I knew that was what she wanted to hear.

Zvichadzokera smiled as she shook her head. "We cannot know it all."

I found my mother by the river. Nearby, the children screamed as they played tag, but Mum seemed oblivious to them. She stared at the water rushing past as if she was looking for something. As if she was ready to jump in and follow it.

Beetroot Salad

Donald Molosi

"Partir, c'est mourir un peu."
– Edmond Haraucourt, *"Rondel de l'adieu"*

*M*onkoki's mind feels like liquid today, moving this and that way, lacking focus. She rolls up the blinds and lets the sunlight rush into the square studio apartment, forming bright rectangular patterns on the beige carpet. Although she is still lethargic from last night's long flight from Botswana, Monkoki feels somewhat refreshed, bathed in the crisp newness that waking up in a foreign city creates. This new city is, after all, in the United States of America – a country where prosperity is rumoured to rain down on hungry immigrants like a dream.

Monkoki gingerly muses on that fantasy, the American Dream, before her mind drifts to a parallel thought: Kitsano's stories of Real America. Stories in which anyone could become anything they desire. Stories in which homesickness is paralysing. Stories in which Americans know too little about anyone else. What will Real America be like, particularly characterised – as it sounds to be – by a collision of deep losses and peculiar freedoms?

Monkoki smacks her lips at the weightiness of that question: *mmp-mmp!* She cradles a coffee mug with both hands and, for strange comfort, she allows its heat to burn her palms. *Mmp-mmp!* She stares down at her feet. The beige carpet is entwined with tiny circles of Kitsano's hair in a Velcro hook-and-loop fashion. Her throat suddenly tightens and Monkoki panics. Her eyes dart to the wooden donkey-brown windowsill, looking without really wanting to see. Even at a distance, she can smell the stale menthol of the window frame. A tear slides down her cheek. *Mmp.*

Monkoki dries her eye on her shoulder. She left Botswana without telling most of her relatives, fearing that they would yank down her airplane from the sky with jealous magic. How else would they react to talk of golden-paved American streets when they themselves were stuck in the fallow backwaters of Mahalapye? In the words of Mma Gabanthate, Monkoki's grandmother, where there is no jealousy there is no love.

A dull pain knots Monkoki's stomach pit and mutes her unease for a while. She misses her pushy relatives: Uncle Barobi, short and combative, from whose mouth vile words slop out too easily at family gatherings; Cousin Raymond, with dreadlocks and a gold tooth-cap, always backsliding from one prosperity-preaching Pentecostal church to the next in search of a "matrimonial miracle"; Cousin David, bald and divorced, who has been not-so-secretly having sex with Cousin Raymond; Uncle Dikgopiso whose dutiful wife, Mma Betty, raised Monkoki like her own daughter; Grandmother Mma Gabanthate whose dim eyes capture the doom of living in Botswana as a woman. The act of missing her relatives instantly defeats Monkoki. She resents missing even the witches and hypocrites simply because a family tie is like a tree – it can bend but it cannot break.

Thoughts of her relatives bring other concerns into focus. She has dared this trans-Atlantic trip for a man she has no desire to marry. She has also never felt the hunger of her empty womb. All her body has is a strong wish to survive.

*M*onkoki's coffee has gone cold. She feels antsy. Pressing her nose to the window gauze like a bored child and – in an attempt to clean up her mind of thoughts – she hums a Setswana hymn that she learnt from Mma Gabanthate when she was little. Monkoki had chanted this cry of an orphan to herself on many nights when guzzling Savanna until she was cross-eyed and weeping in front of the mirror. In this moment, it stops her asking herself if she would have made this trip had Kitsano not come to Botswana for her mother's re-burial last year.

Sala le nna, tsatsi le phirima.

Meriti ya bosigo e tsile.

Lord, with me abide.

Kitsano had just moved to the U.S. for medical school. Three years ago. She used to write him long love poems, to the disapproving amusement of Mma Betty.

"*Uhu!* A medical person is being sent rhymes to read? Just make him pay cows and marry you. And you, with your warm brain must waste no time!"

Those were the days when Kitsano used to adore her books and poetry, even if he thought some of her poems too racy to be morally African. Yet, she had always maintained that to harbour the assumption that an African story must be without sex is to insinuate that nature had not bestowed sexual imagination upon the African. Distance has since rendered Monkoki's relationship with Kitsano less poetic and more realistic. Distance and adversity have mentored them to be individuals in a relationship with each other. Proximity would have melted them into a predictable oneness too early like it did Uncle Dikgopiso and Mma Betty.

Kitsano is still asleep. America must have made him forget that it was impolite to sleep past sunrise, which Monkoki finds sad.

Sala le nna, tsatsi le phirima.

Meriti ya bosigo e tsile –

The humming brings back more memories in a crowded rush. Those were the days when she used to imagine Kitsano living in a Gilded Age mansion with many garages, all American-style and no cockroaches. She glances at him now sleeping on the tiny sofa-bed, swathed in a leopard-print snuggie. The Kitsano she knows from home would never wear a snuggie because snuggies are backward robes: ridiculous.

*W*hen Kitsano hears Monkoki hum 'Sala Le Nna' he wishes that the sofa-bed would magically swallow him; he keeps his sleepy eyes closed to conceal the moisture gathering in them. But keeping them shut invites flashbacks – a new old grave, a re-mourning, a greyish skeletal corpse with leathery skin oozing with liquid. Even when Monkoki stops humming, 'Sala Le Nna' always throws Kitsano back to last year when Monkoki used to drink Savanna and then waffle sadly on the phone. That was before he flew to Botswana to steady her mind, while Mma Monkoki's body was in the process of being dug up and re-buried facing east.

When a Motswana woman marries a Motswana man, she

belongs to her husband's family, and Mma Monkoki had been no different. But the poor woman had had the misfortune of being buried by her own family instead of her husband's because the latter lacked cows to sell at the time. Nine years later, her husband's family won the court case to exhume Mma Monkoki and re-bury her facing east, as was the custom of her husband's people. Even in death, a Motswana woman's body belongs to her in-laws.

Kitsano has never told Monkoki about the nightmares he had during that time or how – in that week of the re-burial – he had turned to smoking weed with Cousin Raymond to sleep better at night. Neither has he told Monkoki what Cousin Raymond said about her.

That evening at Mma Monkoki's house, Cousin Raymond had crouched over the fire next to Kitsano. "She always jokes with you that her mother was once taken to the special hospital in Lobatse, right?"

"O bua eng?"

Cousin Raymond outstretched his arms towards the fire for warmth, "Well, Monkoki is not far from that herself, rra. The girl needs deliverance. That's why you people need to start attending church. You know she has a warm brain. Kana, I am not telling you anything new! You two must go before God's throne and come against any machination of Lucifer in the brain of—"

Kitsano looked at Raymond without blinking, "This conversation is over, Raymond. Don't ever again dare! I love Monkoki, she loves me and that's all that I need to know." Kitsano sucked his teeth after laying into Cousin Raymond. He had then stared at the fire with his nostrils angrily flared, forcing Cousin Raymond to get up and go squat on the other side of the rondavel.

But now on Monkoki's first day in the U.S. and their first day together in the same house, Kitsano strains to act resolute. This beautiful young woman that he is watching through slightly parted eyes has been weeping and grinding her teeth non-stop for about an hour. He couldn't help wondering how long she would keep at it, whether her brain was indeed too warm for comfort.

*W*hen Monkoki stops humming, her own dreamy memories evaporate fast like a breath on warm glass. Her eyes, however, remain moist. Her thoughts are scattered pieces of broken glass.

She finds the Californian wind in Anaheim too warm, too unclean. It smells of old rust. The clumsy grit leads Monkoki to conclude that she must be far from Hollywood where the wind is surely cool and uncluttered.

Below, on Ball Road, blue dumpsters sit randomly along the street, their wide mouths foul and agape with bags of assorted rubbish, usable furniture and broken television sets. The minty but skunk-like smell of marijuana seems to permeate the entire street. Pudgy teenage boys of Latino extraction swagger up and down the street dressed in oversized grey tracksuit pants and tight white vests. They are rattling unintelligible sounds into their cellphones and gesticulating in an unfamiliar language. A homeless man is beating his tiny dog...

"Good morning, ratu. Wassup?" Kitsano groans, opens his eyes and yawns in Monkoki's direction. She is still standing at the window. His head is shaved bald and his gibbous eyes are heavy with sleep. As he smiles, she smiles back. Monkoki muses how Kitsano's beautiful masculinity – his perfect set of white teeth revealed behind his full dark lips – is at odds with his symmetrical face and long eyelashes.

"Morning. O robetse sente?" Monkoki asks while turning away from the window to face Kitsano. She sits down on the sofa-bed facing him. She realises then with heavy guilt how glad she is to be away from her overbearing grandmother, a woman for whom marriage was the goal of one's life. *Mmp!*

He looks up at her and smiles, "Slept okay. And you, baby, how did you sleep?"

"Sente. Are you going to show me the town today, Kitsano?"

"Yes, ratu. I thought that since it is your first day in the U.S. we might do something very American. Like walk down to Disneyland. It's only ten minutes away."

Monkoki silently returns to the window. She closes her eyes. She thinks of her late mother, Mma Monkoki who loved evening walks. She can't help grinding her teeth. Mma Monkoki was always a little crazy. Every morning she would be perched on the metal chair that Monkoki had welded together for her using greasy pieces of metal that Cousin Raymond stole from the scrapyard of Rra Ofodile, the next-door mechanic...

"Monki? Disneyland?" Kitsano asks again, his eyes soft with affection.

"Yes, Kits. Huh?" Monkoki responds snapping herself out of reverie. "Maybe."

She realises then with a tightness in her chest that she is indeed in the U.S. That she will not have fresh beetroot salad every Sunday because there are no decent organic beetroots available here: everything is genetically modified. That she will not even be around enough people who call it "beetroot" instead of "beet", because this is Real America, where everything is manufactured with so many preservatives that bread does not even rot. In this moment Monkoki feels as though a heavy arrow, a barbed and heavy arrow of God, plunges into her chest. She flicks her braids, "For such hot weather I wonder why these boys wear heavy tracksuit pants. I mean, vests I can understand but as for the tracksuit pants!?"

Kitsano gets up and hugs her from the back, "I love you, Monk. I know it is all new, this place. We will be alright, ga ke re? I am here."

"Yes, we will be alright. I also love you, dobenaas."

A few moments of reassuring silence sweeten their embrace.

Kitsano ambles to the bureau to turn on his computer, "Can you believe that here they call tracksuit pants 'sweatpants' and the vests are called 'wife-beaters'? Madness, I tell you."

"Gatwe wife-beater?" Monkoki points with her lips at the boys on the street as though addressing them. "How American to reduce a real word to a cheap popular phrase!"

Kitsano and Monkoki share a familiar laugh. She turns around to fully embrace him and she feels the bulge in his pyjamas. Their giggles bubble up and then burst into comforting raucousness.

In those peals of merriment she hears only his *HA-HA-HA* because hearing Kitsano's deep laughter echo throughout the tiny American apartment is familiar, steadying to her unquiet mind.

When Kitsano walks towards the bathroom door, Monkoki glances at his buttocks and teases, "Nice round buttocks, Ngwato boy! Shàll we take a picture to exhibit in *Laahn-dahhn?*"

She knows that he dislikes it when people remark on his rotund behind. He finds buttocks to be essentially a feminine thing to compliment anyone about. His stress on "essentially" always amuses her as though nature had selectively created women with behinds and men without.

Kitsano turns around to face Monkoki and they giggle until water streams out of their eyes. Their childish joy around each other – even when mocking an otherwise-charged issue like the colonial past – is one of the habits that their relatives in Botswana always looked at with chiding eyes, especially Uncle Barobi.

"*Ah!* Just not serious about life." He often spoke to them with a dismissive curl of the lips. After all, a couple should always act judiciously stiff around aunties and uncles as a sign of serious rehearsal for marriage. What other way is there?

Monkoki grabs Kitsano's buttocks. He grabs hers. They chase each other around the tiny apartment squawking and ducking. The laughter dies out only as Kitsano finally enters the bathroom and shuts the door behind him.

Monkoki picks up her coffee from the floor and puts it on top of the mini-fridge sitting against the wall; she wonders if Kitsano would be better off without her. She walks back to the window, biting her nails. The tiny dog has just broken free from the homeless man and it is running across Ball Road, tongue out.

Monkoki begins to wonder what her grandmother Mma Gabanthate is doing at this moment in Gaborone. She must be having Sunday dinner with Mma Betty, both of them wearing brightly-coloured two-piece dresses and jubilee-wool dress-hats, eating beetroot salad, complete with a touch of mayonnaise. Monkoki weeps again, fast and mechanically as though to save time.

Her cheek-long tears glisten and converge under her chin. Her hand finds its way under her T-shirt. Her fingers caress the outer edges of her right breast, and then the left breast; both firm up.

She skips over to the tiny bureau by the sofa-bed and opens Kitsano's iTunes on his laptop. She chooses a dancehall playlist called "ShowerPower" and plugs the laptop to the speakers. Booming drums blast through, shaking the bureau.

In the bathroom, Kitsano sings along, rolls off his pyjama pants, steps into the shower and allows the hot water to massage him muscle by sleepy muscle. It embitters him as a doctor and even more as a boyfriend that there are too many things that he does not comprehend about depression, like how its victims cannot snap out of it and organise their thoughts. A slender hand grabs his buttocks. He smiles the same crooked secure smile that he had smiled over the phone when Monkoki said three months ago that she was finally willing to relocate to America to be with him.

"I guess I can move," she had texted. "You helped me re-bury my mother."

As the hot water pours on their seamlessly dark bodies, Monkoki's breasts swell firmer. They feel warm against his back and she purrs a little when she begins to tease the whorl at the back of his head with both hands. Somehow this part of his body, the little insignificant bone, always excites her as being wonderfully masculine. Monkoki begins to rub her pelvis on his buttocks in dance-like sensuous circles smoothed by the shower water.

She allows her hands to fall down past Kitsano's shoulder blades and waist, and then shoot frontwards. In them he feels thick and firm. She moves her hands in slow strokes at first and then faster quivers until he hastens his breath, holds and then releases it with his eyes glazed.

Monkoki smacks her lips. "Aren't you glad I finally joined you in America, Kits?" Her voice is rapt and playful. She is still holding him in her hands, "I may not be able to control what my mind wants to discuss. But you know I control my hand very well. Don't you, my honey?"

Without uttering a single word, Kitsano turns around, kneels before her and parts her thighs with his tongue. Right then she experiences the confluence of loss and freedom. As she moans, her mind blanks as though Kitsano, with his tongue, had at once opened her thighs and closed her mind. In that moment she does not parse her femininity, she does not question her feminism, she does not even long for beetroot salad. As the water washes over them, she relishes the peace of a blank mind.

This Land Is Mine

Wesley Macheso

*I*f you still had a name I would have written to you. I don't understand why you decided to get rid of it and renounce your faith in Allah. That was the first step you took. I watched you as you wiggled out of yourself to become a new person. And that person made her way out of our lives to exist only in postcards that fly in from different corners of the world. Father reprimanded you for talking back to him. Then he slapped you when you declared that you no longer wanted to wear the hijab and that you had no time to attend prayers at the mosque five times a day. You told him that modernity was slavery to time and as a modern woman you had no time to waste on superstition and blind faith. How did you muster the courage to tell father that he was myopic and unreasonable? He hated you when you called him a simpleton. You asked him why he was stubborn on settling in a death trap when reasonable people advised that we relocate to a safer place. Father told you that he owned the land and that his ancestors were buried there. "And what do you know about death?" he asked you. "If you want you can leave." So you left.

You told me that you did not need a name because you did not want to be defined. You said names were not for human beings but for simple inanimate things like trees and mountains and buildings. You said human beings are too sophisticated to be called by a single name. You can be a student to one person, a daughter to another, a sister, a Muslim, a drunkard, a whore, and whoever else others perceived you to be. How could all those things answer to a single name? And I understood. You told me that I could call you anything I wished, but that hasn't been easy since you went away. When you were still here, I could just say sister and you would turn your ear to me. There is so much I want to share with you. But I don't even know how to address my letter to you since without a name you have become a void – an empty space that roams across the globe in search of things I can't even comprehend. I finally understood why the world demands that we abide by a few irrational dictates like having names. Names have their place whether we like them or not.

I wanted to tell you that you were right. Father might have been myopic. The invisible python came again this year. It swallowed our food, guzzled my friends, and made away with our livestock. They say the python lives in the mountain, in a big hole, where people used to ditch deformed babies and people with leprosy. But people don't do that anymore. So when this python is hungry, it churns and groans under the surface of the earth, sometimes making the world tremble and shake. When it becomes angry, it creeps through the dark nooks of the earth and finds its way out in one of the rivers that come down from the mountain. It creeps into the flow of the river, manoeuvres in its tide, vomiting volumes of water that it carries in its belly. The python rushes like gushing wind and consumes everything it finds in its way. It wreaks havoc on houses, slashes down trees and crops, sweeps away land, and swallows humans and animals to feed its hunger. It joins the river and runs down the valley to kill those of us who reside in the concave of the country.

As you yelled at father that evening before you left, I heard everything. You emphasised that there was no sense in staying down here waiting for the water to come and sweep us away like it does every year. Father told you that you could not be sure whether or not the python would come out this year. He told you to leave everything in the hands of God. He told you that he was not planning on leaving the land of his ancestors. You shouted at him – telling him to stop running away from reality with his superstitions. You told him that there was no mystical python that brought water down the valley. You said it was a geographical fact that the area was prone to flash floods and it wasn't meant for habitation. Father sneered at you in the fading glow of light, his eyes crimson like burning coal in the devil's furnace.

"So you think you know better now that you let a white man abuse you for his pleasure?"

And you said his outbursts were irrelevant.

"Did I send you to school to become a whore and talk back to me?"

And you told him that he was committing a fallacy; *argumentum ad hominem*. You said you did not understand why he was attacking you instead of addressing the issue at hand. I don't think he understood any of this because he just turned his back on you and banged the door behind him.

Ever since you started going out with Theo, father attributed everything he didn't like in you to your relationship with him.

"Nothing good comes from those people," he said.

He believed it was Theo who made you lose your faith in Allah. He said it was Theo who told you to get rid of your name. Father called you Zeinab, after the granddaughter of the prophet Mohammad, but you did not like this name. "I am a free spirit and I will not be trapped in the confines of a dead woman, be them holy or whatsoever," that's what you told father. After that you went to Sweden with Theo and when you came back a dragon was chiselled on the upper part of your left arm. Father did not want to look at you. He said the spirit of the python was in you and that the demon was passed on to you from Theo. But you told me that having a tattoo was just a way of expressing yourself. It showed that you owned your body. You went on to pierce your bottom lip and your bellybutton, as if the snake on your arm was not enough. Father hated Theo for all this.

"There is nothing good that comes from a white man," he repeated those words. "Aren't they the same people who came with a picture of their friend nailed to a tree claiming that he was God? What God can be nailed to a tree? Isn't it the white man who is bringing strange practices into this country? Aren't white people teaching men to sleep with other men? These people are evil!"

When I asked you about this you told me that father was not always right. You said there were some things that he did not know and others that he did not understand. You said homosexuality had nothing to do with white people but that it was just love as we know it – a lasting affection between ordinary people. You said the problem was that people always wanted to put labels on everything and that they were scared of what they did not understand.

"Do you remember Gwaza?" you asked. I remembered him. He was that man who looked like a woman and people made fun of him. He used to live at the far end of the river and he had no family. He had a beard and he was bald like most men here. But his voice was too squeaky for a man and he had a very big behind and what looked like breasts. People always whispered and giggled when he passed by. They made him run away.

"Was Gwaza a man or a woman?" you asked, and I said I was not sure.

"You see, not everything can be categorised," you tried to explain. "There are some things we cannot understand in this world because the world is much bigger and much darker for our comprehension. We are in no position to judge others."

I wonder what father would say if he heard that you started smoking. Your last postcard almost made me cry. You said smoking was a new experience you were experimenting with. You actually made an effort to squeeze a chunk of words onto that postcard to make me understand how you felt. You said you love how the smoke feels when it descends inside you, scorching your lungs. You like releasing the smoke through your nose or watching the plume of smoke wiggling into space when you whistle it out from the small hole you create between your lips. You said it feels like you hold the smoke hostage inside you only to give it the freedom to melt into open space. You said you love the idea that you are able to free something from the confines of humanity and this gives you satisfaction. You talked of freedom with such passion that your words dug a hole inside my heart. I yearn to experience this freedom that you talked about. You described it as the power to be. I swept the postcard across my nose to smell you and its fragrance made me realise how much I missed you.

With my postcard I wanted to tell you about the strange night when the water came. I woke up around midnight to find drops of blood splattered like rose petals on my white bed sheet. It was a freaky sight and I leapt from my bed in terror. I wanted to wake father up to show him what had happened but that was when I heard a gushing sound like thunder down the valley. It was as if the mountain was crawling downhill to displace us from our land. I rushed to my window to witness the absurdity of the night and that was when my eyes confronted death. Death looks like nothing. It has no face, no shape, and no sense of direction. The darkness of the night was displaced by thundering fog and the wind outside was rushing at the speed of sound, inflicting vengeance on the environment. The water was coming down like it does every year but this time with more vigour and a new determination. The blood on my sheets was a sign.

You see, it had been raining continuously for two weeks. The government warned us that the rain would be heavy this year. They sent trucks and other heavy vehicles to help us move from this area but father and others like him did not listen. I wished I'd left with you when father disowned you but I was powerless. Father told me that I was not old enough to make my own decisions. I knew that this place was dangerous but I was too much of a coward to stand up to father. I would gaze at his thick lips and his thick beard and wonder how I could challenge him. With all the authority and the knowledge that he carried in his balding head, father was God personified.

Others heeded and left before the disaster. We stayed. Father did not want to abandon his land. He would go out in the rain to check on his crops, most of which were now faltering from too much water and no sunlight. He dug gullies around the house to stop water from getting in. He put plastic bags on the roof and on the windows to prevent leaking. He had no idea what mother nature had in store for us. He dismissed the government people, accusing them of plotting to steal his land.

"This land is mine!" he told them. "No one will remove me from it. My fathers were buried here. My yesterdays are in this place!"

They told him that meteorologists had forecasted hostile weather conditions and heavy flooding but father did not listen.

"I have lived here my whole life and I know the python comes and goes, taking what it wants with it. I will not leave!"

They told him that there was no python but that only made him furious. He said he would beg Allah for mercy so that the python spares us like it did every year.

"But science tells us otherwise. This time it's dangerous." The government official tried to reason with him.

"You want to teach me science young man? The white man's wisdom, huh?" Father's eyes were burning coal. "The white man has torn my family apart, turned my daughter into a disrespectful whore. Now you want to use his ways to rob me of my land?"

The government official had no clue what father was talking about. His face looked like a puzzle with a dozen missing pieces. He glanced at me, pity seeping from his eyes. "Child," he told me, "I hope you leave this place before the worst comes."

Father told him off. He told him not to put ideas in my head. The man left.

And on that night the blood foretold the worst. I wonder if there is anything good that comes with blood. It's always an ominous sign. The water cascaded down the valley like it had scores to settle. The river seemed possessed by a spirit that lurked beneath it and had lost its shape and its sense of direction. My animal instinct took control. A strange impulse then seized my rational faculties and I stormed out of the house with nothing on my mind but to run and run and run. My vision was blurred by the enormous fog. I did not know where I was going and it did not matter. The sound of the water grew closer the further I tried to escape from death. Then I felt a heavy force that knocked me off my feet. The water slammed my body against something hard and I lost all feeling. I was unconscious of pain or any other sensations. My eyelids dropped instinctively, embracing my impending death. Before my mind made full sense of my surroundings, the water had already taken what it wanted and I could hear the deafening roar fading in the distance, tearing down the valley.

When dawn broke on the eastern horizon, I found myself hanging on a lean branch of a tree whose trunk I could not see. The water had absorbed everything. Looking at the ground was like perceiving the earth upside down. As if the ground was covered in clouds. There was nothing but water beneath me. I was certain I was somewhere in the Indian Ocean. I wanted to cry but my eyes already beheld too much water for tears to come. I hung there suspended, surveying the nothingness around me. I was at the brink of losing my mind when the helicopter came to airlift me. I could see the relief workers shouting, telling me things, but I could not hear them. They pulled me up and covered me in huge blankets but my body clung to its numbness like a corpse ready for cremation. I tried to remember what had happened but there was nothing to recall. I had not seen things happen. I'd only heard their sounds.

Sitting in this relief camp, listening to the chatter of mellow birds, the chirping of crickets, the groans and moans of frogs churning the mud, all I do is think. I think about the flood and many other things. Most of the time I think about Allah. Why did he let this happen to us? Sometimes I think he sent the water as a punishment for our sins. When I think in these lines you come to my mind. You are the one who said there was no god and that you did not believe in anything that had no proof of its existence. Allah must have punished us because of people like you. Doesn't the Qur'an tell us that "there is no God but God"? And how could a girl like you challenge that? When I have these thoughts I try to find comfort in the holy book. I try to recite some verses from the Qur'an but my mouth fails to form and produce the words. Sometimes I yearn to proclaim, "Truly he is most forgiving, most merciful", but when my eyes behold the water that has occupied the place we used to call home, my heart grows faint. There is no strength left in me with which to proclaim the love of Allah. I gaze upon the vastness of the water down the valley and wonder where Allah might be in that expanse. There is nothing there but death. The mosque is gone, the people are gone, the houses are gone, the trees, and the crops. What can Allah be doing in a place like that? I have thought very carefully over this for some days now. I finally got rid of the hijab and threw it over the cliff. Allah went with the water.

I sit here and think about water – how it has transformed both of us. Water has emancipated you and me in very unusual ways. It was after you crossed the ocean that your attitude towards life changed. You travelled across acres of water to another part of the world and came back with new ideas. Crossing the water gave you the courage to question father. It gave you authority over your body and lit a new confidence in your eyes. It made you get rid of your name. That was freedom for you.

And in a way the water that killed my friends has also given me freedom. The world that I knew has been washed away. When I look around me and search through the faces in the camp, there is not even a soul I recognise. They are all gone and I feel like this has somehow set me free. This may sound strange but I know you will understand. I can walk without the hijab and no one will sneer at me with contempt. Sometimes I wear shorts like a boy and stroll around the camp. Nobody swears or calls upon the name of Allah. I'm thinking of going back to school, hoping that I get the chance when it's all over.

I lost all the postcards you sent me in the flood but I still remember what was written on the last one. It was a comment by a certain woman on time and dancing. I liked her words. If you still had a name I would have written this story on a million postcards hoping that they somehow reach you. But I feel it's about time that I concentrated on me. I will try to find myself like you did and to taste what freedom feels like on my tongue. I want to experience what it means to live. I don't want to just exist in this world – I want to be part of its orchestra. I want to sing along to life's melody and dance to the rhythm of time. By the way, father went with the water. I've been thinking: does man really own anything in this world?

The Tale of the
Three Water Carriers

Pede Hollist

$\mathcal{T}$hey knew crossing the intersection on their water carts was dangerous. They knew one of them would be killed one day. They knew the person would die at the scene, like the gangsters in the Nollywood films they watched in the sweltering aluminium-shack theatres: Pow-pow! Boo-doom, the goon falls. Tight head shot. Blood trickles from the left corner of the mouth. An economic death – no moaning, broken bones, or splattered entrails. No eulogies or memorials. Here one moment, gone the next. That was how they expected the destined one to die. Yet each, believing he was the darling of the gods, felt certain the dead person would be one of the other two. Time proved them all right.

They were the original water carriers: Orz, their leader, fifteen, gold and diamond miner till he caught the cough that had killed many of his co-workers; started but never completed primary school. Timba, his deputy, thirteen, apprentice logger till a saw sliced three fingers from his left hand; almost completed primary school. And Fish, age and origin unknown, a street child till Orz and Timba, and later their families, took him under their wings; never attended and had no interest in attending school.

They lived with their families, and sometimes friends and strangers, in cramped two-room cement flats scattered within a massive compound near the top of the treeless, toffee-coloured hills overlooking overcrowded and water-starved Teneria, a once lush-green valley city on West Africa's Atlantic Coast. Rumours floating around the hills said the city's water problems started right after the Johnson Spring Water Company, adjacent to their compound and owned by their landlord and some government ministers, began operations – that to fill its plastic bottles and sachets, the company diverted water from the city's main supply pipe to its plant.

"Our water comes from springs deep within these hills," a spokesman told reporters in front of the oversized aqua rain drop logo painted on the company's main gate. The denial lost credibility next to the barbed-wire-crowned concrete wall that ringed the plant, the twenty yards of unobstructed view all around it, and the four guard posts with swivelling search lights, manned twenty-four seven by red-eyed, gun-toting men. In fact, the rumours morphed into fact when, a day after the government shut down the main supply pipe for repairs, Johnson Spring began rationing its products, and continued to do so until the repairs were complete. "We want to ensure everyone in the city has access to water," the spokesman explained the coincidence. Soon after, water delivery broke open as a labour-intensive, small-scale business in Teneria.

For a prearranged fee, the carriers filled five-gallon plastic containers with water from Pump Station (PS) 10, located at the bottom of Hill Road, loaded them on self-built Iroko-wood carts called bearings, and delivered them to the lightheaded residents with dry mouths and yellow-coloured urine, trapped in their dust-choked houses on the steep three-quarter-mile tarmac road. To avoid the long lines at PS 10, the carriers gathered daily at the front gate of Johnson Spring at 4 a.m. Once assembled, they mounted their carts and raced down Hill Road, the ball bearings they used as wheels grating bragalagabragalagalagalaga on the tar, producing a roar that intensified as their speed increased. The low-tech carts resembling those of ancient Ghana and Songhay covered the downhill stretch in five minutes. However, fifty yards before they reached PS 10, the carriers had to cross Main Street, a harmless four-way crossing during the day but a death-defying one at night, especially on their carts with no brakes. Even if the carriers could see and hear like bats, they had only a few seconds to decide whether to pull up or cross in front of vehicles travelling through the junction. They chose the risky option, every time.

One inky-blue morning, a car missed Fish by the raised hairs on his forearms. Seconds later when they arrived at PS 10, he shoved his cart to the ground and followed the rusty pipe leading from the pump into a culvert crossing over the central Samba Drainage Canal that emptied into the Atlantic. Inside the tunnel, he pulled down his shorts and expressed his terror in brown squirts his friends heard yards away. Amused by the effect on Fish, the boys named the intersecting streets Kaka Junction. From that day, you showed character as a water carrier if you crossed in front of a vehicle, avoided having your bowels splattered, and did not spill their contents yourself.

Yeah, yeah, I suppose you could call them crazy, but they saw themselves as patriots, Teneria's Mugabe, Rawlings and Mandela, fighting to save the once-green valley city from the people and drought sucking it dry. So, near miss or not, every morning they raced down Hill Road in service to the country.

At PS 10, they followed a routine: Orz, the strongest with six containers, filled three first. Timba filled two of his four next, and Fish, the weakest, filled one of only two. While the containers gobbled the water, one carrier followed the exposed water pipe into the culvert-turned-public latrine to relieve himself. Another took the large metal cup each tied to his cart, filled it with water, walked over to the garbage-laden canal, and brushed his teeth. The third tuned Orz's battery-operated shortwave radio to a station playing local music. But as soon as the nubile girls with their perky nipples came to fill their buckets, the person holding the radio changed it to a news station, and they pretended to be interested in the news reports, mostly about terrorism, global warming, and financial markets, and, on occasions, the public service announcements about AIDS, malaria, and cholera prevention, none of which they cared about.

One rainy morning, a few days after Fish's near-miss, Orz half-listened to a report about micro financing as his eyeballs pin-balled to the bounces of the water-drenched blouses of the girls frolicking around the pump. Later that day, his brain clogged with water-laden bosoms, Orz told his co-workers he had first learned about micro financing watching *The Oga*, a Nollywood remake of *The Godfather*. A micro financier, he explained, "Na a rich man who dey lend money to poor people to start bizness. If the people dem no pay am back, the man go send his gangsters to kill them."

"I like him," Fish said, shaping the pointer finger and thumb of his right hand into a gun and shooting two delinquent lenders. "Pow-pow, boo-doom; pow-pow, boo-doom!" He smiled, blew the curling smoke from the muzzle, and whipped the gun into its holster with a flourish, as he had seen gangsters do in his daily diet of B-rated American, Chinese, and Indian films.

"We go borrow money from this man," Orz said, "make more carts, and rent them."

Timba and Fish nodded in agreement.

"The gangsters call the financier modaforka," Orz said.

"Yes, like black Americans. Wazap, modaforkaaaa!" Fish added.

"No, black Americans call themselves nigga."

"Nigga na bad word."

"And modaforka be good word?"

"Make we call the man mf for short," Timba said, settling the name dispute.

"Okay. Today-today, we dey go find mfs," Orz said.

After delivering their containers, the carriers searched Teneria for mfs. First, they asked their landlord. "He must be a mf," Timba said.

"I am not," the landlord replied, stiffening. "Go try the bank."

"We don't have any," the bank manager said, and added: "You'll find lots of mfs at the Ministry of Finance."

"Oh no, no," a man in a brown Mao-collared suit at the Ministry of Finance said. "You want *real* mfs, go to the NGOs."

"Nein, nein," a middle-aged, blonde-haired lady at the first NGO said. "Vee had vone, but the mf left vithout notice and now vee can't do our vork."

"Yes, we have a mf right here," the sister at the second, faith-based NGO said. "But he specialises in battered women and child brides. Though you are cute, you don't qualify for his help." She flashed Fish an assortment of misaligned teeth. He cringed.

That day, they realised that, though Teneria overflowed with mfs to give loans to carpenters, fishermen, night-soil workers, prostitutes, and even ex-combatants who had cut off the limbs of some people and murdered others, they found none that would give them loans – *they* who delivered life-giving water to the residents of Teneria. The carriers became angry, and the next morning they got even angrier when a voice on the BBC said the Tenerian government should make laws to stop children under eighteen from working.

"Bastards! You get wok for give us?" Orz said.

"You go give us chop money?" Timba echoed.

Unperturbed, the radio voice pressed on: "Children must be protected from harmful work... exploitation... injury... death..."

"Astafulai! I go kill anybody who want take bread from my mouth," Fish said, grabbing his cart with the fury of a boy safeguarding his self-made toy at the approach of a coveting stranger.

The next day the carriers continued their work, filling containers and pushing their water-laden carts up Hill Road, their veins stretched under their skins like the branches of dry season baobab trees. They performed their work with pride, chuckling at the pedestrians who panted and groaned from carrying bags of groceries, and scoffing at the drivers tooting their horns like children at play. For the carriers, real work made your muscles scream; it involved pushing, straining, and sweating up Hill Road until they could push, strain, and sweat no more. Exhausted, they would stop, sometimes in the middle of the road, defying the horn-blowing cars and lorries to hit them, and would pour water from the containers into their metal cups. Then they would chug the lukewarm liquid, like fufu down the gullet of a hungry man. Many times before they finished their deliveries, they would have drunk four or five cups.

Noooo! The water carriers did not have a death wish. They understood the science of crossing in front of cars: it involved scanning for light, distinguishing headlights from flashlights and from the winking street, house, and security lights, powered by the fluctuating voltage from the Teneria Power Authority, with its slogan "Lighting Teneria one bulb at a time." The science involved knowing the difference between the vroooooommmm of smooth running motor cars, the pre-keh-lek-keh-lek-keh of oil-starved okadas, motor-bike taxies, the vraaammm of diesel-fuelled lorries and responding to these sounds either by slowing down or speeding up. They disciplined themselves to estimate vehicle speeds and factor for distortions of wind and rain before deciding whether to pull up or cross. They had turned crossing in front of vehicles into a skill, if not an art.

Yes, they realised a near-miss might one day result in a death at the scene, but that's not at all the same as being reckless. In fact, they agreed to stagger their downhill runs and rotate the lead driver. Twenty yards from the junction, this person would shout "Kaka Junction" several times and wave his hand to warn the others. But, dear-oh-dear, their safety efforts led to two deaths.

The first was that of Pa Johnson, a near deaf eighty-year-old suffering from acute constipation. He was also a lifelong student of Greek and Roman culture. He lived in a brown, two-story wooden house named Villa Roma on the northwest corner of Kaka Junction. His second-floor bedroom window overlooked the crossroads. Every night, Pa Johnson opened his window to allow fresh air to flow in, but, as bad luck would have it, the water carriers' warnings sallied into his waterlogged ear as "Kaka Johnson." Believing the carriers had found out about his condition, he became depressed. His stomach swelled and pain ripped through his body. He complained to their buxom housemaid, who many mornings collected water from PS 10 and was the only person in the household who even pretended to listen to him: "Even the Almighty has abandoned me," he said. "Tell these illiterate, good-for-nothing boys to stop calling me names and go back to where they belong. They have turned my junction, this Elysian field, into a bloody fish market."

The housemaid, nursing grievances of her own about being underpaid and disrespected, nodded to please the old man but ignored his complaints as soon as she disappeared from his view. Two short weeks after the water carriers started calling out warnings, Pa Johnson suffered a fatal heart attack. Choking back tears, the eldest son eulogised his father: "He died peacefully in his bed, looking out through the window at his beloved junction, his faith in the Almighty as steadfast in his last moment as on the day he was born."

The day after the funeral, the housemaid who smiled and giggled at Orz in the mornings at PS 10 stopped the carriers as they trudged up Hill Road and told them what she knew. They agreed to honour Pa Johnson by suspending their warning calls for one day.

That very morning a lorry struck and killed Timba.

One moment, Orz, followed by Fish and Timba, zoomed in on Kaka Junction, the cool morning breeze lathering their faces; the next, a metal mass popped out of the darkness. Orz and Fish remembered pushing down hard with their feet, crossing the junction, and seeing the metal mass swerve left, lurch as if about to topple, right itself, and melt into the distance.

Timba died in the abrupt, inevitable way the last wisp of cool morning breeze disappears at the arrival of stifling day heat. An economic death, it seemed. No groans, broken bones, or burnt flesh. Except: drip... silence... drip... silence. They spun towards the sound. Sure enough, above them, in the house at the opposite corner from Pa Johnson's, they saw Timba, his head lodged through the yellowish-brown banisters of the upstairs verandah, blood dripping from his head like a faulty tap.

Scared they might get into trouble, Orz and Fish raced down to PS 10, grabbed their carts, and, for the first time since the station opened, pushed empty containers back up Hill Road. They did not go home but parked their carts against the wall of the Johnson Spring plant. Then, without telling their families of the accident, they walked down toward Kaka Junction. By the time they arrived, dawn's sapphire-blue light had lit the first scene of the day: a sombre crowd forming a semi-circle in front of the house, staring at Timba's dangling body. A chorus of voices from one side of the crowd chanted:

He was one of the water carriers.
Brave boys, faithful servants of this nation.

Their water relieved our suffering:
Cooled our parched throats
Washed our food-encrusted pans
Watered our penny vegetable gardens
Cleansed our grime-covered bodies.
He must have been killed by sorcerers, jealous devilish people
They want to see us suffer.
Farewell, boy child, son of patriot, Jerry
Till we meet again on that beautiful shore.
Where are his friends, the other water carriers
By their wits trying to make a living?
Dear God, help us to protect their future, our present!

But another chorus of other voices intoned:

He was one of the water carriers.
Unruly youth, faithless, bane of this nation.
Their noisy carts blocked our restful sleep
Left us tired all day
Scared our children
Defiled our holy Sabbath
Turned our streets to markets.
This is a hit and run.
Good riddance, boy child, son of traitor, Charles
Wild uncouth, killer of your own!
You had this death coming, showing no regard for our law, our civility.
Where are his friends, the other water carriers?
Arrest them, every last one of them, and remove this scourge on Teneria.

The prospect of jail, if they escaped street justice, roused Orz and Fish from their stupor, and they melted from the crowd as if an untested egwugwu had selected them to be candidates it would cut in halves and join back again in living humans. The two remaining carriers walked back up Hill Road, arm in arm, their tongues swelling, ears and noses clogging. The world contracted into oblique aqua droplets.

By the back wall of the Johnson Spring plant, they sat beside their carts, glad to be away from the judging voices. They rested their heads on the wall and let their minds go back – to the beginning, the moment the idea for their water-delivery business burst from the screen of the sweltering movie theatre like piping-hot oleleh bean-cake from its banana-leaf wrapper.

They remembered their barefooted walks on hot tarred roads in search of boards, old and new, they could salvage or steal. They remembered the first one, a discarded, easel-mounted blackboard they found in a school compound, a math equation and other scribbles of knowledge faintly visible on both sides; how they carried it like a hard-won championship trophy to their compound, set it up against the wall of the common outdoor kitchen, and dreamed about how it would free them from menial work for pocket change and leftover food; and, strangely, how all three of them woke up earlier than usual the next morning to secure the board so their mothers would not think they had brought it home to be used as firewood.

They remembered the other boards – thick, thin, sturdy, saggy, smooth, coarse, grainy, wavy, reddish-brown, brownish-red, yellow, creamy, off white – that, along with nails, they scrounged from furniture workshops, wood depots, building sites, backyards, churchyards, schoolyards and cowyards. They remembered their efforts to take out the bearings from the wheels of junk cars: how they had stuck their hands into greasy brake drums and wiped them on their sweat-drenched shirts; how they had poked, turned, twisted, hammered and grabbed to pull out the bearings – three-inch oily steel disks – and had set sixteen of them next to the boards.

They remembered the boards, bearings and ropes strewn about the yard without form – their blueprint an oil-stained magazine picture of a go-cart, their untrained biceps and triceps the power tools to give shape to the formless. They remembered how for six days inexperienced hammers missed their marks and smashed into fingers and toes as they'd nailed the front and rear axles to the main chassis; how chisels jabbed the flesh between the thumb and pointer finger as they'd shaped the ends of the front and back axles to fit the bearings; and how deformed fingers tied the ropes to control the front axle.

Aaaah, they remembered the day they rolled out the finished carts and how their siblings clapped, mothers cried, and fathers glowed; and they remembered the young men who sneered and said carrying water was women's work and how Timba, fire in his eyes, said he would rather do women's work than be a man who did nothing all day but scratch his balls.

They had rested on the seventh day and began their deliveries the following Monday, their ball-bearing carts rolling down Hill Road decades after motorised vehicles began plying Teneria's streets. The city's young had clapped, some had even marvelled at the carriers' ingenuity; but their compatriots, struggling with cataracts, rheumatism and dementia, had sighed, confused, no longer sure of time or place or progress.

The carriers recalled their mothers' smiles when they slipped crumpled bills into their hands to buy the corn porridge that made the hungry girls smile and revealed their sisters; the cold Star beers that wiped the scowl off the faces of the men with the dirty finger nails and pockmarked bodies and revealed their fathers; and the books that kept their brothers in school and promised a future better than their own.

Even though their Timba had been taken from them, felled at the scene, the two remaining carriers determined that nothing, nothing, would ever stop them from delivering water.

Two days after he was killed, the families returned Timba to the soil, unmarked, from which he had sprung. They had no money for headstones or slabs. No time for eloquent eulogies. After a few coughs, sniffles and snorts, they walked back to the firestones and mortars of the treeless compound. There, the mothers pleaded with Orz and Fish to stop delivering water and do something safe, but the fathers, their faces frayed with worry, made no such pleas. It was, after all, an economic death.

So, yes, at 4 a.m., the day after Timba's burial, the two remaining carriers raced down Hill Road, again. They understood what few others did: that for five glorious minutes every morning, the breeze of independence, of freedom, coursed through their pores, puffing their hearts and swelling their lungs. They became Olurun, Mulungu and Atala, masters of the universe. As they crossed Kaka Junction, *they* – not their parents, the radio voices, or Teneria's mfs – controlled their fate. With a right or left tug of their axles and a scan of the junction for light and sound, *they* decided their destiny. Nothing else mattered – not the partisan politicians blaming each other for the water shortage or the well-fed people condemning lawless youths. Orz and Fish knew they not only had to fly down Hill Road every morning to honour Timba, but they also knew they had to do their part to help the people of Teneria.

Unfortunately, they died less than a month after Timba.

Their bodies warned them though. Aches, chills, dizzy spells and deep-inside-the-stomach rumblings accompanied them like vengeful ghosts. Their minds, too, signalled the need for change. They wondered how long they could continue pushing the carts uphill and tempting fate crossing Kaka Junction. They had even begun thinking about their future, especially after the buxom housemaid became Orz's girlfriend and her hand raced up and down his trousers inside the dark aluminium shack theatre. Pow-pow, shots rang out. Boo-doom, a body fell, except this time it was not a gangster on screen but Orz, experiencing a high that sent his right leg flailing, tugging the cord that supplied power from the generator to the video player, and ending the movie.

Even on the morning of their death, Teneria's Independence Day, nature also warned them. Storm clouds growled over Teneria, foretelling of angry waters to come, as if Heaven decided it had had enough of this self-inflicted drought, and would now shower Teneria with enough water to return her to her once lush-green state. When they arrived at the gate, a prickly drizzle had been falling and hefty wind bands swooped down the hills. Anticipation charged the atmosphere, as in their neighbourhood churches before the charismatic thunder-fire prophets exploded into sermons about the evils of sorcery. That morning, Orz and Fish did not talk much to each other or to the two new carriers – Patrick, a boy, and Musu, a girl built like a boy – who had joined them.

As they were about to depart, Orz vomited. Fish rubbed his back until he stopped. Then, he shook the dregs of water from one of his containers into a cup and gave it to Orz. Fish suggested Orz should go home, but the idea amounted to asking the sun to return to bed at the start of a cloudless morning. So, instead, they agreed to a slow, side-by-side ride down Hill Road, with Fish helping to steer Orz's cart, and, if necessary, to jump off rather than risk crossing in front of a vehicle. Fish relayed the instructions to the recruits, and the four left the school gate, Orz and Fish never again to return.

As they approached Kaka Junction, thunder rumbled, followed by lightning. It illuminated the cross streets – swept clean of the debris of day life, perhaps the way Pa Johnson would have liked – for a brief moment. Darkness smothered the junction as the four carriers entered it.

No, they were not killed by a car. They off-loaded their containers, arranged them around the pump, and sprinted to the culvert. Moments later a massive storm assaulted Teneria. Within minutes, the water flowing through the culvert had reached their shins and had enough force to make them grip the walls of the canal. Then the rain stopped, dead, like loud music when electricity goes out.

They hurried back to the pump. Orz, however, stayed behind. He needed to go. Fish, feeling dizzy himself, tightened the caps on Orz's containers, loaded them on his cart, and helped Patrick and Musu load theirs. The newcomers said goodbye and pushed their carts up Hill Road.

Fish's chest tightened as he walked toward the culvert to check on Orz, who squatted on his heels off to the side, his head bowed. Sensing he was being watched, Orz raised his head and waved to convince Fish he was fine. Though not assured, Fish returned to his cart and trekked up Hill Road. He might well have been Sisyphus.

He'd push forward but the cart would roll back. His back and arms ached. He trembled. Sweat soaked through his white singlet. The world became silent. Hill Road swayed from left to right. Then it leapt and slammed Fish in the forehead.

"Epidural hematoma precipitating cause of death," the man behind the blood-smeared apron said, pointing to Fish's body. He had millions of the cholera bacteria. Enough to kill an elephant two times. He spun to his left and pointed to Orz's body. "Same cause. Millions and millions of vibrio cholera. You people should boil your water. Don't you listen to the radio?"

The carriers' parents, siblings and neighbours looked on, puzzled, befuddled. They did not have an answer for him, did not know what questions to ask, or even think they had the right to ask questions, let alone to demand answers. In fact, because they had no money for burials, they did not want the apron-wearing man to tell them to take the bodies away, so they hotfooted out of the mortuary, the strange words describing their children's deaths offering a vague realisation there were stories and worlds to which they did not have access.

That night, the surviving parents watched the silhouetted forms of their children playing around a small bonfire and wondered: how could they protect them, their resources and only source of wealth, when they could not protect their Orz, Timba and Fish? Who would care for them when they got older? The bonfire sputtered out, unable to provide them with either an answer or comfort. With heavy hearts, the parents clambered on the straw mattresses that poked them into a listless sleep. But when, at 4:05 a.m., the bragalagabragalagalagalaga of bearings woke them and echoed around the toffee-coloured hills like the call of the muezzin, their hearts grew wings, and they soared along with Patrick, Musu and two new water carriers down Hill Road.

The Worme Bridge

Cat Hellisen

*W*hen I was old enough to walk by myself to the shops to buy my mother her cigarettes, she decided I was too old to believe in rubbish like Santa Claus and the tooth mouse and fairies that live at the bottom of the garden. Instead, I would learn the real stuff, like what really happened to Pa and my older brother Matty, and what was going to happen to her.

Why ever since Pa had died she'd made me take him as medicine, ground up into my food to ward off the sickness.

Ma couldn't walk properly because her feet pained her now that they'd gone all boneless and scaly with sickness, and no one would serve Matthias because of the stink, even if he could have walked to the shops himself. Which he couldn't. Matty was born like that though, Ma told me, with his legs all melted together like two candles lit too close to each other and forgotten.

The trips weren't so bad. I liked the walk past all the square little houses with their concrete ox-wagon wheel walls, with their laundry and their chimney smoke, flicking the lighter in my pocket and thinking about things to burn. I liked to pretend no one saw me, walking up to the corner shop where the Indian men would sell me cigarettes even if I was only ten, because they knew my ma and I guess they felt sorry for her. The walk there and back took twice as long as it should have because I had to go to the second-closest shop. The closest one meant going riverwise and crossing the foot bridge built in 1809 and named after some dead man, I guess the one who built it in 1809. Or maybe he just had other people build it in 1809. He was very proud of it because he put a big stone right by the front that said *Built in 1809* so we would never forget. The man was called Matthias too, but they called the bridge Worme instead.

By the time I got back to Ma, I'd always be wishing she didn't have these rules about the bridge and the river. Some days it could get so hot the tar would melt under your feet and give you new soles for free, and sometimes it was so cold you wouldn't even be sure you had feet and would have to check at the door before going in to the house. *Are these feet inside my shoes? Or have I got the sickness too?*

Let me tell you for nothing it was a great relief to find all my toes in the right order and with the right amount of skin and bone. You miss them fierce when you don't have them.

I would open Ma's cigarette box for her while she shivered, wrapped in dog blankets she bought cheap at the Pick n Pay. The skin on her hands hurt too much to do it herself. I loved that crinkle of the see-through plastic, thin as sleep, the slow tear. I loved peeling back the silvery paper and finding the twenty sticks, all neat as soldiers. The smell of new tobacco, before the fire ate it. I would breathe deep, then pick the bottom middle one to draw out. The virgin straw.

If it had been my box of smokes, I would have taken that one and turned it over and placed it back in, filter face out. I am old enough to know about virgins, but too old for fairies.

Ma was always like that – telling me what it was time for me to believe in. I knew about virgins because one time she decided I needed god, or we all did, so she took me and Matty to the church – rolling him all the way there on a low wooden trolley with wheels from a pram. We had to sit on cold hard pews and listen to the man at the top tell us stuff from the Bible. This was when Matty was alive, of course. We didn't take his stinking twisted body to church after, even though they seem to love believing in dead guys.

It was boring in the church, and because Matty couldn't sit properly, he was rolling around on the pew and flopping about and just being a general nuisance, so people kept looking at us and whispering and shaking their heads. It was also because Ma was single. I had a dad but he died before Matty was born so it was hard to explain to people how that worked. They thought Ma was a whore. Another word I was old enough to know.

Except for all the idiots, there was one nice thing, and that was the singing. During the boring bits the man at the top would say *every body rise and turn in your hymn-books to page* and every person who still had their body would shuffle up with whispers and cracks and rustles through their pages until they found the right one. Not

Matty, he just rolled about, gasping because he already couldn't breathe properly then. But I would stand up, and Ma next to me, and we would share this hymn-book which was a thick book with pages made of fairy wings. We joined together in praise of our good risen lord, who I guess was Jesus or his dad, since they were actually the same person. And this Jesus guy was dead and then alive again, and all the church people were okay with that and made songs about it. So you can see why I didn't understand when they couldn't deal with Pa or Matty.

The music was slow and sad and filled with water, and it was like drowning, but nicer. There was an old lady who would play this organ, which was a big thing like a piano but with a different sound, a sound of waves. It made music that crashed down right over your head. Then all the cold deep men's voices rose up with currents and little waves and eddies of higher sounds, like water that is warm in the sun.

And I would sing too, catching the tune and letting it pull me on, the notes flickers of fish, shoals of bright sounds that raced through the river of the organ swell. And that's how I know about virgins because they kept going on about Jesus's ma being a virgin and my ma had to explain it there in the church because I kept asking.

And then one day Ma decided we didn't need god after all and we stayed home on Sundays again. She had to drown Matty and there's no way to explain that kind of thing to church people.

"Sanette? Is that you?" Ma called from inside the house even though no one else ever comes to us. I sighed and kicked off my shoes so I could unroll my socks and check my toes. It was winter – the third after Ma took Matty to the river and the second after her own feet gave in. All my toes were present which is what you say at school when the teacher calls your surname in home class.

I always get called last: "Worme."

And my answer is to say: "Present, mejevrou." Like I am giving her a gift, which I am not, unless it is the gift of my presence, which is a pun, Matty says. Also I must call her *mejevrou,* even though it is an English school, because she says *mis* is what cows make.

I wriggled all my toes, one by one. "Ja, Ma," I said. Then I frowned, because the one pinky toe was stiff and a little blue, but I couldn't tell if that was because of winter, or because I was going down the road of illness. Ma had always said that I would be fine because my legs were straight and strong, and it was only the boys who have to be drowned and brought back. But that was before her feet went, so now I am extra scared all the time.

Quickly, I covered up my toes, rubbed them hard to make them warm, and shoved them back in my school shoes, which were black and pretty with a strap and a floral cut-out and were more expensive than plain Mary Janes. I had feet, so all the shoe money went on me.

"I got your cigarettes, Ma." I grabbed the plastic bag back up. Cigs for Ma, a Kit Kat for me and a tin of sardines for Matty. I hopped over the little ridge of wood on the front door step, and went inside.

The smell was very bad in my house. Partly it was because of Matty, but also Ma who sat with her feet in a black plastic tub of hot water and her dog blankets wrapped around her, hoping to stay human, and partly it was because she kept Pa's bones. Though they were dried out now, they still had a funny stink to them, like the skin of a snake or a lizard. They were in a box covered with sea shells and lined inside with red felt. A very expensive box – almost a hundred rand – but not very big, because there weren't so many bones left. Ma kept grinding them up and feeding them to me.

"Here," I said, unwrapping the box of cigarettes as slowly as I could. I folded the silver paper neat and tucked it in my blazer pocket, took out the first virgin straw and lit it with my yellow lighter that I keep only for Ma's cigarettes, and not for anything else, like setting fire to the school dustbins. The smoke tasted like the death of fairies and Santa Claus. The smoke tasted like learning the truth and it always made me choke. I handed her the lit cig and crouched down to look at her feet.

They were going wrong. I didn't need to be a doctor to see they were turning long and thin and see-through like Matty's. The skin at her ankles was rubbery, melting together. There were raw bits shining pale red where she'd pulled the skin apart. It didn't matter. In a few months Ma would be as bad as Matty. She was already starting to smell rotten. Worse than cigarettes and not-washing. "You okay, Ma?"

She nodded, and blew out smoke so I couldn't see the expression in her eyes. She only started smoking when her feet started changing, and I think it was because she believed that the stink of the cigarettes covered up the other smell. Which was definitely getting worse. Maybe she and Matty couldn't tell because they were wrapped in it all day like a duvet, but I still went outside and knew that healthy people with two good strong legs did not smell like cod liver oil rotting inside a bottle left on a windowsill in the sun.

"Ma, where's Pa's old trolley?" I said, because at thirteen I was learning to be practical. We'd used the trolley to take Matty to school, and to church, and then, right at the end of his first life, to take him down to our family bridge built in 1809, which is probably when the first Worme had to drown someone in their family.

Ma coughed, choking on her stinking cigarette. "Don't need the trolley yet," she said and waved at her feet. "I'm fine now, the water's helping."

The water would only help with the pain for so long, we both knew. Towards the end, we kept Matty in the bath, trying to slow everything down with clean water, scraping off his scales and trying to cut his fingers apart. He used to cry when Ma took the little vegetable peeling knife and slit through the skin growing thin between his fingers, gluing them together. He never cried loud, but he turned his face to the wall and his shoulders would shake. Ma dropped the bits of skin in a plastic bowl that I held out for her, and then I buried them in the garden.

But even with all that cutting and burying, we couldn't stop his insides from changing, or help his lungs work. We had to drown him. It was the quickest way to set him free, in the end.

We'd gone at night, Matty crouched and covered with a sheet

on his trolley, and rattle-bounced down the gritty tar road that was always full of potholes because of the summer rain, all the way to the river and the Worme Bridge.

Ma had drowned him. I had just sat on the edge of the river with my knees right up against my chest and cried because ten is too young to know that sometimes your parents have to do what's best for you even if it hurts you. Even if it hurts them.

Afterwards we had dragged Matty back home, wrapped in his sheet again, and three days later he'd said he felt much better and he was sorry that Ma was so sad.

I watched Ma smoking her cigarettes and smelling like rancid fish, before I left her and went to the bathroom. The door was closed, so I knocked, and after a while Matty said to come in.

"How was school?" he asked. He could still talk, though it could be hard to make out the words unless you knew what he was saying. Also, he was really smelly. Not in a rotting way, like Ma, but like a harbour full of seals and seaweed.

"Okay," I told him. "You lucky you missed all this, I think this is the hundredth time we are learning about the Great Trek." Which is basically the story of how a bunch of Dutch people in the Cape got mad at the English and missioned off up the country, and mostly they had a horrible time of it but they said god was on their side so he helped them kill a lot of black people, which seems a bit unfair to the black people, really. This god guy, I don't know.

"I brought you something," I told him, and peeled open the tin of sardines.

Matty took them with a wide grin, which was horrible because all his teeth had fallen out and his mouth was full of needle white splinters. I was used to them, but I could imagine if anyone else had seen him they'd be grossed out. And scream, and probably try bash his head in with a spade.

I waited till he finished his meal, dripping the last of the fishy oil down his throat, and handed me the empty tin before I told him about Ma.

He frowned. "I was wondering why she never came to visit

me any more," he said, and I could hear how sad that made him. "Thought maybe she was sick of seeing me." He waved at his legs, which were under water, fused all together and silvery green and scarred with white ridges. In the beginning Ma had tried to scrape the scales off with the back of a knife, but she gave up after he died and now they've grown in funny. Some scales were beautiful, silver and the size of my thumb nail, others were twisted and small and a dull grey. In places the scales never grew out at all, and the skin was white and puffy-raw. I knew they hurt him, those raw scars. We would never do that to Ma, but we couldn't stop her doing it to herself.

"She's definitely going funny," I said. I curled my toes in my shoes, and felt the one twinge and ache. Not me. I wasn't going. My legs were fine. I wasn't going to die. But Ma was. "I'll dig the trolley out of the garage tonight. We'll need it soon."

Matty didn't say anything after that, just swirled his webbed fingers through the little bit of water he could move in, and sighed deeply. Every now and again he would shift his body so that he could put his head under water for a moment to wet his gills. He could breathe out of water for a little while if he had to but preferred it the other way: gillwise.

I pulled the plug to drain some of the water, and ran in fresh cold water from the taps. Matty didn't feel the cold like I did. He said it was better, the cold. Being warm made breathing hard, even though he tried holding on to it, because it made him feel human still. "If I have to drown Ma," I whispered to him, "you're going to have to move out to the river." There was only one bath in the Worme house. The Wormes who had died couldn't survive out of water. Just look at Pa. Or what was left of him.

"It won't be so bad," Matty said, which was a lie. Matty would be in the river, and Ma would live in the bath. And I – I would have to keep grinding up what was left of Pa and sprinkling him into my sandwiches to keep me from turning. I would have to buy Ma sardines with the little bit of money she kept under her mattress, and change her bath water, and watch her be alone and dead.

"If it happened to Ma," I said, "Chances are it will happen to me."

Even Matty couldn't lie that much, not right to my face. "Perhaps," he said. "But Ma is old, it only took her now. You've got years to live."

Years. A whole lifetime of living in the Worme house, with only my dead ma in the bath tub for company, and being able to spend time with my big brother only when there was no moon and I could pray to the dead Jesus who rose again that no one would see me sneak down to the river.

I took Matty down to the river first. Three months had gone past since we'd talked about killing Ma, and winter was softening a little at the edges. Ma could hardly breathe most of the time, and she'd stopped sending me out to buy her cigs. She'd turned down the last pack I bought, and I kept it now, sealed and new. Like a reminder. "It's time," I told him. "There's no moon tonight, and it'll be dark enough." I could wheel Matty down on the trolley, wrapped in his sheet. He could breathe long enough for me to get him to the river, we knew that much. If people heard the midnight rattle of the pram wheels, they would just think it was some homeless guy, looking for junk, rooting through the rubbish bins. No one would come to see what I was doing.

We waited for the dark to fall and for the stars to light up. When there is no moon, the stars shine much brighter, as though they're trying to make up for all the time the moon takes from them. *When the cat's away the mice will play*, I thought, and pictured the stars as little bright mice leaping here and there, looking for crumbs in the night. It was better than thinking about what we were going to do.

It was better than thinking about the toenail I found in my sock, and how my pinkie toe had started growing long and thin, and how I could see the bone through the skin, how it bent easily as the quill of a small feather. How spongey the skin on my legs felt.

I carried Matty, half-dragging him out to the trolley, and when he was firmly wrapped in place, I grabbed the thick plastic twine

189

of the pull, feeling it bite into the softening skin of my palm, and tugged him down the road to the Worme Bridge. Matty went easily into the water, and stretched out, flicking the long bones of his feet. Of his tail. He belonged here. It would take a blind idiot to think he didn't. And Ma did too.

"I'll be back," I told him. He nodded. He'd promised to do the drowning. It would be easier for him, already there in the river. No sense getting me all wet and I'd already had to do all the heavy work of hauling both of them down to the water.

Ma didn't argue with me. Her legs were mostly grown together by now, and her feet were gone. Just a big split tail like a fish's stuck on all wrong. She'd given up on scraping away at her growing scales sooner than she'd given up on Matty's, so she was already silvering. Her legs were bare and sexless, but she wore a big loose T-shirt.

"I'm not about to go around naked like a whore," she told me. "I'll go to my death with dignity."

She was much heavier than Matty, though at least she was able to help me more. After a bunch of heaving and swearing we got her on to the trolley, and I started the final trek down, the trolley practically racing me so that I had to run to keep up with it and Ma, so that they didn't career off into the pavement and send Ma rolling downhill like a giant dead tuna.

I pulled the trolley to a stop near the bank, tearing open the puffy skin on my palms, and hobbled over to Ma to help her down to the water's edge. My new toe was paining me, crushed up in my shoe. Luckily we'd talked it all through before, the three of us, and Ma went to the water like a woman going to John the Baptist, who was a friend of Jesus and also had to drown him first.

It didn't take long, though she thrashed a fair bit while Matty held her under.

During their struggle, I kicked off my shoes and sat on the bridge, my bottom getting soaked through with early dew, and my legs dangling over the edge of the water, as I leaned between the railings and watched. My toe shimmered in the starlight, silvery pale and new. I pressed my knees together hard, and felt the skin give slightly, the blood and veins underneath calling out to each other, moving toward a joining.

Matty's head bobbed up, and his needle teeth shone as he smiled.

"Done?" I asked him. In my pocket, I closed my fingers around the box of cigarettes and pulled it out to slowly unwrap the thin plastic, to fold the silver paper and choose my virgin straw. I tapped it with one fingernail, waiting. A moment later, Ma's head came up alongside Matty's. She was staying in the river, there'd be no three days of rebirth for her. It was better this way. Better to let your dead go than to try hang on to them.

I took the yellow lighter from my pocket and thought about how quickly the Worme house would burn. By the time the fire department came, I'd be gone. They'd have no idea where to find me. I slipped Ma's cigarette between my lips and closed my eyes. The fire sparked and even through my closed lids I could see the warm redness of it. I breathed in the smoke from my final cigarette. It tasted like acceptance of growing up.

Drowning would hurt, I knew. But first, I had a house to burn down.

Nyar Nam (Daughter of the Lake)

Florence Onyango

*T*heir silhouettes, cast against the purple-red of the rising sun, were like the chiaroscuro illusion of a visual masterpiece; a painting telling the story of fishermen preparing to set out for the morning. Auma savoured the brevity of the sunrise. Warm whiffs of freshly fried mandazi floated through the air. A low vibrating chatter nudged the world awake.

Auma cherished mornings like this. The fishermen sat on the small, crooked wooden chairs, leisurely drinking tea as they observed the hyacinth weeds suffocate the surface of the lake. It was going to be another slow day unless the wind picked up and blew the menace away.

"Jajuok!" Atis, who had been squatting by the basin washing plastic cups and plates, pointed a soapy finger at a lonely boat moving languidly over the water. "Atis!" Auma warned. Chastised by her grandmother's glare, Atis obediently resumed with the dishes. But the damage was done; the fishermen had turned their idle attention to the man struggling to push his boat through the hyacinth.

"There's that crazy old man." One fisherman commented, instigating gossip of Mahe's maligned tales. Atis slowed her washing and her ears twitched with glee. The fishermen always enjoyed their tea with a hefty dose of sigana – village tidbits. It was the only thing that made washing dishes at five in the morning bearable.

Mahe was known as the town's crazy old man. His real name was Odongo, but everyone called him Mahe after the unlucky man in the Luo legend of Nyar Mgondho; a fisherman who hooked a beautiful woman, married her and became wealthy, but let his mind become poisoned by greed and alcohol, until the woman marched back into the lake with all his riches, leaving him poor and humbled once again. For the adults, Odongo was a crazy old man whose fate was eerily similar to Mahe's. For the children, Odongo was more like a jajuok – a night runner; a possessed man who runs around naked at night causing a ruckus.

Atis was quite a shrewd girl, a captivating storyteller who would charge the children a shilling for a thrilling tale – and Odongo was her source of spooky bedtime stories. She would listen attentively to the fishermen and then give their stories a good twist of horror. Whispers of Odongo the jajuok delivered delicious shivers under the gleam of kerosene lamps during long dragging nightfalls.

The fishermen were all chattering about the old man. "Do you think Mahe had something to do with those two missing girls that were in the news?" one asked. Atis's eyebrows pricked up. *What missing girls?* she wondered. Wild tales of ritualistic murders and witchcraft circulated in her head.

"That's enough!" Auma hissed at the fishermen with more asperity than she had intended. "Are you so idle that you'd turn a lonely, grieving man into a joke?"

The fishermen exchanged glances. Much to Atis's chagrin, they changed the subject to the water hyacinth and what a nuisance it was. Sensing Atis's annoyance, Auma turned her attention to the lanky girl washing dishes. She was treating the dishes carelessly, throwing them about and splashing water everywhere.

Auma's mind drifted back through time to the shy child Atis had once been: a tiny and brittle girl, like a dried leaf that would crumble if not handled gently; the result of her father suddenly abandoning her one evening with her grandmother. For years Atis would pitter-patter behind Auma, watching the world, hiding from behind her long flowing skirts, her little eyes wide and round as if she could absorb everything with them.

When Auma got too old to farm her land – and when Atis was still too young to help her – she began to sell tea and mandazi to the fishermen by the Lake's shore. The journey to the Lake from home took about half an hour and so every morning she was up long before the crack of dawn. She had left Atis behind the first time she made the journey. She had thought that the commute and early hours would be too strenuous for the frail child, so she left her in the care of her neighbour's cousin. But when Atis had woken up and Auma was nowhere to be found, she panicked and decided to go look for her grandmother. Auma had arrived home late in the evening to find everyone out with their lamps looking for Atis. It took two hours to find her; the two worst hours of Auma's life, as visions of Atis being mauled by wild animals filled her mind every time she heard the hyenas' distant, deranged laughter. By the time Atis had eventually turned up, Auma was prepared to unleash the full fury of her pent-up worry on her. But Atis just stood there, smudged by dust and adventure, her eyes shimmering. She rattled on and on about a leopard with eyes like pearls that had escorted her all the way home. That night, under the attention of relieved villagers, Atis overcame her shyness like a hatched chick.

The fishermen were long gone by the time Auma brought her mind back to the present. Atis was done with the dishes and seated on one of the chairs sucking on a sugar stone, thoughtfully observing Odongo. Auma followed her gaze to where Odongo was struggling to anchor his boat.

"Atis?"

"Yes, Nyanya?"

"Tomato? Who are you calling a tomato?"

Atis, giggling, turned to face her grandmother. It was a little joke they always used to break the ice: "nyanya" meant both grandmother and tomato. Atis then addressed her grandmother properly, in Luo: "*Yes*, Dani?"

"Why did you call the old man 'Jajuok'?"

"I heard the other children calling him that."

"He's not a night runner. He is just a very sad and lonely man."

"But he acts funny. He's always talking to himself."

"That's because he is sick."

Atis did not respond. She looked at the old man walking aimlessly about, flipping his arms up and down as he muttered to himself. Auma's brows furrowed with worry as she studied Atis. She knew that it was Atis who had started that jajuok rumour: she had a flair for drama, basking in the attention that came from exaggerated fibs. It had begun with the lie about the leopard. In truth, Atis had gone looking for her grandmother, but when she couldn't find her, she had come back home. One of the villagers had spotted her climbing up the mango tree where she had fallen asleep till the commotion had awoken her. Not wanting to rain on her parade, the villager had not told anyone but Auma. Children are known to exaggerate a story here and there to make it more interesting, but what made Atis such a captivating storyteller was that she actually believed everything she said. This worried Auma greatly.

Odongo was now on his way towards them. He made as if to walk past but instead stopped and turned towards them. Auma's gasp caught in her throat. She had always been too afraid to go near him. Seeing him like this, a scruffy-looking man with the unkempt hair and wide vacant eyes, her heart bled for him. His mind had long been captured by his demons. He fixed his eyes on Atis with an unnerving gaze; he stood so still he seemed unreal, as if he was made of stone. Atis met his eyes with a mix of intrigue and fear in her own. From hell and back, that was the transition Auma saw unfold in Odongo's eyes. It began with a gleam of recognition through his hazy stare, like a fogdog. "Atis," he let out her name in a soft breath before his demons snatched him away again. Abruptly, he turned and hastened away. Auma's entire body felt like it would melt from the intensity of the encounter.

Her son had returned, even if for a fleeting moment, he had returned.

Neither Atis nor Auma would recall the walk back that evening. Their weathered bare feet carried them and their heavy thoughts home. Something was stirring in the pits of Atis's memories, fragments of a person weaved in and out of her thoughts, cudgelling her mind. Auma recalled the moment over and over, invoking hope within her. She had always believed that Atis had the power to bring her father home. Atis was so much like her mother, if only Odongo could see it, he would come back to his senses.

When they got home, they made brown porridge and pan fried peanuts. Auma asked Atis to sit with her. She had placed a lesso over the woven cypress mat just outside the hut. She sat on it with her back against the mud wall, her long slim legs stretched out. Her bony feet, sticking out of her long dress, were crossed at the ankles. Auma always sat this way when she was about to explain something intricate to Atis. Auma looked up at the sky. Far away from the city lights, the stars shone in all their glory. Auma smiled as she remembered when Atis had tried to show her the constellations.

"Atis, do you see that star?" Auma asked, pointing to a star twinkling on its own near a cluster.

"Yes."

"Doesn't it feel lonely to you?"

Atis stared at the star but did not respond. She wondered if stars were like people. If they felt sad or left out.

"That star reminds me of Odongo."

Odongo had called her name and called forth her past. She couldn't understand it yet but in that moment she knew that Odongo was the father that had left her.

"Why is Baba that way?" Atis wondered.

Startled, Auma turned to her. "Do you remember?"

"Not really, but I know. Now."

"Your father is a very sad man. He lost something precious to him in the lake."

"Did he lose Mama in the lake? Did she return to the lake like Nyar Mgondho?"

Not exactly, Auma wanted to respond, but she only nodded.

"If Baba found Mama, would he stop being sick?" she asked.

"Mama is not coming back, Atis, but if Baba finds you then he will become better."

"But I'm not lost."

*A*tis had fallen asleep on Auma's lap. Auma mulled over life, and how sometimes truth was stranger than fiction. Akello, Atis's mother, was like a siren to Odongo. Short of catching her like a fish, as the legend goes, he rescued her from drowning. Or had he? Akello was a beautiful Nairobi-bred girl who had fallen in love with Odongo – or thought she had, at least. To her, Odongo was a knight in shining armour, or, more fittingly, the frog that had turned into a prince. Enthralled with their whimsical romance, they married, and Odongo left to live in Kisumu with her. Akello's father was then the Governor of Kisumu. He took Odongo under his wing and mentored him. He placed Odongo in charge of a thriving electronics business. Auma had met the governor once. His eagerness towards Odongo had been unsettling. He was a furtive man who hid his secrets behind a booming laugh and firm handshakes.

It was only a year after Atis was born that Akello began to unravel. The cracks of her beauty began to reveal the tormented soul hidden beneath. The mist of a fantastical love began to clear. Akello wanted to possess Odongo: every look, every smile, all his attention. She would call him in the middle of the day with a fabricated emergency just for the assurance of having him run to her aid like a knight in shining armour. Two weeks before the night that would ruin their lives forever, Odongo arrived home with Atis. Auma looked at her son and felt a strong premonition. He was vapid, his Achilles' heel exposed for all to see. He was exhausted by the demands his wife was making on him. Auma wanted to beg him to leave Akello but she knew of his devotion to her. He would never abandon his siren.

Odongo should have heeded the warning signs. On one particular occasion, Akello was more restless and sensitive than usual, any wrong word or tone could send her off the ledge in a tempest of fits. They were hosting the governor and close friends for dinner. Odongo had shared some light, innocent banter with a friend. Akello distorted the exchange as flirting. She became convinced that Odongo was having an affair. She accused him of taking her for granted and threatened to ruin his life, to return to the Lake just like Nyar Mgondho. She ran out into the backyard, and kept running till she fell into the lake. Odongo had gone after her but it had been too late to save her.

At first Odongo had held on to his sanity by the thread of his love for Atis. For a while, everything seemed like it was going to be all right, but slowly the thread unravelled and finally snapped.

There were murmurs about witchcraft and people began to avoid Odongo.

"Mama, do you know the time I met Akello? She wasn't drowning, you know, she was trying to kill herself." Odongo had confessed the last time Auma saw her son. He then covered his face with his hands. "They never told me."

When Auma asked what he was talking about, Odongo abruptly got up and said he had to leave Atis with her that day. He promised to return.

After a couple of days Auma began to search for him. He had not been back to his home and no one had seen him around since that night. It would take Auma a long time to accept the morbid reality that her son could have met the same fate as Akello.

There was a nephew of Auma's who had lived in Kisumu around that time. He came to visit her one day with a peculiar story and a spark of hope. "Everyone in Nairobi knew about Akello, that's why her family came to live and marry her off here." He had informed Auma.

"Is that why they rushed the wedding with my son? You know, Odongo said something about her trying to kill herself the last time I spoke to him."

"She wasn't well, Auntie, she hadn't been for a long time. Did you know that she once tried to suffocate Atis?"

"What are you saying? Her own child? Why would she do that?"

"She believed Atis wasn't her child."

"My poor boy. My poor, poor boy. What life did he lead?" Auma lamented, understanding the reality of her son's marriage for the first time.

"There's something else I wanted to tell you about. There's been some chatter by the lake about a crazy man looking for his wife."

That was how Auma found out about the crazy old man called Mahe by the fisherman. She may as well have found his bones for he was nothing but a remnant of a once cheerful, carefree man.

Atis had walked in then. Her nephew had stared at her. "Look at those wide eyes, just like Akello's," he had noted. Auma looked into Atis's eyes as if seeing them for the first time. With dread she could sense Akello's soul reflected in those dark brown eyes, liquid with fantastical notions.

*M*emories weaved through Atis's dreams the night after the revelation by the lake. Images of a laughing man lifting her to the sky. Her father's rusty smell of sweat and the image of his horn-rimmed glasses swelled her heart with longing. She dreamed of a snake wrapped around her throat. It had her mother's voice. A voice calling to her.

Atis awoke to the loud bang of the wooden door kicked open. Outside the hut, fear was the soul of darkness. Two glittering eyes stared at her again. The leopard had come for her. Auma slept soundly beside her. Careful not to wake her grandmother, she stood up quietly. She knew where the leopard was taking her.

"Have you come back for me?" she asked. She remembered it all now, how she had waited and waited for him to come back for her when she was a baby. "Are you looking for Mama? If we find Mama will you come back home?"

He did not respond. She walked over to him and took his hand. "Let's go find Mama."

Together they walked, holding hands. In the distance they heard the hyenas laughing. Atis told him about her encounter with a real leopard. She asked him if it was true that jajuoks dance with hippos.

They reached the shore. The lake was hidden under the shroud of darkness. Atis thought of her mother beneath the rolling waters. Odongo made to pull his hand away but Atis held it tighter. "Where are you going? Are you going to get the boat?"

She let go of Odongo's hand. He didn't understand. He would never bring back Mama like that. Bracing herself, she slowly walked towards the water. She knew what she had to do. She would bring Nyar Mgondho back and everyone would be happy.

Atis first felt the slimly wet leaf of the hyacinth before her toes grazed the icy water, and then she was sinking into the cold. She thought, before she comes back, she must push away the hyacinth to let the fishermen fish. The cold numbed her. She felt herself being pulled further and deeper in. Then she was light, soaring high.

*O*dongo lay with his back to the hard wooden floor of his boat. He was vaguely aware that he had met his daughter that day. Had that been real? Some days he knew himself, most days he didn't. Could he really go back? Would Atis remember him? These thoughts weighed heavily on him before sleep took over. His eyelids began to shut. In the distance, he thought he heard a ripple.

Were

Louis Ogbere

*T*he Atis wanted, more than anything else, a perfect day. It was their seventh anniversary after all. But that morning, they woke up to a new tenant in the compound. She had taken residence in front of the house where the grass, low and trimmed, gave way to a square patch of earth. Her possessions consisted of a once-white wrapper hanging from her rakish body, two rusted beverage tins (the contents unknown), and an empty carton of a transistor radio. She wore two different colours of slippers, the corners of their soles chopped round. Her clothes were of one who had attended an expensive party on an island some years ago, and had since been looking for the road home.

Their son, Morenikeji Ati, was the first to step outside after the family prayer. He was the second-born child, and the only one alive.

He saw the compound covered in fog, the landscape of Mopa an even spread of white. Morenikeji thumped the bottom of the broom with his left palm ready to sweep. For no justifiable reason – as he and his mother had argued more than once – he liked to start this chore from the back of the house. As he sliced into the morning, the fog parted like silk curtains. His wet feet broke twigs that had fallen off a mango tree. The noise drew chirruping from the birds. Some of them flew away, others chose to stay. His face was damp, his eyelashes heavy with dew. He gathered a heap of garbage at the middle of the compound and continued with his sweeping.

He was close to the edge of the garden in front of the house when he heard something stir. He stopped and listened. The woman sprang from the wrapper. Morenikeji took three steps backwards unsure of what was approaching, but when he saw her ragged hair, torn clothes and the mismatched slippers he screamed and ran back to the house.

Margret Ati was in the kitchen singing a familiar song, one of lost love and redemption; the theme song of a Bollywood film she'd watched the week before. It was her obsession with everything Indian that had kept the spice in her marriage. She oftentimes spoke spats of Hindi to herself during chores. Most of the expressions were gleaned from the movies she watched. Ade Ati was in the shower, having turned down his wife's offer to get in with him that morning. Aside the fact that she spent time probing for histories about the scars on his body, Margret Ati was a good four inches taller than him: he just hated being looked down on. And for the seven years they'd been married, they had only tried taking a shower together twice – once during courtship and the other in their third year of marriage.

Morenikeji skidded into the house in sand-covered feet. He cut through the corridor to his parents' bedroom.

"Daddy? Daddy?" He banged on the door. "Daddy! A mad woman is outside."

The water ceased in the bathroom and Ade Ati unlatched the lock and stuck his head out. Soapsuds like cotton wool covered his ears.

"Daddy! A… a mad woman is outside our house, daddy. She is playing…"

"Margret!" Ade Ati yelled at his wife in the kitchen. "*Margret!*" She was in a trance, the full scene of the song playing before her: two young lovers singing and dancing in a cornfield.

Ade Ati re-tied the towel around his waist and stepped out of the room, shoving Morenikeji to the side. He stopped at the kitchen door, stuck his head through as if fearful of a sniper.

"Margi! The boy says there is somebody outside. Please check who it is."

Without waiting for a response from his wife, he made his way back to the bathroom. On his way he passed his son, still stationed at the bedroom door.

"Your mother will see who it is now." He patted the boy on the head and closed the door behind him.

In the kitchen, Margret peeped through the window that overlooked the front yard, but she couldn't make out any figure.

"Mummy…" Morenikeji called when his mother refused to move.

205

"Okay then," she said. "Let's go see for ourselves." She wiped her hands with the towel by the sink and packed her hair into a ponytail. The hair, long and thick, grazed below her shoulder blade – a trophy of a lifelong dedication to Dark & Lovely relaxer and Indian Hair Growth. She stretched her right hand out to her son. His hand fitted right in.

Outside the fog had begun to dissipate, a clear morning emerging. Margret wriggled her hand out from her son's grasp and picked up the broom he had thrown away earlier. She instructed him to wait on the pavement.

The woman had moved her belongings to the side of the house, close to the shrub fence. She was bent over arranging the items: the two tins of beverages positioned on both ends of the wrapper, the transistor radio carton placed in-between, and other paraphernalia of madness scattered on it.

"Hey!" Margret raised the broom like a club.

The woman turned, her face contorted in a grin.

"My customer!" the woman shrieked, clapping her hands. "What can I offer you today?" Her voice was like sandpaper on rough wood, her English impeccable.

Confused, Margret lowered the broom. The woman smiled widely, and moved toward her. "Hey!" She lifted the broom up again. "Hey! Pack these things up and look for somewhere else, now." She used the broom to emphasise the *things,* an afterthought of the initial poking in the woman's general direction.

The woman looked from side to side, then back at Margret, who felt her heart fluttering. There was a trespasser on her property. Morenikeji, frightened, hid behind his mother. The woman looked like one of those mad women who scavenged the dumps and landfills; one of those people Margret had seen herself around Oshodi, turning over packs of expired sausages, biscuits, and diapers covered in baby poop. The filth and smell and disease that came with her kind had just begun to manifest. Margret thought she could see yellow blotches of eczema on her dark skin. Yet, every time the woman smiled – which was unnervingly often

– two dimples appeared at the sides of both cheeks. Margret Ati noticed this and the woman's thin eyebrows and angular chin. To think she spent every other morning tweaking her own eyebrows made her slightly envious of this woman. In her sane life, thought Margret, she was probably a pretty woman. She seemed to her the sort of woman who had a history, a good one: a dutiful wife whom the stress of maintaining her motherhood had overwhelmed. Or maybe a one-time successful business woman who travelled to exotic locations like Dubai, Singapore, Mumbai. Whoever this woman was, life had chosen to punish her.

The woman went back to rearranging her things. Margret stood there watching her for a few seconds then turned to leave. She bumped into Morenikeji and shoved him aside. Morenikeji followed his mother into the house. They both went to Ade's room to give a situation report.

"She seems stubborn," Margret Ati said. She sat on the bed while Morenikeji stood by the dressing table. "I even threatened to call the police, but…"

"The police is of no use here."

She knew he was running late for work and hated such distractions. As a bank manager, his temper fluctuated like the balance sheet of his branch – some months he made profits and on others, losses. One wrong word from her and he might explode. He glanced at her through the mirror and threw one end of his tie over the other to complete a perfect Windsor knot. Ade stood up from the dressing table stool and walked out of the room.

Outside the house, the woman had made the place her home. Her legs were outstretched, with one of the rusted tins wedged between her feet. She stirred the content of the tin with a stick, singing along as she kept busy. The end of a stick pierced her from behind, the sharp point travelling through layers of cotton to draw blood. Before she could flinch, the stick landed on her head. *Thwack.* Twice. *Thwack.*

Ade kept hitting her on the head.

"Move now. Move. Move!"

A twig broke off the stick with which she was being struck and fell into her clothes. She wriggled and scratched her body from the discomfort.

"You will not leave me in this house, 'brebre? How many times have I told you to leave me?" She threw her hands in many directions like an octopus.

The beating intensified.

"Leave me, leave me, leave me!" She cried out in that sandpaper voice, but she did not move, only flinging her hands.

Margret ran out into the yard. "Ade! Please, let her be!" The husband turned to his wife. "You are late for work already, besides the rains are coming. People like this are scared of water. Trust me, she will leave when it begins to pour."

Ade saw the wisdom in his wife's words. He threw the stick away.

"I will talk to the environmental people when I get to the office," he said as he walked past her and into the garage. A moment later he drove out and parked the car few metres away from his wife.

"Don't come out until this nuisance is off my property," he called out. "And keep Morenikeji away from her, please."

Okay boss, she wanted to say, to make light of the situation. Instead she nodded and walked back into the house, drawing the curtains of the parlour windows, and locking the front and rear doors. When the hum of her husband's car drifted from the compound and became a distant rev, Margret closed her eyes where she stood in the kitchen. She crouched over and felt a sharp sting in her heart.

Seven years already and she was still here. Seven years, and she is still sane.

Her mind wandered to the second year of their marriage when she lost her first child. During one of their fights, she had woken up one early morning, the cold pinching her skin till it triggered goose bumps. She went into the kitchen to boil water for Ade's bath. She saw him sweating as he got out of bed while she dropped off the water in the bathroom, next to the tin bath they had then. Then five minutes later, he was screaming down the roof.

Why did you make the water so hot?

Why will you even heat water in this hot weather?

You do not use your initiative, and that is my biggest problem with you!

Then he banged the bathroom door, freeing a screw from the hinges. But that was a long time ago, she told herself. Today was their anniversary and she had to stay sane – sane for her family; well, for Morenikeji, for he was her family. She thought about the woman outside. How did she end up like she did? What if the woman outside had faced the same issues as Margret did in her home? What if Margret faced the same trials that the woman did? Would she be that woman now, with no one looking for her, with no husband, no child, no relative to ask of her whereabouts?

Margret Ati felt a hand wipe off her tears, smearing them all over her cheeks. She opened her eyes and saw Morenikeji standing beside her. He wrapped his hands around her neck, his hands tucked behind her back in an angel's embrace.

*I*t was now mid-afternoon, the sun behind the darkening clouds. The Environmental Agency officials had still not shown up. Margret Ati got up. She looked out the window, but immediately closed her eyes when she did, as if to shut out the world that was playing in front of her house. She went back to her seat, and flicked on the television.

Like the movies she was addicted to, Margret translated all life's conversations and actions into single words. During her child's illness, she had translated life at that time to *trying*. All that she could see and feel was a test to her existence, her purpose as a mother and a wife. Now she looked outside the window and all the happenings fell into a single translation, a Yoruba word – *were*.

Madness.

Her routine had been distorted. Were it a normal day, she would have sat by this same window taking in the empty road, counting the cars that passed through. Other times, she would sit here, her hands and legs busy working the sewing machine.

"Yuck!" Morenikeji made a soured face. He was on the couch

looking out the window. Margret came closer and peeped, her lips slightly parted.

"She looks dirty!"

"Hey," she whispered to her son. "Don't say such things about other people." She reached out and patted his head.

They both watched as the woman moved from the shrub fence. The clothes made her movement sluggish, like a man walking in a bee suit. She stopped by the almond tree at the middle of the compound. The leaves of the tree had browned, the impending harmattan evident in its shrunken fruits. She picked up a fallen stick and aimed it at a half-red-half-green fruit. Failing at knocking it off, she placed one hand on her waist, the other in a mock salute to block the sun, completely oblivious to the two people watching her from the window.

A siren blast from the TV drew Margret's attention back into the house. On the screen an old Peugeot was chasing a silver Toyota through a street of grocery stores, the product of an elopement gone awry. She knew how this scene would end. She played the rest of it in her head as she walked into the kitchen to see to the last of her chores for the day.

The first hint of rain finally appeared in the sky. The almond tree shook in the gathering wind, dropping its dried fruit. They thudded on the ground like pebbles. Dust lifted off the ground. The woman's possessions were caught up in the gust, the tins toppling over. The woman stood up, then stooped to rearrange her things.

"Morenikeji!" Margret called from the kitchen. "Go lock your windows before this rain floods your room."

She heard him shuffle in the parlour, then run through the kitchen down to his room. He returned a minute later and kneeled on the couch to resume his post at the window. He strained his eyes through the threads of rain that fell from the roof. He couldn't see the woman. Alarmed, he opened the front door and stepped out to the verandah. He glanced around where the woman was earlier in the day, then walked around the side of the house. The woman sat there, on the ground, in her heap of clothes and matted hair, her hands folded across her breasts. Morenikeji ran into the house and almost knocked over his mother, along with the plate of steaming jollof rice she was carrying.

"Mummy! Mummy! The woman is shaking!"

He waited to be chastised for going outside. Instead, his mother wordlessly dropped the plate on the dining room table and wrapped herself in a purple shawl that was lying on the couch. Morenikeji tried to follow her outside.

"Go back inside and put on your jumper," she said, and by her eyes Morenikeji knew not to disobey her. Alone, Margret surveyed the compound, her eyes travelling the length of it to the roadside. She saw the soaked wrapper and the rusted tins collecting water on top of them like an offertory tray.

"It's this side," she heard Morenikeji's voice behind her. She threw her hand at the air behind her and missed his head by an inch.

"I thought I told you to stay inside? Get back inside! This boy."

It was the way she said *This boy* that frightened Morenikeji. It meant punishment would be soon to follow.

Still, without her son's help she might not have found the woman. Margret searched by the side of the house and saw the woman in her heap, her body moving in rhythmic spasms. She stood there for a while, the words in her throat bloating, unable to spring forth. In all the years they had lived here, the neighbourhood had offered Margret no practice for the easy words or re-assurances of friendship: almost two kilometres away from their closest neighbours, the Atis' house stood in a thick of vegetation. There was nobody she could call for assistance. The closest houses were occupied by grass growing where a parlour or bedroom or kitchen would be. She couldn't call her friends, she realised, for the majority of her friends had grown to resent her family – mostly her husband, who they were quick to pick on. Telling them her predicament would have generated a lot of bashing and too little help. Besides, they were tens of kilometres away: they all lived in the Lagos mainland now.

Nevertheless, Margret went back inside the house and picked up her mobile phone. She had to remind her husband of their visitor and ask for the environmental officials. But the signal bar on her mobile phone was blank, the name of the network gone. Why today? Why must it always be her to be inconvenienced every time something important happened? She bit her lower lip. She dragged a chair to the dining table, and dropped her head onto the flat, cold wood. What would Neena Abhay do in such situation? She didn't know. Morenikeji came into the parlour with his sweater on, and Margret lifted her head and looked over at him. Outside, the woman had walked back to her items as if she'd just noticed the rain now. She was about to sit down when she did a somersault, landing headfirst, then falling flat on her wrapper. Morenikeji could see her begin to convulse again.

"Mummy?"

"Mm?"

"She is shaking again, on the grass."

Margret got up from the chair and ran outside, only to halt by the verandah stairs and run back into the house. She ran outside again, this time with an umbrella to shield herself from the rain. As she got closer to the woman, she noticed a thick foam of spittle gathering at the corners of her mouth. Margret stood over the woman, raindrops dripping on either side of her body from the fronds of the umbrella. She nudged the woman with her foot. No response. She then stooped down to try to gather her off the ground. She cast aside the umbrella – she couldn't carry both. Morenikeji, who had run outside, picked up the umbrella and then began to gather the woman's belongings.

"Don't touch those things!" Margret shouted at him as she tried to get her hands under the woman. She tripped on a twig and both women tumbled down, the woman spread-eagled on top of Margret. But even this emaciated body was too heavy for her to carry. She dragged the woman to the backyard instead, to the old shack that had served as a kitchen during the times they held parties for their friends. It was detached from the main building and made of corrugated sheet that had begun to rust on the sides. The ground was not tiled, nor concrete; just bare red earth embedded with pieces of charcoal and dead beetles and ants. Stacks of firewood were heaped on the side and a wire-basket, where she kept smoked grasscutters and fish, dangled from a string attached to what passed for a rafter. Margret propped the woman's back against the wall. She twitched her nose as the woman sighed, and set her head straight as it kept drooping to the side. She stood away from the woman as if assessing a piece of artwork, then ran out the room.

Inside the house Morenikeji was struggling to fold up the umbrella when his mother walked in. Margret snatched the umbrella from him and ran again into the rain, picking up each end of the woman's wrapper and folding it, creating a neat, round package of all her belongings. She took this to the shack and dumped it beside the woman. She then took out a raffia mat from the garage, along with a teaspoon and plastic cup that she didn't mind burning later, as well as the container of baking soda from the kitchen counter. This was a trick she learned the hard way, she remembered, from when her daughter had her first seizures. Inside the shack, she laid the woman on the mat, her deep breath resounding between the thin walls. The rain had begun to subside. Margret made a mixture of baking soda and water, and lifted the woman's head. Their eyes met, the woman's bright with only the irises visible; hers red with tears and fatigue. She blinked back the tears and emptied the mixture into the woman's mouth. White froth dripped down her chin. When she began to belch, Margret released her head. She stood up and rested her hand on the door ledge, monitoring her patient. When she was sure the woman was stable enough, she closed the door behind her. Inside the house she dished out jollof rice into a plate and carried a container of drinkable water to the shack.

The woman was still in the position she had left her, her breathing punctuated by hiccups. Margret pushed the plate with her leg toward the woman's side, then as an afterthought, stooped to position the spoon near her clenched hand. The sight of her new tenant made Margret want to cry. She didn't just want to cry for the helplessness of the woman, but also for the reprimand her husband would give her if he found out what she had done.

She shut the door behind her.

*I*t was dark when Ade arrived home from work. Morenikeji was waiting for him by the garage door, offering to carry his suitcase. As the two of them made their way into the house, and Ade into the bedroom, he asked his son where his mother was.

At that moment Margret came out of the kitchen, and set the plates of food on the dining table. She then joined Morenikeji in the parlour as he watched a cartoon. Minutes later as he tap-danced past her seat making a 'come here' sign with his index finger, Margret inhaled the after-scent of Ade's soap, which contrasted with the baking soda, still heavy on her breath. Ade threw glances at his wife and son, trying to make out the cause of their sullenness.

"How was your day today?" she asked him as they sat down together at the dining table.

"Fine," he said. "Fine." A morsel of fufu made its way down his throat. He took a sip from a glass of water. "Sorry I couldn't get through to you earlier today. Your number was not reachable." He took another bite of food. "The environmental people said their men were on strike for something something," he mumbled with his mouth full. Ade could be sweet and childish when he knew he was in the wrong. Margret liked that about him. It softened him.

"So," he then said, straightening his shoulders and clearing his throat, "when did the *were* leave?"

"Oh! Um, since…"

"She left on her own, Daddy," Morenikeji interrupted, covering up for his mother.

"I hope you did not touch her?" It was a question for both of them. *We don't touch such mad people in our place*, was the message he expected them to hear.

Oh!, thought Margret instead, *there he goes again with his people-talk*. It was just like their courtship days all over again, when he would pontificate about people doing things this way and not that way. Why their women wore this kind of clothes and not these kinds. When, when, when. She tried to suppress her indignation. *Breathe in. Breathe out.*

"She looked harmless," Margret finally said, despite herself.

"Even with that. Her madness is the type our people call *were afise*. Just look at her. She is a cursed mad woman, and such curses can be transferred to whoever touches her."

Margret wanted to say something else to her husband, but thought otherwise. She instead let the music from the cartoon nibble at their silence. She felt the smell and the taste of the baking soda rise up to her throat, so she got up and went into the kitchen to drink some more water. Clearing his empty dish from in front of him, Ade looked at his wife and smiled. "If you touched her," he only half-joked, "she would probably be displaying her madness in you by now."

*I*n bed that night, Ade Ati snuggled up to his wife, his hand wrapped around her waist and his lips grazed the lope of her ear. In a whisper so soft she initially passed it off for his breathing he muttered, "I know I have messed up, arguing with you in front of Morenikeji and all, but I will make it up to you. You just wait and see." Then she felt the tug at her wrapper. She let him untie it and raised her hip as he dragged it underneath her. She winced and raised her hip further to ease his penetration. And as he pounded and huffed away beside her, she feared she would have to be the one to make it up to him; if he ever made the discovery.

*M*argret Ati was woken up by a knock on the door the next morning. It was her son. She understood why he was there, but she did not want him to follow her. She greeted him and went into the kitchen to drink water. When she returned, he was still there.

"What?" she asked him.

"Nothing," he said. She thought she noticed a smirk on his face.

"Oya go na."

But the boy stayed put.

They both understood that they were accomplices, neither of them willing the other to shoulder the responsibility. They both stepped into the morning, to visit their tenant. When they got closer to the shack, they found the door ajar. The woman's belongings were strewn about: the two rusted beverage tins, the empty radio carton, an empty plate, plastic cup and spoon, and a container of baking soda. There wasn't any sign of her. Part of Margret was relieved that the woman wasn't there, and the other part worried that the woman might someday return. She drew her son closer, more of a reassurance of her own sanity that he would not run from her or scream. It was over now, she thought to herself.

She planted her lips on Morenikeji's head and whispered, "If she were truly a cursed mad woman, she probably would be displaying her madness in us by now." Then she began to laugh, and laugh, and laugh, so much that Morenikeji had to distance himself from her, observing from a few feet away.

Mother's Love

Dayo Ntwari

"*F*orce-feed the heretics! the monotheists, the abominations, all of them! let them know the taste of freedom!"

The Archbishop's thunderous voice shook Anointing Square, his words slightly out of sync with the movement of his lips and the rest of his face, as it glared down from the video screen that covered the entire north side of the Bishop Charles Mbamalu building, the headquarters of Pastor Olumide's West Niger Gigachurch.

Little Chris pointed up at the screen.

"Look, mummy!" he tittered. "His mouth is confused again!"

Mama Chris's hand struck the boy's face so hard, that the impact sent Little Chris reeling. Lucky for him, his mother's grip on his wrist was as tight as it always was. She pulled him through the city crowds.

"Are you daft, you dis stupid boy?" she hissed at him. "Do you want to kill your mother?"

Little Chris giggled at her despite the fresh stinging on his cheek, and Mama clamped her free hand over his mouth. Little Chris knew better than to misbehave, but the excitement of coming to West Niger on their supply runs every month was always too much for him. This was, after all, the biggest city on the Atlantic Coast. It was overwhelming: the jarring launch alarms, the columns of bright yellow and red flashing from the shuttle stations; the air crafts filling the sky, shooting into space; the glossy megastructures encrusted with video screens; the elevated hyper-rail system. And the people, oh the people! The incessant tidal waves of city dwellers and commuters rushing, pushing, bumping, shoving, yelling, grunting, sweating, laughing, scowling, and always pushing and shoving, pushing and shoving. Perpetual human migration. One hundred million bodies roaring into motion around him. It would seem like a dream if it weren't already real.

The Purge was particularly grim this month. There was another execution of Bultungins scheduled to take place at the Square in about an hour, which meant in ten minutes the Council of Prophets, the Evangelical Realm's secret police, would commence a full security lock-down of the area surrounding Anointing Square.

Little Chris, a six-year-old Bultungin, was not yet in full control of his body. Being half human made Chris particularly unstable as a shapeshifter. Over-excitement and high stress situations often caused unintentional shapeshifting into his hyena form. As an adult Bultungin, Mama Chris would only involuntarily shapeshift under the most extreme physical duress, for example during the agony of childbirth. Intimate inter-species relationships between humans and Bultungin shapeshifters were punishable by death under the laws of the Evangelical Realm. Church doctrine dictated it was biologically impossible for a human and Bultungin union to procreate. Little Chris's very existence was heresy manifest, and a negation of the infallibility of the Ultra Archbishop.

Time was running out. Mama Chris needed to get them away from the Square, and then to North Badagry as soon as possible, to get more Mother's Love from the Old Woman in the ocean. Without Mother's Love, Mama Chris had no power to suppress the involuntary shifts of her child. Mama led Little Chris into the foaming rapids of passengers bursting out of the hyper-rail station. A big screen showed the arrival and departure times above them, a psychedelic symphony of time and place and colour. Mama leaned against the crowd to the Red Line platform, violently dragging her son behind her, lifting his feet from the floor. Only the dark vice grip of her hand was visible to her son through the curtaining blurs of fabric and skin towering around him. Her fingers were practically fused to his wrist-bone. Chris hummed to himself as he watched, fascinated by the never-ending flow of warm bodies, a torrent of rush-hour commuters, that might, at any moment, rip him from his mother and drag him away, into the street where, surely, his little body would be crushed down into the waste grates.

"Plenty, plenty people," he sang to himself. "Plenty, plenty people dey here o! Plenty, plenty people. Mmmm-hmmm hmmmmmm mmmm." He grinned at all the breaking waves of commuters' faces washing over him: the grim, the indifferent, the preoccupied, the harried, the frustrated, and the tired and angry, all flashing past him like fleeting memories from a past life.

Eventually, they reached an automatic door, and the rush-hour flood subsided. He stood with his mother. Little Chris was very small compared to six-year-old human Topsiders. He would be about average height for an Underland Bultungin of his age, short enough to tuck himself beneath his mother's skirt – in between her muscular, hairy legs – as soon as they entered the train. The Red Line's heavy doors rattled shut. The big screen display started oscillating blue and white: the security lock-down was about to go into effect. Outside, the world of the platform warped into a blur and disappeared, as the hyper-rail shot out of the station.

The compartment was packed, ankle to ankle, shoulder to shoulder, chest to chest, cheek to cheek. No seats on the Red Line. Seats were for the Green Line, for people going to Zone 49 or closer to the city centre. The Red Line served only triple digit Zones. It took Mama Chris every bit of her strength not to collapse under the crushing weight of the passengers in the carriage as the momentum of the train shook them from side to side. She always struggled to keep her mind from visualising her body buckling under the load of the rocking passengers and collapsing on her son. They would likely get trampled, and the ensuing tumult would terrify the boy and trigger his shapeshifting. Her sweaty, scarred knees threatened to crush her son's body. Little Chris, oblivious of the knife-edge his life balanced on, winced at the pain at his temples every time his mother's legs banged into his skull. Still ensconced in his mother's skirt, he dug into his shorts for the avatar he had pick-pocketed from someone during the rush to board the train. He switched it on, and immediately the avatar connected to the Live Stream. The Archbishop's voice roared from its tiny speakers. He couldn't turn down the volume quickly enough. Mama Chris heard the noise coming from below her and looked around, only to see all the other passengers staring at her quizzically. In one movement she flung her arm under her skirt, grabbed hold of Little Chris's ear and twisted hard. The boy's vision exploded in agony and he frantically tapped the avatar against her arm until she let go of his ear and took the tiny device in her hand, obliterating it in her fist and dropping the pieces to the floor.

Chris stirred the pile of broken glass and metal with his shoe. If only it weren't for the Archbishop, he'd still have a shiny, new avatar. He'd heard his mother talking about the Archbishop, the man who had authorised the Purge. It began at the request of the Pastor of West Niger, who had now spent a year rounding up Monotheists, as well as other enemies of the West Niger Giga-church. Like people who did not pay up on Tax Day, or people who missed church on Tax Day twice in a row, or papists who still swore allegiance to Pope Gregory xvii. Like Anglicans, or Methodists, or Baptists, or Muslims. Or Hindus, or animists, or pagans, or witches. Or, worst of all, Abominations, as the Evangelical Realm referred to the shapeshifting Bultungin. This was only the latest of a number of purges the megacity had seen since the Realm's crusade first began against the old woman in the ocean, and her followers, many years ago.

"*W*hat are Aboninators, Uncle Gbenga?" A few days ago, Little Chris and his mother's oldest brother were clearing away rubble and rubbish from a lot in their neighbourhood in the Underland. The city's excavation works had caused another tremor earlier that week, which partially collapsed a small building, as well as a tunnel leading out of their Zone.

"Abominations," Uncle Gbenga corrected Little Chris. "Where did you hear that word?" He picked up a boulder almost as big as Chris and dumped it into the cart.

"The Archbishop said all the aboni… all the amoni—"

"Abominations…"

"That all the Abominations will be caught, and anybody that hides them will be arrest, too."

"*Arrested*."

"Will be *arrested*, too. To protect the Realm."

Gbenga sat down on another boulder, this one much bigger than Chris, and scratched his head.

"Did your mother not tell you to stop listening to the Live Stream?"

Little Chris dropped his chin to his chest and pouted. Uncle Gbenga put a thick, hairy finger to the boy's chin and lifted his face back up.

"The Archbishop is a dangerous man, Chris. Do not listen to him, and do not go near him or his people. If he catches you, nobody can help you."

"Not even you, Uncle?"

"Not even me, Chris. Not even me."

Little Chris's furry little tail brushed against his uncle's leg. Gbenga's gaze went cold, the hair on his hyena head bristled. The effects of the monthly dose of Mother's Love that Mama Chris took seemed to be wearing off again.

He snapped at the boy. "What do I always tell you, Chris?"

"No shifting, especially in Topside," Little Chris said, eagerly. "When in Topside, always look like the people in Topside." His reddish eyes quickly turned white again, and his tail shrunk and disappeared.

"I don't want you to get yourself or your mother in trouble, my boy. Try to be disciplined about it, even down here."

Chris nodded. The dim lighting from the tunnel's ceiling cast their shadows against the wall: the massive torso and head of an adult hyena, and muscular arms and legs that looked human, standing next to a little 6-year-old "Topsider". In order to suppress her son's accidental and careless shapeshifting, Gbenga's sister would need to meet with the old woman in Badagry to replenish the Mother's Love. She refused to let her boy out of her sight. Without the potion, she could not take him out in public, to her work in Topside each day. Not without running the risk of Little Chris's excitement getting the better of him, and finding themselves strapped to a stake awaiting execution at Anointing Square. Gbenga frowned to himself. He wished he could make these dangerous monthly trips on his sister's behalf, but the old woman would not deal with anyone other than Mama

Chris. The old woman was paranoid about being infiltrated by the Evangelical Realm.

"Uncle G."

"What is it, Chris?"

"Are we anonimations?"

$\mathcal{T}$he train was nearing North Badagry. There was a bit more room now in the compartment. Mama's legs no longer threatened to cave in Little Chris's skull. She allowed herself to breathe just a bit easier. Her son peeked from under her skirt and tried to see if he could catch a glimpse of the Hall of the Council of Prophets as they approached the coastal suburb. But from down there, all he could see between the shoulders of passengers was the roof of Prophets' Hall, topped like a wedding cake by a hundred foot high, gold-plated bust of His Holiness the Ultra Archbishop Chris Chukwu, the head of all the gigachurches in the Evangelical Realm, and his namesake. Or his pretend namesake, that is: Chris's real name would give away his Bultungin heritage. Pastor Olumide began the Purge shortly after Chris was born, and his mother thought it wise to change his name to a regular human name, befitting of a member of a gigachurch.

Rumours had been circulating for a few months running up to the beginning of the Purge. A human and a shapeshifter had born a child somewhere in this megacity. It did not take long for the Council of Prophets to start the round-ups and interrogations. Bultungins were barely tolerated in the Realm as third-class citizens, so long as they knew their place. For the most part, the shapeshifters had been confined to the subterranean dwelling, the Underland caverns beneath the megacity's sewage system, once they were first discovered almost a century ago. The law of the Evangelical Realm came from the Ultra Archbishop, worshipped as God in Human Form. The Realm's doctrine stated only humans, plants and animals were creatures of God. The emergence of the Bultungin, a people who could transmogrify into hyenas, was problematic for the integrity of church doctrine. To minimise their visibility, the Realm used the shapeshifters for menial and hazardous work only, and they needed a Day Pass to enter Topside, the city of West Niger.

Little Chris was humming again, now that they were out of the carriage and back on the streets again. They walked along a swampy road near the Ocean Wall, a giant rampart behind which the Atlantic foamed. The roar of the ocean racing in and throwing itself at the Ocean Wall was much louder in this rundown part of the city. The Wall was in disrepair, somewhat. Tiny rivulets snaked from small breaches in the Wall, forming mossy ridges in the reinforced concrete. Green puddles festered at the base of the Wall. Little Chris looked up and imitated the high-pitched hiss of thin grey streams of poisonous, pollutant-heavy water arcing from the fissures in the Wall. He puffed his chest as big as he could, to imitate the sound of the raging sea.

In the distance, a group of boys was coming up the street toward them. They waved at them, and Little Chris, seeing his friends for the first time in a month, waved back, and jumped up and down with excitement. As she had expected, her son couldn't stop himself from partially turning into a hyena. "Sorry, mummy," Chris said, grinning sheepishly and shifting back into his fully human form.

"It's okay, my son."

They stopped by a row of trees lining the Wall, and Mama Chris let go of her son's hand and reached to her afro. Or her "fake-fro", as she liked to say. She undid the knot hidden inside it, and three fat red-brown dreadlocks uncoiled and tumbled down her back, stopping just above her ankles: the trademark of a healer. And an unsanctioned healer, at that. But here, in the slums, where mostly shapeshifters and other undesirables lived, it didn't matter. Even though Pastor Olumide ruled over all of West Niger, the Security Commission seldom bothered to enter the slums. That is, as long as everyone paid up on Tax Day, every week.

The boys had finally reached them, and greeted Mama Chris politely. Some of them walked with the hind legs of hyenas. This was their neighbourhood. Still, she did not want Chris getting in the habit, and preferred he stayed in his human form at all times, whenever they left Underland.

Mama patted Chris on the head. "Okay, my son," she said. "You can go and play now, but don't go far. Stay where I can hear you o!" She smiled at him. He looked like such a lovely child, she thought, when he looked like a Topsider.

"Thank you, mummy!" Chris's excitement made his voice a bit louder than necessary. Immediately he and his friends ran across the street to the playground.

Mama Chris sighed to herself, satisfied. It was time for her to go to the old woman inside the ocean. She turned to the trees. They were tall and dark, misshapen like giant, crooked old men, petrified for eternity. Long-dead trees defying the twin sickles of time and decay. Fireflies danced in the void between the black branches where their leaves should have been. Mama Chris moved her feet silently over the ground beneath the trees, barren and patterned by cracks and gaps in the dirt. She began to sing, and the fireflies began to stir. Hundreds of them. Thousands, now. Their yellow and white glow cast on her a soft shimmer. She closed her eyes and heard them singing back to her, as if from far away, while they floated down from the branches surrounding her. She let a small smile creep to her lips: walking through the Veil always made Mama Chris feel beautiful.

The cloud of fireflies tightened around her, and the ground started to moisten, and then turned swampy. She opened her eyes and watched the dead trees creak and groan as they soaked up the black, oily water bubbling-up from the swamp widening at her feet. Dark veins swelled just below the bark of the trees, as if they were pumping black blood from their roots, to their trunks.

Plump with the swamp water, the branches coiled around themselves, reaching slowly downward and toward Mama Chris. The ground bubbled more ravenously, and started to give way as the branches reached Mama Chris and pushed her downward, downward, into a place unseen.

*M*ama Chris found herself behind the Veil, in front of an octagonal clearing, bordered by neatly arranged groups of black and green tents. These were occupied by the priestesses and followers of Yemoja, after they had been driven into the ocean by the Ultra Archbishop in their conflict against the Evangelical Realm. Yemoja, the Old Woman inside the ocean, also known as The Mother of Gods, was the arch-enemy of the Ultra Archbishop and the Realm.

Here behind the Veil, in the Unseen, the air was fresh and dense with humidity. Mama Chris moved across the clearing, her legs suddenly sluggish and her body suddenly weightless, as if she were diving in a calm lake. A school of long, brightly glowing fish, some as long as her leg, swam in the air above her, disappearing beyond the horizon of tents. Dark green shrubs and weeds swayed on the ground, as if caught by a current. She too felt the current around her legs, and whenever her feet touched the soaked earth, bubbles spluttered up, tickling her toes. The Old Woman, Yemoja, sitting by her fire, called out to Mama Chris by her son's Bultungin name.

"Use his Christian name!" Mama Chris snarled. "Please! Is it every month I have to tell you, Yemoja?"

"Sorry o. No vex. Mama *Chris*." Yemoja cackled as she always did, and waved dismissively at the bandages on her leg. Mama Chris stared at her for a while, then shook her head and sighed.

"How body?" Yemoja asked.

"I'm fine, thank you. How is your leg? Are you taking the medicine?"

"Medicine, ke?" The colossal woman's breasts bounced and rippled with her laughter. Unperturbed, Mama Chris gingerly unwrapped the bandages on Yemoja's leg to get a look at her wounds. The old woman threw her head back and laughed her dirty laugh. "Medicine? Who dash you medicine? Ordinary witch like you."

Mama Chris remained stoic. Yemoja's wound seemed to be healing gradually. She reached into her pouch for clean bandages and a jar of Borgum Spider jelly. The theocracy of the Realm only permitted church-sanctioned televangelists to conduct religious activities, and the only gods officially acknowledged by the gigachurches in the Realm were the Ultra Archbishop and his Archbishops. During the Realm's first purge, after the Ultra had risen to power, the gigachurches had slaughtered hundreds of thousands of Yemoja's followers. The remaining survivors fled into the ocean, here into the sanctuary of the Unseen, where she provided them with shelter behind the Veil.

Through the torture of her captured devotees, the Realm had managed to learn about some of Yemoja's weaknesses. The Ocean Wall was soon erected, all the major industrial sewage of the megacities along the West African Atlantic Coast were rerouted and discharged into the ocean. Natural rivers and water bodies within city limits were artificially dried out, and soon, the Veil began shrinking as the ocean's pollution increased. Yemoja fell ill. In recent months, sores had appeared on Yemoja's legs, and they seemed to drain her of more and more of her power. Mama Chris had found a way to heal the wounds, but whenever they completed the healing process, a fresh wound would appear in another place.

"You are funny, Mummy Chris, honestly," Yemoja wiped tears of laughter from her eyes. Silently, Mama Chris rubbed the jelly over the wound. The woman winced and glared at her, "Softly, now! Ah ah!"

Mama Chris took no notice, and wrapped the bandages slowly and firmly, whispering the formula and carefully fastening the clip.

The Old Woman motioned at a bowl that was floating by. Mama Chris took hold of the bowl and handed it to Yemoja, who coughed up phlegm and spat into the bowl.

"How is your son?" Yemoja asked, as she proceeded to lubricate the inside of the bowl with her spit.

"He is fine, Yemoja. Have you heard anything from the Council?" Mama Chris asked. Despite her weakened state, the old woman still had spies inside the Council of Prophets, and Mama Chris relied on her information to keep herself and her son safe from the Realm's secret police.

"The Council? Hmm, no," Yemoja took one of her breasts in her hand and squeezed. Inky black Mother's Love squirted into the bowl until it was full. She then handed it back to Mama Chris.

"Mama Chris. Why you no tell me say na Pastor Olumide be Little Chris papa?" Yemoja's voice was like ice. Mama Chris held the bowl of Mother's Love in her hands, frightened stiff.

"Drink," Yemoja said. "Drink." She gestured at the bowl. "Drink first, before you answer my question." Yemoja's expression had turned belligerent, and Mama Chris had no choice but to acquiesce. She drank quickly, hungrily. Her eyelids fluttered involuntarily with every gulp she took. When she finished she released the bowl and a current sent it drifting away.

"You go fuck the Pastor," Yemoja accused Mama Chris. "Come my house dey find Mother's Love to hide your son? Who you dey hide am from?"

Mama Chris snapped at the old woman. "Watch your mouth, Yemoja! I no fuck anybody, you hear? Do you understand?" Yemoja closed her robe furiously, covering her breasts.

"Stupid woman," Yemoja said. "If you no fuck, how you come get belle? Hmm?" Her flabby arm swung out and she slapped Mama Chris's mouth. The irate ocean goddess jumped to her feet, growing and now a towering behemoth looming above Mama Chris.

Mama Chris's dreadlocks floated around her lowered head. "The Pastor raped me!" she growled, her hands balled up into fists barely as big as Yemoja's pinky toes. Little Chris's cheerful voice echoed from outside, drifting into the Unseen. A little green octopus came cartwheeling through the palm fronds and gently played with Mama Chris's bobbing locks. The goddess Yemoja and Mama Chris stood silently.

"Kai. Come here, my daughter." The goddess sat back down, not much bigger now than Mama Chris. She held out her arms, and Mama Chris reluctantly approached. Hot tears streamed down Mama Chris's scarred face, and she rubbed her sleeve across her nose. Yemoja's rumpled fingers tenderly wiped the tears from

Mama Chris's face and they sat. Mama Chris laying on her side in the goddess's lap, Yemoja rocking her soothingly. She reached into her robe, pulled out one of her breasts and tucked the nipple into Mama Chris's mouth.

"So, Mr Pray-and-Rape know wetin you be?" Yemoja asked. Mama Chris, still laying on her lap, was washing her dreads with swamp mud. Mama Chris nodded, yes the Pastor knew she was Bultungin.

"And him know say Little Chris him son?"

Mama Chris shook her head.

"Hmm." Yemoja stared into the distance, "No wonder you dey always ask of Council of Prophets."

"The Council discovered a member of a gigachurch in one of the cities committed the sin of bestiality, and a half Bultungin and half human abomination was born," Mama Chris explained.

"And na why Senate of Elders dey investigate gigachurches since last year?"

Mama Chris nodded.

"And na wetin cause the Purge. Olumide wan cover him tracks. How many wey him rape?"

Mama Chris shrugged. "I don't know. Maybe just me. Maybe more. There are over a hundred of us cleaners and gardeners at the Church," she sighed. "And he's using Monotheists to cover it up. If he only killed Bultungins, the Senate might get suspicious and order a Spiritual Audit on West Niger."

Yemoja broke open a coconut and sprinkled the water over Mama Chris's head. Her locks iridesced as the goddess rubbed the liquid into Mama's scalp, and rinsed out the swamp mud.

"Mother's Love alone no fit keep your son safe forever, my dear. You hear?" Mama Chris nodded.

"All this while, you dey come Badagry, dey risk your life, your child life. Why you no yarn me since?" The goddess frowned at her.

Mama Chris sighed and got up from the old woman's lap, "What good would it have done to tell you, Yemoja? You know your power ends at the Wall."

"Na wetin you think? You think say my power no pass these people? Hmm?" Yemoja asked, scratching her own head. Tired. The old goddess's gaze slowly moved from side to side like she was looking for something. Her big lips pouted in confusion and she mumbled something to herself. She looked at Mama Chris and seemed to stare right through her. The vacant look in Yemoja's eyes tugged at Mama Chris's heart: the Mother of fishes, the Mother of gods was dying, and her memories seemed to rise and fall with the tides, coming back weaker each time Mama Chris visited.

Mama spoke softly now. "There are no fish outside the Veil, Yemoja. The way the Pastor has been hunting me, is the same way the Ultra Archbishop has been hunting for you since even before I was born." The goddess's head snapped back to Mama Chris, her eyes wide and lively. She greeted Mama Chris jovially, as if seeing her for the first time today.

"Please, Yemoja. His name is *Chris*. Please try to remember."

The old woman giggled. "Sorry o! No vex, Mama *Chris*! You wan treat my leg, abi? Siddon, siddon. How body?" Yemoja motioned to a moss-covered rock.

Defeated, Mama Chris put a satchel of herbs on the old woman's shelf, "Drink this in your tea every morning."

"What is that?" Yemoja asked, shooting Mama Chris a quizzical look.

"It's your medicine, ma."

"Medicine, ke?" Yemoja bent over and slapped her good knee, laughing hard. "See this witch! You be doctor?" She laughed hysterically while Mama Chris embraced her warmly and kissed the Mother goddess on the forehead.

"Thank you, Yemoja. See you next month."

*T*he hyper-rail was virtually empty on the way back home to Underland, as it always was this time of the morning. In the distance, the strobe lights of a Prophet patrol corvette flashed, as it prowled through the empty sky. Its dark hull sliced through the tall dawn mist, while the vessel scanned the waters for smugglers. When the rail tracks bent eastward, it gave the illusion the hyper-rail was outrunning the patrol. Little Chris pressed his nose against the grimy window, humming his melodies. On the overhead screen in the compartment, Pastor Olumide came on:

"Good morning, my children. Happy Tax Day. I expect all of you in church today for service. May you continue to be blessed and may…"

Mama Chris looked at her son. Usually, Bultungin shapeshifters gained full control of their bodies around the early to mid teens. However, with Little Chris being an unprecedented hybrid human-Bultungin, there was no way for her to know when her little boy would come of age. What Mama did know, however, was that Yemoja would be long dead before then. The old goddess would probably not last another year before the Veil was breached. And when Yemoja dies, the ocean and the Mother's Love would die along with her. Mama Chris and her boy would be at the mercy of the Council of Prophets. Maybe, by the end of the year Mama would have saved up enough of her wages to pay smugglers, and flee the Evangelical Realm. Lately, these smugglers had been selling out the undesirables to the Council of Prophets, taking money from both sides and getting rich off the spilled blood of the Bultungin.

"Look, mummy!" The tube at this section rose above the Wall. Little Chris pointed at the pale orange sliver on the horizon. She spat on her thumb and cleaned off some dried mud from his earlobe. Mama Chris nodded. She pulled her son close and together they watched the rising sunlight reflecting on the rippling ocean's surface like a blanket of dancing fireflies. The ocean waves were breaking against the Wall, slowly, like an old collapsing elephant. White mist sparkled in the sunlight.

"Plenty plenty water. Plenty plenty water dey here o. Plenty plenty water. Mmmmhmmm hmmmmm hmmmm." Mama Chris put on a brave face, and laughed and sang along with Little Chris. They watched and sang together until the hyper-rail descended below the Wall again, hurtling back towards the city centre.

How We Look Now

Christine Coates

*I*t's 5:30 a.m. and there's a pewter angel sticking out of my mouth like a figurehead on the bow of a ship. How did I get here? I was in the sea off Mouille Point one minute and now I'm lying on the grass on the Promenade. Words explode in my head because I can't get them out past my lips; past her – the angel. She's taken up residence, the bitch. I can't say a thing. People stop and stare – it's like I'm a bloody Rolls Royce or something.

I'd forgotten what abuse felt like; I've been avoiding the land lately. It's much better under the water. There are people there who understand me. Ingrid, for instance. We've become good friends. Like sisters, you could say. Poor girl, she was treated badly too. People said she was crazy; but the way she was treated, I would have gone mad as well. No one helped her, they just used her. "Some lithium would have gone a long way," she says. She lured men, she knows she did, she admits it. "They were like fish for sex; couldn't resist the bait." When she was high, she was lus, like a nympho. Her eyes shone, her whole being shone. The men came like moths, but she was the one who got burnt by the fire.

We sit on the rocks at night talking, Ingrid and I. She tells me things. Things about her father – Abraham. She says his name means "father of many", but he couldn't be a father to any. "You're a poet an' you don't know it," I say, but of course she knows it. What she doesn't know is that she's famous now. So I tell her how Nelson Mandela read that poem of hers about the child in Nyanga. "You're known the whole world over," I tell her. "It's too late for that," she says. I say it's never too late. Some nights she speaks her poems to me – always in Afrikaans, and always I love it. We speak English in the day, but Afrikaans is the language of the night and of poetry. She utters some beautiful things, also sad things. I wish she could write them down. She makes me cry, but then she also makes me smile. She says I make her laugh. "We have to have something to laugh about," I say. There are many things we wish for. We wish things had been different, but then we think we're lucky to be here, living under the sea, and to have one another. We're the best companions we've ever had, each other and the fish.

Back to her father, the father of many, the censorship man. Can you imagine? Writing like an angel and having a father like that. He forbade her writing. He threw her away, like a piece of rubbish. Even so, with all that passion, all her ideas grew. Her vision grew. She saw things others weren't seeing, she said things others weren't saying. Like the child in Nyanga – who else would sing for him? She wonders who sings for him now. She still had many songs to sing. She's sad that it's ended for her up there on the land, but, like I always say, who knows what the wind carries?

We have to accept this life under the sea, though it's not bad. We can do things from here, from the depths. We are mermaids, we are harpies, we are sirens. Together we sit on the rocks at night and sing high, sweet songs. And we say poetry. She tells me things I would never have known: stories of mermaids, like Atargatis, whose beauty could not be concealed by the waters. Even the angels were jealous of her. "Beware of angels," Ingrid once told me. She is educated this Ingrid, not like me who left school at fifteen. Ingrid has read books, she's travelled. I've never been out of Cape Town. Well, once I went to Bellville. But Ingrid's seen rock paintings in the Karoo; paintings of mermaids. The Khoisan thought fish were sacred. They never ate them. Mermaids, Ingrid believes, were forced into hiding because men would not let them be. They always want to catch one and take her home and put her into a tank and keep her, like one of those silicone sex dolls. Ingrid tells me of a Greek mermaid, Thessalonike, who posed riddle-questions to the sailors she encountered. Like, "Is King Alexander still alive?" They never had the right answers.

We took to that idea. When the men of the night bring their women here – girls they just pulled off the street, girls plied with brandy, girls who show their legs on Main Road; even when they are busy with them, they hear us, those men, and then they can't help themselves, they want it all. It's the quick pomp with the bitch-in-the-ditch, love her and leave her. Wham-bam-thank-you-ma'am – but they also want what their ears are calling them to. We know men like that, Ingrid and I.

So we sit on the rocks and sing. We sing sorrowful tunes, tunes

they can't resist. They drop the girls they have with them and come
to the rocks. "Come, come," we sing. We are Lorelei, we are sirens,
we are harpies. Come closer, closer. See our young breasts, firm,
nipples standing to attention. Yes, this is for you – look at her pink
breasts, firm like cling peaches; and mine, bronze and gilded, shimmering in the moonlight. Our hair hangs down our backs, a lock
over one shoulder. "Come and see, come here, come closer."

And they always do. It's our revenge. We dive down, they
follow. Deep down under the water we ask them the question,
"Is King Alexander still alive?" We feed them to the white sharks
that swim by at dawn. There are a lot of bottom feeders here – not
only the sharks but the poachers who come at night and net the
crayfish and tie the bag to a rock to be collected later when no one
is around. We loosen those bags and the crayfish swim free. But the
abalone are almost all gone now – stripped, the ocean floor raped
like the women on the shore. And to think this is a marine reserve.

But we are her rangers. We protect but we also wreak our
revenge, for the fish, for the seafood, for the women. The ones they
have raped, the ones they fuck up and beat up, and the ones they
leave at home.

*T*here are some curious things here under the ocean. On the
seabed there is the Seafarer, the ship that crashed onto the
rocks nearby. It happened not long after Ingrid died. She died
close to our rocks here. At first it was awful for her. Talk about
post-traumatic stress, having a great big ship like that almost crash
into her and drag her to the deep. Back then she was just getting
used to being alone and quiet, getting used to the winter storms.
But by now she is used to it all: the stress, the storms, the wreck.
We swim in and out of its hull. The windows are empty sockets.
No pearls, but we've found the odd coin. Ingrid says she wishes
the ship was the Titanic. Then at least we would have some stylish
stuff: carved balustrades, silver, china, a dancefloor.

"We need some beauty," she says. "Think about it. We could waltz."

"What?" I chuckle. "With our fish tails?"

All night we watch the goings-on up on the Foreshore. The whispering drug dealers, the corrupt policemen. Sure, there's a lot going on under the sea, but all the human activities are on the land. We've seen how the bergies and the street-children crowbar off anything that's metal to sell for a quick fix. We saw how they took the brass plaque that commemorated Darwin's visit to the Cape. Ingrid knows about Darwin. She told me how he came around the Cape of Good Hope long ago looking for the origins of life. There's not much hope here anymore, but perhaps he saw something in it. "This is a pretty and singular town," he wrote. "It lies at the foot of an enormous wall, which reaches to the clouds, and makes a most imposing barrier – Cape Town is a great inn…"

An enormous wall? A great inn? I ask you – or I ask Ingrid, she's the only one here. The survival of the fittest. *Kyk hoe lyk ons nou.* Darwin should see the inns today, I say – the Grand Westin, the One and Only, the Table Bay. They've even turned the old jail into a hotel – like there isn't the need for more space for all these crooks and villains. I ask Ingrid what she thinks Darwin would say about the city today. She says Darwin was no poet. That's for sure. But still they should have left his plaque.

Nothing is sacred. A few years ago, when the world soccer came to Cape Town, an artist put up a line of beautiful sculptures. Each was of a young woman on a platform, each time standing in a different position, dressed in a red and white bathing suit, with a bathing cap and goggles on her head. Some nights, on a blue moon, I can walk for a few hours. How I loved back then to get out of the water and wander along next to them. It was like I was walking her story. The first one shows her arms outstretched, as if she was dreaming she could fly. She looks up at the sky, seeming to say, "Yes, perhaps I can." In the next she reaches her hands out before her like a beggar, asking for mercy, asking for change. Then she's sitting on her haunches, holding her face, looking out to sea. In another she stands like a diver about to plunge off into the water. But it's the sky that's calling her. That's where her true dominion is. She opens her arms, wide and then wider, hoping perhaps her dreams will come true. She wheels her arms, like one of those cricketers when they take a wicket, hands whirling this way and that. Now she's bending and looking half up as if seeing a gull against the setting sun. But it isn't a gull: it's a dragonfly, and the dragonfly is hovering above her. She reaches out to let him take her hand. "Yes, come," the dragonfly seems to say. "Come and fly with me, let's fly away. I can show you the world." "Yes," she seems to say back to him. "Fly me to the moon, let me play among the stars." But they're still on the promenade, still fixed by gravity. Yes, I think. They're all the same – the men. They promise you the world, the moon, to take you to heaven and back. But it never happens quite like that.

Now our bathing beauty shifts, she stops, looks up and around. It's as if something's dawned, a realisation that she can be as free as he is, the dragonfly. She just has to let go. And as she does, she begins to grow wings. Oh, and what joy! Now her arms are wings, wings just like the dragonfly's. At last she is free and she flies.

One night I was telling Ingrid the story I'd seen unfold on my walk. I was telling her and using my arms spread out to demonstrate it. She was impressed. "It's beautiful," she said. "I hope it's true for her."

Early the next morning I took Ingrid's hand and we moved to the edge of the Promenade wall, we looked up to see the bathing-suit girl. We had to make sure that no one was watching. People are always trying to capture mermaids. Then I saw it. The sculpture closest to me was bent right over and buckled. Dangling. Her legs were smashed, two iron rods where they had once been. It was as if she had fallen over in a drunken mess, assaulted. Chunks of concrete lay shattered on the ground, her face staring right into it. I looked further down the row of bathing girls. One had been removed completely, others were smashed to pieces. We couldn't breathe. We couldn't move. It was as if we had been attacked ourselves. It brought it all back: what had happened to us, as if it was yesterday. It felt as if all our songs, the poems Ingrid said, that all these had crashed into the sea and drowned. Numbed, we sat on the bricked paving. It was a rough sea that day, the north-wester was coming up. Soon the swells grew huge and pounded the sea wall. Mammoth clouds blew across the sky and colossal heads of foam brewed up against the stone fortifications. We looked up at the mountain, and it really did look like a colossal wall that blocked everything: the light, the hope, our dreams. We retreated back to our rocks and slipped into the sea. It isn't easy being a mermaid in north-wester storms, especially if you have to stomach your own history. The water battered us back and forth.

Our songs to each other became wretched. We hardly laughed anymore. We wondered what was going to happen to this country. What kind of society hates the female form so much that it vandalises and destroys even the sculptures of young women? We asked this of one another.

We seldom went up to the Promenade after witnessing the spectacle of the sculptures. Not for a long time.

So I don't know how it happened, how that pewter angel hooked me – but it did. And now I am on the grass, lying there gasping like a fish. A fish with a sculpture in its mouth. "That's beautiful," an old woman says. She bends and stops to touch the angel. "Fuck off! Leave me alone!" I want to say, but I can't. I stare daggers at her eyes instead. "I beg your pardon," she says and slinks off. I'm not Kate or Leo, I'm not the king of the world flying on the front of the Titanic. I'm hooked. And then I see it – a rhino looking at me, a steel rhino where the girls had been, with a great long horn coming out of its head. The girls have been replaced with a rhino. That's rich, I think, at first. But then I realise it's the same thing: the rhino is just like the girls. It too is under threat. It too is molested, its life not honoured. But this horn won't get poached for medicine. The poachers here are not noisy nose-eaters. No, the poachers here are on tik. They will steal the metal to sell for scrap. The ones who destroyed the girl who wanted to fly like a dragonfly; the ones who grab any girl who just wants love and money for her baby; the ones who drive a poet into the sea because they can't commit themselves to her. I wish Ingrid was here and I could ask her what she thinks

– would Darwin say this too is the survival of the fittest? Even the last rhino, the last young woman – a scream in the silent universe.

I don't know what to say anymore. Even if I did know, the angel is blocking my mouth. I've tried being a fish, to hide under water, to go back to my origins, but now this fucking angel has hooked me. She's flown me right out and landed me like the coelacanth. A boy points at me. I hiss. He skittles off to his mother.

*M*y heart is cleft. Half of it lies at my feet. A trail of blood pearls its way to me. Everyone can see it's my fault. "She stinks like a dead fish," a passer-by says and I hiss again. It feels like steam escapes my nostrils. A pressure release.

I remember it all now – how he pushed me, how I grabbed the steel bar as it broke and I managed, somehow, to hit him hard across the head as I fell into the sea. I don't know how I did it but I'm guilty as hell. There's blood on my hands, blood that the whole ocean couldn't wash away.

People cluster around. It's how he got away with murder. I told Ingrid the whole story, how guilty I felt pulling him down here with me – but she saw things differently, she saw it as it happened. She's my only witness. But it's all my fault. My blood is what's on my hands and I can't even tell them the truth. A policeman is coming – he parts the crowd like he's some fucking Moses. He takes hold of my arm to lead me away, but I buck and he misses. He hasn't even noticed my tail, but he shouts into his walkie-talkie, "She's a slippery fish this one, and she stinks like one too."

Don't they have cellphones these bastard cops? I could scream at him, but my mouth is full of angel. My teeth hurt. Teeth, I wonder about them. Have they survived? I once had nice teeth – the one nice thing about me, the one thing my boyfriend was jealous of me for. His were like bad mielie pits.

But here's the hero Moses again, parting the waves, with fucking Joshua with him. They've brought their chariot. I suppose they will now take me to the Promised Land. I try to laugh to myself. In court my only question for them will be: "Is King Alexander still alive?"

Traces
Megan Ross

I can't count the times I've wished him dead. Grey. Lifeless. That smart mouth shut for as long as there is and there being not a damn thing he can do about it. If you were me you might worry about these thoughts, maybe to the point of talking quickly and quietly to your psychologist in that lunch-hour appointment your husband doesn't know about.

But me, I'm not that fussed. I'm just the same as every other woman on this street, numbers twenty-two to thirty-eight. Not many things are certain in this life, but one thing for sure is that men will be men. And in this neighbourhood, that means men will be arseholes. Sure, you can protest, set your hair on fire all you want. But around here they wouldn't waste a second before soaking their dicks in whiskey and finding somewhere to put 'em. Look around. Crumbling walls. Crippled front gates. Every last smudge of front lawn ironed to strips 'cause we don't have driveways and we can't afford tarmac. And if you bother to look further, you'll see woman after woman crying herself to sleep night after night. Black-bagged and weary, we once shone with youth. We dreamed. Danced. Imagined the happily-ever-afters that never came, slowly succumbing to the children that weighed down our hips. We turned to shadow, dissipated, saggy-breasted, with memories now just the fodder for dreams. Never thought it would be like this. Nope. For one, I imagined a whole universe outside this shithole. You kind of have to when you grow up in it. But when a man with a charmer's eyes and a pastor's mouth puts his hands on you at midnight, it's only a short wait until your period's late and Daddy's walking you down the aisle.

Hard to resist, men like Jo. Dreamers. Big mouthed. Poetic and broken down in just the right places. Overripe fruit with bruised flesh, soft and bitter at the core. It wakes the mother in you, you know? Stirs her in the night. Nipples all pert. Heart hammering hard. Lunar tides swishing around her. A soft slice of moon losing panties to the floor. Womb spilling open in a '95 Opel Kadett.

Almost every woman has a Jo. Difference is, a wise woman shags him twice and sets him loose. Blames it on the Aquarius full moon, books a pap smear and tells no one. But the fool? She wants to drown in him. And nine months later, she does.

Sometimes Jo makes me so mad I shake. I used to calm my nerves with smoking, but there's a second stirring in my womb and death sticks aren't ideal when you're pregnant. Placental abruption, premature labour, stillbirth. Technically you shouldn't smoke at any time, but when you're carrying it's an even worse idea. Says so on the box, all black and white and finger-wagging like those ladies outside church.

My hands are shaking something stupid and I pray to God for strength. There's a box of ciggies in my drawer but I just can't. I can't. Would you? Stefani's five years old and already asthmatic. Nothing to do with me, I assure you. Her father's got lungs like a parakeet – poor genetics, that's all. But I don't take my chances. Despite everything I am *not* a bad mother. There is nothing good in my child that didn't come from me. If you met Jo, you'd understand why.

He should be home already. Phoned earlier, though. Said there was a burst pipe in Cambridge that the boss-man wanted him to see. Absolute nightmare, apparently. Water everywhere. He's just an appi, so there's not much I can say. And besides, we need the money. But he was really apologetic, too, which is what got me suspicious in the first place. That and the SMS that followed five minutes later: *FNB :-) R500 drawn from S. Save at Hemmingways Casino.* Man's like clockwork. Can't get a week's wages without walking into the devil's den. Grocery money getting all slick and wet in some gaudy machine. The straw that breaks the camel's back, although I didn't know I had any more bones to break. But men like this? Ingenious. Always another way to hurt you.

As of now I want to chop his snake-head off and watch that liar's tongue writhe on the stoep. But I'll wait for him to get home. Let him in, all smiles and *love-yous* and my little-wife eyes. And then I'll pull out my phone and show him what a dirt bag he really is. I'll watch that bastard face turn bright red and then I'll kick him out.

This time, for good.

I walk outside to wait for him. Stefani's inside, acting out an imaginary cat fight with two cardboard dolls. Esmeralda (who is really Lee-Ann Liebenberg) and Jasmine (that black girl from *X-Men* – Zoe something?) are fighting over a non-existent Ken doll. Her toys are furry around the edges where I cut them from the *YOU*, but she doesn't seem to mind they're not real Barbies. Immediately on stepping out onto the stoep I hear an emphysemic clearing of phlegm from the flats across the road. A rotund arrangement of curlers and nicotine stares at my belly.

"Sho, you huge hey? Wow. *Sho-weee!* When you due?"

"December," I grunt, unwilling to specify the date.

"You're big in the backside. It's a boy," she shouts down from her balcony. Bitch has a sea view. There's no justice in this world.

"I've been told," I reply. Old people love misfortune. It takes their minds off death. I hear the wash machine beeping inside like a nagging child. Can hear it all the way out here, whining like a baby. *Beeeeeep. Beeeeeep.* I head back inside to tend to it. You love your kids but they drive you nuts. Right? Always changing. Sizes, clothing, tastes, moods. What they eat, what they like, what they do. Worst was Stefani, with the breastfeeding. Chopped and changed her mind. Bottle, boob, bottle, boob. Didn't want a formula baby, you know? Increases the risk of ADD, and seeing that Jo isn't exactly a sterling sperm donor, I got to do all I can from my side. There I was, though. Bang on twenty-one, all chewed up and stretched like stale gum you've been gobbing for hours, praying to God that life will get better, when without warning the little thing ups and leaves the nipples she cracked to broken stars and takes the bottle. Furious I was, but also secretly relieved. Couldn't take her eyes anymore, those big Caramel Treats, open wide like the dawn, every inch of me disappearing into that gaze of hers, feed after feed.*Beeeeeep. Beeeeeep.* Housework, hey, it's tiresome, but at least it stays the same. Day in, day out. There's clothes to be hung up, taps to shine, dishes to wash, rubbish to put out. A hook for sanity, someplace to rest the mind. No thoughts, just water and detergent. I think I'd go nuts without the routine. Saint Mark's nuts. Crazy-crazy. Padded walls, restraints, all that shit. Give me dirt and a sponge any day. Maybe even that Verimark squeegee I should never have bought – have you *seen* the streaks it leaves?

Or just add water. Like cereal. Morvite or Pronutro. Sure, okay, you're supposed to add milk but try getting home from the café without it going sour. Heat's a killer. Used long-life for ages but Jo's not a fan. Makes funny patterns in his coffee, he says – no jokes, this is the man-child I married. When he comes with shit like that, early in the morning when I've got up specially to make it for him, two heaped sugars, water just boiled and snapping at the mug, body aching and tired cause he snored all night, that's when I want to kill him.

Instead, I clean. Helps me smooth out my life. Like mental ironing, you know? I go over the kinks, the seams, the creases. And I wipe it clean. Chop-chop, spit-spot like Mary Poppins. There's alchemy about it. Something instinctual. Starts with that funny itch you have when you're nesting. Nine months pregnant and waving a vacuum cleaner around. Dust, sweep, polish, mop. You think you're just tidying up but before you know it you're in the back of an ambulance while a brand new human splits you open like the sun.

At first, you can't fathom how a baby can wear so much. Shit so much. Need so much. And all of it clean and hung in the sun to dry. But then it takes on a rhythm. Soft slosh of soapy water, gentle brush of mop across tile. Transformation becomes yours. One minute you're on the wrong side of short and six months pregnant, next you're the reason the windows sparkle and a child has clothes to wear. Magical.

Did I tell you I never had a wash machine before Jo? My parents were too poor. Hand washed everything all of my life. Even in winter when the geyser turned off and we had only a hosepipe for washing. When I moved in with Jo I still thought he could afford a maid. Images of bossing and preening wafted through my mind. Thought washing was the *girl*'s job, you know? And I didn't have patience for those knobs and dials. Hieroglyphics to me, I told Jo.

But those promises deflated like a balloon after a birthday party, all pap and skimming the bedroom floor, the ribbon still all silk and tied to where your heart should have been. In the end I surrendered to the mundane and found in it my salvation. Sacrifice, ritual, rite. Never been religious before. Sure, there's a St. Christopher that's hung between my breasts for six years, *and* I let that pervert pastor from the Baptist church dip me in his paddling pool. But I never experienced transcendence or the mystery of Jesus, not in bread nor in wine. Miracles meant the rent went unpaid and the landlord didn't kick us out. That Jo still came home to me, night after night.

But this changed me. Okay, okay. Mother Mary never showed up in the cutlery. No, I didn't see her halo in the spoons or the Sacred Heart in our bathroom mirror. Mine is a magic distilled from desperation. Call me superstitious all you want. Laugh at me, Crazy Natalie, *ja ja,* heard it all. But I learned how scrubbing Sunlight flakes into your husband's shirt cleans more than smudges of unfamiliar lipstick. That hot water and cold can pull the sadness right out your clothes. And that wringing out your bedroom sheets shakes more than dust mites from the fabric.

With Omo and StaySoft I became my own liberator. A secret goddess of my home, a water-bearing maven of all things domestic. To this day, I erase indiscretion. Replant dignity. Remove the human stain of forbidden flesh and wandering eyes. I restore the moral centre to our home.

Every pair of underpants hung like limp skin across the wash line he'll never fix. Proof of my goodness in navy, red and white.

The Made in China key is struggling inside the Made in China lock. Plumber's hands. Thick and rough and best sent down toilets and blocked drains. My face is red and hot like December. Jo steps inside. No entrance hall here. Just four white walls and a damp patch the size of Port Elizabeth. In one breath he has kissed Stefani, patted my belly and headed straight for the kitchen. He smells like desperation and sweat. The gambler's scent. I imagine the well-worn tread of his shoes in the casino. Red and gold thread clinging to his heels.

He's helping himself to leftover bobotie. *That's for Stefani!* I want to scream, but my tongue is twisted and sore and every word keeps curdling in my mouth. He's oblivious to me, to my anger. Doesn't even look up when I'm just standing there, watching him pick raisins out the bowl, putting them plump and meat-crusted on the counter. He piles the fork high with mince, mouth open while he chews, grunting like only an overweight man can, oblivious to the glob of Mrs Balls on his chin. Stefani's singing a nursery rhyme. "The Wheels on the Bus". The fridge hums. Outside a hadeda calls, and shits on the washing I hung up earlier.

Goes round and round.

Jo slurps and smacks his lips, swallowing loud with so much saliva I find myself turning dry-mouthed in reaction. I clutch my cell phone to my stomach and watch in shock. *You liar!* I want to scream. *Fucking-bastard-son-of-a-bitch! You utter piece of shit!* Instead, I stand still.

Round and round.

His entire chin is shiny with sauce. I'm about to attack him with a serviette when a mouthful of mince falls square on the distended boep he expects me to find attractive. On the shirt I washed and dried and ironed. In the fabric I folded my love. A *white* shirt.

"Ah, babe, can you wash this for me? Please?" His fat hand dabs at it with a dish cloth. Dish water mingles with egg, mince and rice. Grease slides into the damp. The stain sets. Ruined.

"Babe?"

He stares at me like I'm Jesus when suddenly something snaps and I've picked up the fork and thrown it at his face. Time stops. A horrified expression crawls across his face, then sets. The tines wobble sedately in his forehead. Slowly a drop of blood trickles down his nose, halting just above his cupid's bow. I wonder when my aim got so good.

"ARE YOU CRAZY? What the *fuck* is wrong with you? You fucking bitch, you stabbed me! *Stabbed* me." An unknown calm sweeps over me. I am Lot's wife. A pillar of salt and rebellion. "Who the…

how… you BITCH. You stabbed me, Nats. *Stabbed* me." He sounds like he might cry. Tears gather in his eyes. I wobble. The mother in me rising again.

But something stops her. She steps quietly back, suddenly clear of mind.

"Don't be ridiculous, Jo," I say. "I didn't *stab* you. That's a fork in your forehead, not a knife." His eyes are flashing something mad and I'm nervous he's about to swing. He's never laid a hand on me but there's a first time for everything and this might just be my turn. "You're a whore. A good-for-nothing whore. I'm done. You– you a-a-and Stefani. I'm done. I'm out of here."

He doesn't bother with a bag. He leaves the fork on the sink, its four prongs glistening with blood. The rest of the kitchen is still spotless, save for the unfinished dish of bobotie and the raisins he picked out of it on the table. I decide to leave the fork there. It will be a talisman. A charm against more lies.

*I*t's been a week now. He hasn't fetched clothes or called or even got his brother to pick up his things. I can't let this crush me. Not with a five-year-old and another on the way. While he may come and go like the seasons, I will in all weather remain. Babies tucked safe in my pockets. Curved and flattened against the skull of this house, a copper pipe threaded from geyser to tap. Detoxifying, warming, loving.

The fridge hums. The wind has died to a breath in the trees and Stefani is settled on the grass next to me. Her skin shines like polished milk, the violet veins visible beneath. I hear her sigh, not out of frustration or tiredness, but because I sigh and I put my arm around her little shoulders and pull her towards my belly. It's not all bad. The rent is due and Jo's left again and I'm not sure if this time's for good. But like every dawn the moon will tuck itself into the folds of the sky, gently resting until the sun takes her place.

I resolve to phone Jo's mother. Tell her enough is enough and she can expect demands for child support soon. I'll do that straight after Stefani's down and the floor is mopped and I've properly washed my hair. It's right up there with legal aid and changing bank passwords and scrubbing the smell of Jo out of the walls.

Once I've told her exactly what I think, I'll hang up. Won't even give her a chance to argue with me. No, not this time. Then I'll walk around my home. I'll pick up toys and straighten cushions and pour myself a tall glass of water. I'll pretend it's wine and drink it slowly, imagining with each sip that things are going to get better. And when I've finished my pretend-wine and put the glass back in the cupboard, I'll get into bed with my daughter, her little body warm and sweet and curled around my belly. With eyes closed I'll reach to every corner of my being. I'll gather what I find and sew it all together, a quilt I'll lie under night after night, until I am more than just traces of my old self. Until I am me.

The washing line spins on its axis. A carousel of socks and panties and tights. It's easy to forget who you were before. It's a simple job stagnating, calcifying. Right now I'm like blood that won't clot, platelets wall-flowering around a wound. But things will change for me, for us.

For a moment, the entire world is still. In the coral tree, blossoms signal the springtime. The garden is alive. Listening, waiting for a next move. But I think I'll get a start on those dishes. Woman's got to keep it together, you know?

Inyang

Mary Okon Ononokpono

I was stirred from my dream by the song of a mosquito. I had dreamed of a drop of dew that contained a world, a moon, an ocean. In my dream, the world within the dew drop drifted towards my face, and I could see clearly that its ocean and moon were red. The red world disquieted me, provoking a feeling of deep unease, then I heard a high note, felt a sharp prick, and the image of the crystalline drop turned to one of a drop of blood. Agitated, I slapped at the mosquito, finding my cheek instead, as a drop of what I took to be rain, rolled down my face. I opened my eyes and looked around, in an attempt to place my surroundings. It was black as the pitch used by my father's men to seal his canoes. For a moment, I was unsure of where I was. I could hear the roar that signified the presence of a large body of water close-by. This was creek country, cloaked in night. I had fallen asleep outside. As I sat up, shuddering, memories of the day returned in a tangle, from which I unravelled a thread.

T he dawn had broken as the dawn before it. The sun rose high, lifted on melodic notes provided by a solitary sunbird poised for flight; her ascent, as the oozing of a ruby yolk, whose bleeding essence warmed all it touched. We had escaped the house early, my sister and I, to catch the sunrise. Being the elder by three years, I was charged with her keep. I took my responsibility seriously, for though we had many, many, siblings, we were mother's only children and therefore shared the strongest of the bonds of blood.

I called her my little shadow, and she lived up to the title, mimicking me as I absorbed the colours of the changing sky, which softened from charcoal to the same blush as the flamingoes which erupted now in flight. We inhaled at the same time, breathing deeply the heady scent of sun-ripened fruit mixed with the unmistakable pungency of the sulphurous creek.

Soon the morning was peppered with the sounds of logging, the floor of the surrounding forest groaning beneath the weight of old majestic trees, felled by men who wielded their blades with the same precision as they wielded their brand new muskets. The sweltering night rolled into sweltering day, the stillness punctured by the sigh of the dying trees, a sound which had become all too frequent over the course of the last few weeks. Mother had told us that the mosquitoes were increasing because the trees were being felled. Because the creeks were drying up and once-sacred pools were stagnating. Because spirits who carried fell diseases brooded and roamed. As mother was fond of embellished words, we paid them little heed; that is, until we noticed a marked increase in the amount of bites on our skin, until one day our bodies resembled the spotted coats of leopards, not dissimilar to the pair of cubs that we had recently befriended in the bush. The sun's rays became prickly, and an intense blanket of heat that drove practically all residents of Afaha Obutong to the edge of the coast.

The rest of the women rose early, scenting the air with prayers to Abasi Urua, God of Trade – for it was market, on the eighth day, in the morning. We bathed in the yard, having collected water the previous day in anticipation of market, before running to join the other children, our bell-skirts chiming, alerting the world to the approach of innocence. We ate hot, sticky dodo as we ran, a blur of brown bodies, laughing and goading, leaving our compounds to explore salt-water swamps and the dense tropical forest. Babies wailed while women gossiped as they set up their stalls by the edge of the watery superhighway.

The length of the coast was soon bustling. We watched as toned men ferried bales of sumptuous cloth on large canoes. I didn't realise then that those canoes had been carved from the felled, ancient trees, even though evidence of their second life was all around us: their transformation into a harbour and small piers, and strange, angular, two-storied houses, imposing and decked; things of peculiar character, built of wood and baked ochre mud bricks. I yearned to enter such a grand house, if only to taste its forbidden treasures for myself. But I was a child of caution and was naturally distrustful of the pale-faced men who frequented the rival trading houses by the harbour. We, the children of the creek, knew all too well of the peril that lurked in the haunts of merchants.

The men ferried whisky and brandy and exotic trinkets for yams, grains and bronzes. A cannon boomed and I jumped as the noise scattered my spirit, until I realised that another winged-vessel had anchored downstream, off Parrot Island, in the mouth of the great river. I held my breath for the replying cannon, fired from our own harbour, the signal that a man would be sent from the big house to begin comey negotiations.

Afaha Obutong had changed. The water was our lifeblood. It was the road that had opened all roads. But now the wetlands and plains of the surrounding areas had been altered irrevocably by the God of Trade. The pace of life had quickened and even we children were aware of it. Our quiet corner had been unshackled. It felt as though the whole world lay on our doorstep.

As we sauntered toward the bank of the creek, mother called us back to her stall, handing me a manilla that she unhooked from the many heavy bangles that adorned her arms. I stared at the copper ring with reverence. My older brothers regularly boasted about their hordes of the recently introduced currency, but they had never deemed me worthy enough of entrusting with one. Mother interrupted my thoughts.

"Nne, take your sister and fetch a barrel of sea water," she said. "I need to replenish my salt. Tell that greedy Asukwor that he must send the remaining barrels promptly, or the women of Iban Isong will hear of it. There is more than enough for eight barrels there but I need you to bring one for me now. I need to boil salt. Don't tarry, sobidem!"

She waved us away. We wove through the tightly clustered stalls, all overflowing with the bounties of Abasi Urua, absorbing the sights and smells. The enormous platters piled with fresh fish, baskets spilling with plantain and newly imported cassava. Tomatoes, grains, nutmegs, and spices from exotic lands that lay far across the spirit sea – all these populated the market. Abasi Inam, God of Wealth, had been generous.

We delighted in the variety of colours, ignoring the hawkers that attempted to force their wares. We picked our way through a group of men arguing outside the Ekpe lodge, distinct in feather-plumed cavaliers and robes patterned with Nsibidi. They easily switched their vernacular, mixing the language of our forebears with foreign, nasal tongues; languages that I would later learn were Portuguese, Dutch and English.

"Eyen akpara!" said one of the men, as we walked past, and I paused, thinking up an equally disdainful retort, until I realised that his gaze rested upon a group of boys dressed like the strange white men. Ignoring them, we lingered and gawped at a stall that sold coral beads, combs, and bridal adornments of rose-bronze and solid gold; that was, until we were shooed away by the proprietor, her painted face contorting, ample breasts swinging like sun-baked gourds as she reached forward to give me a sharp slap. She had been more surprised by our presence than anything, for she had been distracted by the white man nearby dressed like a peacock.

He stood leering at her full breasts, ripe for the plucking, with his filthy trousers bulging and straining, his blood level rising, as she expertly reeled him into her net. I smirked as I saw her swipe the pocket watch that dangled from his velvet burgundy doublet, and laughed as his wig slipped while he lunged at her fleshy, chalk-patterned thigh. Seizing the chance, I snatched a golden comb from her stall and ran, pulling my sister after me, pushing through bodies that smelled of sweat mingled with spices and perfumed oils, only stopping when the woman's foul-mouthed curses had been swallowed by the noise of the market and the cries of gulls that circled above.

"Akpara o! Akpara o!" I shouted as I fled from the stall, until, satisfied that she was no longer following me, I slowed to a walk, grinning as I tucked my prize into my newly threaded hair. I made my way further through the riverside market, my sister firmly in tow, sidestepping women with babies tied to their backs, hopping over chickens and spilled stock. At one point I spotted a mother-of-pearl button, forced by someone's foot into the bank. As I stooped to pluck it from the mud, my mother's manilla fell from where I had hooked it onto my wrist. My sister retrieved and examined it, running her small index along the smooth copper curve.

"What are we supposed to do with this apart from wear it?" she asked. "Eat it?"

"Trade it," I said, "for yams or salt or whatever you desire."

"Why can't I just trade something of mine for something of yours?"

"Because you get more of what you'd like for one of these than for any one thing that you own."

"It's silly," she said. "It makes more sense to just give me a yam if I give you some salt."

"That's what they used to do. Old Edet told me."

"So why do we need these things?"

"They're called manillas."

"Ma-*nil*-la," she repeated, palming the small bracelet, feeling its weight in her small-girl hand.

At that moment a sand-coloured streak grabbed the manilla from my sister's outstretched palm and took off like a wind sprite in the direction of the creek. I didn't think twice, nor did I consider my sister, who stood wailing in the street as I took off after the thief, her cries fading as I pursued him into thick undergrowth by the trees. He was all legs and arms: as strange a person as I'd ever seen. But he was fast.

Though, not as fast as me, for this was *my* playground, and I knew it as intimately as kin. For years I had frolicked upon the hidden paths through the trees. I knew which roads led to watery chasms that housed families of pythons. I knew which paths the crocodiles were fond of crossing. I knew which herbs could heal the sickness brought on by the tsetse and the mosquitoes that increased without ceasing. I knew which plants brought pain and those that brought healing.

This was my home. I had felt acutely the pain of the dying trees. I could see the coming destruction that would spell our demise.

Although I had not used my sight for many seasons, I recalled now the playground of the Gods. In chasing the crook I noted our

passing of the place where Old Ukana still dwells, sleeping, undis-
turbed by the troubles of this world. We passed the place where
Atim Okpo Ebot is said to roam, attempting to restore sweetness
to waters that have long ceased flowing, turning their sacred, life-
giving nectar into spirits of destruction, whose deathly fingers stretch
far and wide. We passed the place I had first seen a mermaid who
had questioned me angrily before putting scales on my eyes. She had
told me to run in a straight line, unsighted, which is precisely what
I did, and I had found myself on my bed the following day with no
recollection of how I had got there, other than knowing I had no
desire anymore to consume any type of river creature.

The thief and I retraced the footsteps of the Gods, his flight
drawing me deeper and deeper into the forest, deeper than I had
ever been. I cursed him for we had long passed the threshold that
mother had forbade me ever to pass, long passed the beginning of
the road to the fabled Spirit Sea. I pursued him through the place
where the very old trees dwelt; the place the heartless loggers were
fond of frequenting. We passed sacred sites littered with ageing
Ekpu, passed Nnam stones crowned in lilies and effigies erected
for Abasi Inam. I was surprised at how many shrines we passed.
Scores of them, even: creek country had grown fat, enlarged by
the fingers of the Gods.

*E*ventually the thick brush began to waylay the thief. As he
moved deeper into the forest his movements grew increasingly
burdened, limbs trapped and slapped by branch and bush. He
began to slow. Grave peril was but a misstep away, it lay all around
us, and the thief seemed to know it. I too knew it: that the forest
was a thing alive, a dangerous thing, a bristling thing. From that
point I tracked the thief easily. He left clues strewn about like toys
spilled in the tantrum of an overgrown child. Following his path
I soon heard the familiar tinkle of a brook, and as I emerged into
a sun-dappled clearing, he was upon me, appearing as if from thin
air. He leapt from a tree and straddled my back, furiously trying to
bring me down.

"Ino!" I yelled, the feather-weight, impish thing clawing at my shoulders. "*Ino!* You will not slay me today, thief."

He was roughly my age, but I overpowered him easily with a move I had learned from one of my many senior brothers. As he lay on the mud near the brook, I picked up a stick to strike him. He would not get up for a while once I was done with him. But soon he whimpered, and I took pity on him, casting the stick aside and wresting mother's manilla from his pale grubby hand. I stared at his face and hair. He was a strange looking creature, with skin the colour of the golden sand found on the banks of azure inland pools; eyes the colour of their waters. His loosely curled hair looked soft as silk and as bright as golden flame. I felt a prickle of friendliness within me.

"What is your name, thief?" I asked.

"They call me Robin," he said.

I helped him to his feet, eyeing him as he eyed me right back. He wore pale-coloured stockings underneath breeches with stripes that seemed to elongate his legs. He wore black leather shoes, with bronze buckles singing in the sunlight. His puce shirt was torn near the throat. He would look like a vagrant were it not for his beautiful brocade doublet that was stained the colour of the waves. This creature appeared to have emerged from the fabled Sea. He was altogether odd, altogether delightful.

"Why do you stare at me?" he asked, cautiously.

"Because you stole my mother's manilla," I said. "*Ino.*"

"I beg your pardon, I truly do," he said. "But you can stop calling me thief."

"But you are a thief," I said. "What does a person who looks like you want with thieving?"

"What does a person who looks like *you* want with thieving?" he retorted. "I saw you steal the comb glittering in your hair. It's not as though you need it. I know who your father is. He could buy you the entire market if you asked him."

I felt my shoulders slump and my demeanour change. "And what do you know of it?" I asked, though it was apparent that he knew an awful lot about me.

"I'm sorry," he said, knowing he had gone too far. He looked me in the eye. "What is your name?"

"I don't give my name to thieves," I snapped. I had had enough of this probing child, so I turned and began retracing my steps. My sister would be worried by now, but if she had any sense – which, admittedly, she didn't always exhibit – she would make her way to my mother who would now be livid with a combination of fear and rage.

I stayed close to the sound of the water on the way back. I could hear the thief with wildfire for hair was following me, but I ignored him. He probably only needed to know the way back to the river. I tried to distract myself from his presence, and the fraught interaction we had just had. So as I walked I recalled the stories that my mother used to tell us about the forest, and about the guardians that roamed these sacred woods: of leopards and sprites and other indwelling spirits; of the sylphs of air that diverted the paths of wars and the migrations of our peoples. I thought of the fabled Ocean, the great bridge that separated our world from that of the spirits, of which I had heard many tales, but never seen, though I was told it was but three days' march away.

I walked until I was weary. Standing at a fork in the river with which I was not familiar, it dawned on me that we were lost. I sank to the earth at the river bank and lapped at the water, quenching a thirst I didn't know I had. Exhausted, I collapsed in a heap where I knelt, wondering how many miles I had followed the river in the wrong direction. The shadows were beginning to lengthen.

I turned to the boy, who was still following me, but keeping his distance. "Do you know where we are?" I asked him.

"No," he said. "I was hoping that you did."

I put my head in my hands and sighed, letting the noise of the river – a great, oddly distant roar – fill my head. How could I get so disoriented? I had to restore myself somehow to find my way home.

Something thudded beside me. I turned and saw that Robin had thrown a mango at me. I took it in my hand and regarded it, until he sauntered up to me and produced a flick-knife like the one I had spotted my brothers playing with. He carved up the sweet flesh and handed chunks to me, which I consumed ravenously as his face reddened. I wondered at his change in demeanour as he sat down next to me and proceeded to portion up another few mangoes that he had procured from somewhere.

We sat quietly, savouring the succulent fruit. When we had our fill we cleaned the sticky juice from our fingers in the stream. The day was beginning to darken, but the heat of the sun only gave way to a damp humidity. Robin stripped to his britches to cool down after the day's travelling. He folded the rest of his clothes into a neat pile, and sat down on top of them, facing me.

"I hope I haven't caused you too much trouble," he said, "with your mother and all."

I laughed at him. "Well, Mma will give me a scolding to last at least two market weeks," I said. "I shall never hear the end of it." I turned to him and frowned. "What do you care anyway? I abandoned my sister because of you. I've never done such a thing before. She must have caught a fright."

His face betrayed no emotion. "You shouldn't go round thieving from people's mothers if you don't want them to thieve off you," he said, matter-of-factly. I was stunned. When I found my words again, they came out in a tumble.

"Uyai? The one the women call *akpara*?" I could hardly believe what I was about to ask this pale-skinned boy. "*She's* your mother? How? She's dark and she's a beauty and you're, you're…" My voice was swallowed by the thunderous sound of the water.

"I'm?" he coaxed me.

"You're… you're one of us?"

"Yes," he said, not smiling. "But I don't look it. I take after my father."

It dawned on me. "That was your father? By your mother's stall? Did he arrive on winged ships that crossed the face of the Spirit Sea?"

"No, no," Robin said, abruptly, his eyes downcast. "That man is my father's first mate. My father is a captain."

"Oh."

His voice was suddenly soft. "But he did arrive from across the sea."

I stared at Robin. Immediately I felt guilty. "Were you outside the Ekpe lodge earlier?" I asked.

"Yes," he said.

"You shouldn't let people call you eyen akpara," I said.

"They say it anyway," he said.

An awkward silence ensued. From the corner of my eye, I saw a red ant scuttle across his doublet.

"That cloth is beautiful," I said, breaking the awkward silence, as I pulled the comb from my threaded hair. "Here, take it," I said, and returned the comb. He placed it carefully into his breast pocket as I wondered out loud. "But why wear all that cloth in this heat?" I asked, puzzled. "It makes no sense."

Robin laughed. "I know," he said. "They're ridiculous. But my father says that they're the mark of a distinguished gentleman, which is to be my destiny, so I had better become accustomed now."

"Why do your father's people dress like peacocks?" I asked.

"Because it is cold across the sea," said Robin.

"I've always wanted to see the sea," I said. "I've heard of it but never glimpsed it. It sounds like a marvel."

"But you are close to it," he said, suddenly jovial. "You're so silly! Don't you know we have followed the road to the sea? You can hear them now, the waters."

"But that is the sound of the great river." I pointed to the fork in the river. "Right there."

"No it isn't," he laughed. "That stream can't make all that noise by itself. It's the sea. Listen to her. She's breathing." I stood and listened as the waters breathed evenly in and out, as Robin walked to the base of a very tall palm. He scuttled up it as one touched by the God of Lightning, his speed stunning even the lizard that traced his steps. He reached the top in a blur.

"Can you climb trees?" he shouted from his place among the fronds.

"Of course!" I shouted back. There were many climbable trees around. I selected an old, enormous iroko, easily scaling its sturdy trunk, hauling myself up by branches heavy with leaves. The leaves restricted my vision, so I proceeded with cautious steps, until, all at once, the leaves gave way at the top and I could see out over the canopy. The view took my breath away. It was something exquisite. I had emerged on the side of the tree that overlooked an ancient creek, which watered the river that spread out and broadened before me. In the estuary I saw them perched: these majestic, winged vessels, mirrored in the multicoloured waters that danced with enchanting lights. Their wings stretched tall and white, their bodies sleek and dark, bobbing gently in the cool, glassy waters.

I followed the line of the bank with my eyes and then I saw her, vast and regal. One who inspires awe. And dread. I surveyed with my own eyes one of the Mothers, the ancient ones; she who watered the earth at the dawn of days; her terror, might, and splendour only matched by the fullness of her beauty. Life-bearer, life-taker, I glanced upon Abasi Inyang Ibom herself.

God dwelt in the waters, and I looked upon her face.

Dusk descended as the dusk before. But never had I glimpsed a dusk as spectacular as this. We watched the light of the sun fill the great, vast sea and I let out a peal of delight. It was just as I imagined it. A redding sun I had dreamed of countless times, slowly being swallowed by the ocean. I laughed, for what was the world if not an enormous drop of dew? And what would our precious home be if not sustained by her life-giving waters?

"Abasi Inyang Ibom," I whispered. "Sosongo, Abasi sosongo." At that moment I locked eyes with Robin as he perched in his palm, and the fire of kinship was lit. In that instant the two of us sealed our fate and became inseparable. As the sun set and night fell we descended our respective perches and slept entwined within the arms of the other.

*W*hen I woke night had long fallen. I felt another drop of rain on my face. I had dreamed I was a drop of dew that would raise the floor of the ocean. The sky above me swarmed with mosquitoes, attracted by the scent of mango skins still strewn haphazardly next to me. I started as a voice called down from the tree closest to the bank of the creek. It was Robin. He was dressed once more in his torn shirt and sea-coloured doublet. I made my way towards his perch, half-crouching, aware that there were more dangerous things than wild beasts that roamed this wood at night.

"Stay away from the water." Robin said. "She's deep and her current is powerful." I joined him on a neighbouring bough.

We lay face down, stretched out on branches that overlooked the waterway which raced along below. It was pitch black, and we were blinded awake, but the voice of the water betrayed its proximity. My bells tinkled and clouds gathered overhead, but the moon hovered over the face of the ocean at the point where the waters had swallowed the sun.

"I may be wrong," Robin whispered, "but I am sure that there are traders that anchor nearby."

"But won't they take us for miscreants?" I wondered out loud.

"*Shh*, speak quietly." He placed his finger to his lips. "The trees have ears and eyes." We watched the surface of the creek as it danced with the sprites of the moon. "There are voices on the water," he said as he stiffened upon his branch. And he was right: the water carried a variety of voices towards the vessels that barricaded salt water from sweet. I stiffened as Robin had done, growing aware of the sound of a vessel cutting through the face of the water. There were voices carried upon the wind, too. The moon shone upon the creek below.

It appeared unexpectedly, the body of a tree of gigantic proportions. Bark still covered most of its trunk, which was hollowed to accommodate a vast number of bodies, borne swiftly on a current that poured into the waiting ocean basin. Wind whipped my face as I heard the bodies' muffled whispers carried on the currents of angry air. A storm was approaching. Electrum-hued ribbons caressed the skies, but no thunder followed. It dawned on me that something was askew, Abasi Obuma was silent.

I saw them when the first rain fell: faces in the water. Faces carried in the canoes that cut across the face of the deep, causing their faces to appear as scores upon scores of small dark islands, dotted in pitch waters illuminated by the distant lights that troubled the heavens. Some of them saw me as they passed beneath: a small child, suspended amid overhanging leaves and clothed in nothing but the bell-skirt and bangles customary for girls of my age-set. But the faces could not call out, for their mouths were bound. As my heart thundered in my ears, overcompensating for the chilling lack of sound coming from the heavens, they implored me with their eyes. Never had I seen a more pitiful sight than that of these creatures, shackled by little more than crude twine and interned in the water that had once been their lifeblood.

How cruel are the webs of Abasi Atai to ensnare us in the very things that would give us power, but from which we are unable to draw. These were people of the creek, powerful fishing folk, who, for a living, harnessed these self-same waters with which they shared an affinity.

As the first canoe glided towards the estuary I counted the ensnared. Eighty-nine, mostly men, but women and children scattered among them, notwithstanding the retinues of slaves which rowed the monstrous boats, or the drunken potbellied men attired in white man's clothing, swigging brandy and palm wine from large drinking horns and polluting the skies with the crudest of songs.

There were roughly one hundred and forty on that first canoe, but it was not the last. I counted eight boats, then lost count, as the flotilla kept coming. I had seen unfortunate captives before – our homestead was practically run by them – but this was different; these were destined to be taken across the face of the Spirit Sea, to the realms of the living-dead, never to return to the land of their birth. A fate worse than death. Among the bound I saw faces that I recognised: many of my senior brothers, twenty, forty, all garbed as white men and overseeing the rowing of the great canoes. A mother and her boy from a neighbouring town, who had that morning come to Afaha Obutong to trade. Greedy Asukwor, from whom I was supposed to fetch a barrel of seawater. Unbeknownst to me, he had been grabbed as a pawn for defaulting on a payment, at the moment my mother found him, to knock him and curse him for waylaying her eldest daughter.

Among the bound lay the unmistakable figure of my uncle, my father's junior brother who had recently provoked a war. He implored me with his eyes now, trapped between the water in his canoe and the relentless flood of the heavens. I wept as I watched him drowning and looked away from the rowing slave boys scrambling to reduce the water. They propped up the bound who still struggled to breathe as the God of Rain emptied the heavens. There was wailing on the water, a wailing carried from the belly of the deep. I was shivering but I couldn't feel it, entranced as I was as the source of my family's great wealth was laid naked before me.

And there he stood. Proud. Regal. Surveying his newly acquired wealth with the eye of an eagle. Etubom, Father of the Canoes, his new title never more befitting than at this precise moment as he surveyed his vast domain. A great chief and his wealth. I watched him. Attired as both Obong and white man. My father. As the blue moon emerged from a thunderous cloud he seemed to intuit me, glancing in my direction and meeting my eye. Lightning struck our tree. My father's face turned aghast as I shrieked and fell. Horror was stamped upon his expression. My father's grief-stricken face was the last thing I saw before hitting the raging waters.

Our lifeblood had become my doom. I was swiftly pulled to the mouth of the estuary. Locked in a powerful current from which there was no escape. I struggled, choking, drowning, my life force ebbing, against the ferocious tide, as I was churned in the rough swell of the seas. I resisted until I could resist no more, and I surrendered, but not before thanking the lady of the waters. In my surrender to Abasi Inyang Ibom, I discovered I could breathe.

I became the ocean. I became the watcher of the water. I became the mother of the wellspring of life, she whose waters house constellations and multiverses yet unknown to humankind. I became the keeper and releaser of souls, she who has swallowed civilisations unnumbered, whose ruins populate her depths which spring from the core of the earth. And I saw figures in the waters. Figures rising from the bottom of the deep. They called for vengeance for the desecration of their bonds of blood and they implored the Lady of the Waters. As they cried, sending up a shout to the heavens, they began to ascend. I became them, tortured souls, a million strong, even as the ocean was turned to blood, victims enmeshed in the great web of Abasi Urua, whose wheels would keep spinning no matter the ultimate cost. But the God of Trade is the offspring of the Lady of Waters, and her mother's flesh cries out with the blood of the children of Abasi Isong.

You must return and stem the tide. The voices repeated their instruction even as I was spewed out of the ocean and onto dry land.

"I dreamed I was a drop of dew that raised the floor of the ocean." I said to to the strange boy with wet flames for hair.

"You caused me an awful fright," he said. "You should be dead."

I sputtered, vision still awash with the imprint of enormous stone effigies, temples of gems and precious metals, wrought, perished and swallowed by the waves, the last vestiges of civilisations long forgotten.

I became aware of a commotion approaching. It was my father and brothers.

"I never told you my name." I whispered.

"Well? What is it?"

"Inyang."

"The name is befitting of you."

"God is in the waters," I said, as he brushed the weeds from my face.

BIOGRAPHIES

Efemia Chela was born in 1991 and is half-Zambian, half-Ghanaian. She studied French, Politics and Classics at Rhodes University, South Africa and at Institut D'Etudes Politiques in Aix-En-Provence, France. She enjoys eating pizza, playing croquet and watching black-and-white films. Her first published story, "Chicken", was nominated for the 2014 Caine Prize For African Writing.

Christine Coates is a poet, writer and art-maker from Cape Town. She has an MA in Creative Writing from the University of Cape Town. Her debut collection of poetry, *Homegrown*, was published in 2014 by Modjaji Books. Her short story "The Cat's Wife" was highly commended and published in *Adults Only,* the 2014 National Arts Festival Short.Sharp.Stories anthology.

Louis Greenberg is a writer, editor and recovering bookseller from Johannesburg with a doctorate in post-religious fiction. He's published novels, stories and poems under his own name; as S.L. Grey, he co-writes horror fiction with Sarah Lotz.

Cat Hellisen is a South African-born writer of fantasy for adults and children. Her work includes the novel *When the Sea is Rising Red* and short stories in *Apex, F & SF, Shimmer* Magazine, and Tor.com. Her latest novel is a fairy tale for the loveless, *Beastkeeper.*

Pede Hollist is author of *So the Path Does Not Die,* named the African Literature Association's 2013 Book of the Year for Creative Writing. His short stories include "Foreign Aid", which was shortlisted for the 2013 Caine Prize, and "BackHomeAbroad", anthologised in *The Price and Other Stories from Sierra Leone.*

Thabo Jijana is a writer from the Eastern Cape of South Africa. He has published two books: a memoir, *Nobody's Business* (Jacana, 2014), and a collection of poetry, *Failing Maths and My Other Crimes* (uHlanga,2015). His short fiction and journalism have appeared in several publications in South Africa.

Fred Khumalo is an award-winning novelist, short story writer, and the author of *Bitches Brew, Touch My Blood,* and *Seven Steps To Heaven,* among other titles. A seasoned journalist and a 2012 Nieman Fellow at Harvard University, Khumalo also holds an MA in Creative Writing from the University of the Witwatersrand.

Alex Latimer's debut novel *The Space Race* was published by Umuzi in 2013. His next novel, *South,* co-written with Diane Awerbuck, will be published by Corvus in September 2016. Alex is best known for his picture books, which have been translated into a variety of languages and sold globally.

Wesley Macheso, born in 1989, is a Malawian writer currently teaching creative writing and literature at Mzuzu University. He is also a columnist with the *Daily Times*. He won the 2014/2015 Peer Gynt Literary Award for his children's book, *Akuzike and the Gods.*

Siyanda Mohutsiwa is a 22-year-old writer from Botswana. In her spare time she studies Mathematics at the University of Botswana.

Mark Mngomezulu is a writer from Swaziland. His work has appeared in Africa Book Club's inaugural anthology, *A Bundle of Joy and Other Stories*, and the *Kalahari Review*.

Donald Molosi is a classically trained actor and award-winning playwright of *We Are All Blue*, a volume of two off-Broadway plays exploring the role of race and borders in the identity of Southern Africa. He holds an MA in Performance Studies from UCSB, a Graduate Diploma in Classical Acting from LAMDA, and a BA in Political Science and Theatre from Williams College. He divides his time between Botswana and the United States.

Chido Muchemwa is a Zimbabwean writer currently pursuing an MFA in creative nonfiction at the University of Wyoming. Her essays have appeared in *Tincture* and *Apogee*. Find her on Twitter: @ChidoMuchemwa.

Nick Mulgrew is a British-South African writer, editor and publisher. He is the author of *the myth of this is that we're all in this together*, a collection of poetry, and *Stations,* a book of short fiction. He is the 2014 winner of the National Arts Festival Short.Sharp.Stories Award in South Africa, and a 2015 shortlistee for the *White Review* Prize in the U.K.

Wairimu Muriithi is a not-yet-writer, an all-time-reader, a secret blogger and a student at the university currently known as Rhodes. She lives in South Africa and Kenya, and spends her time thinking and reading about memory, diaspora, grief and the 1973 film, *Touki Bouki*. She has written previously for brainstorm.co.ke, *Wiathi* in the *New Inquiry*, *Will This Be A Problem?* and the *Kalahari Review*.

Dayo Ntwari is a Rwandan-Nigerian writer whose short stories include "Devil's Village", which was shortlisted for the 2015 Writivism Short Story Prize, and "Nomansland", which was shortlisted for the 2015 Huza Press Award.

Louis Ogbere is a Nigerian-born short story writer, self-confessed gastronaut, and unapologetic introvert. His short fiction has appeared in online and print magazines in Nigeria, South Africa and the U.K. He is currently at work on a collection of short stories.

Mary Okon Ononokpono is a Nigerian-British writer, artist and illustrator. She is the winner of the 2014 Golden Baobab Prize for Early Chapter Books, and a 2015 shortlistee for the Miles Morland Foundation Scholarship. Mary is the author of the children's book *Talulah the Time Traveller* (African Bureau for Children's Stories, 2016). Currently, she studies history at SOAS, University of London.

Florence Onyango is a Kenyan scriptwriter chancing her hand at short stories and poetry. She's a media jack-of-all-trades, working in everything from PR to journalism. She loves to bottle up little pleasures. Her greatest fear is a prosaic mind.

Megan Ross is a South African writer, journalist, graphic designer and mother from the Eastern Cape. She worked as a feature writer before quitting to backpack through Asia. Her writing has appeared in *Prufrock, Aerodrome, Itch* and *Incredible Journey*, the 2015 National Arts Festival Short.Sharp.Stories anthology. She is about to begin work on her first novel.

Karina Szczurek is the author of *Truer than Fiction: Nadine Gordimer Writing Post-Apartheid South Africa* and the editor of *Touch: Stories of Contact, Encounters with André Brink*, and *Contrary: Critical Responses to the Novels of André Brink* (with Willie Burger). Her debut novel, *Invisible Others,* was published in 2014.

Alexis Teyie is a Kenyan poet and feminist. Her work is included in Jalada's Afrofuture(s) and Language issues. She has also featured in *Q-zine, This is Africa, Black Girl Seeks* and *African Youth Journals.*

Mark Winkler has spent his working life in advertising, winning over thirty local and international advertising awards. He is currently creative director at a leading Cape Town agency. Mark's first novel, *An Exceptionally Simple Theory of Absolutely Everything,* was published in 2013, and his second, *Wasted,* in 2015. Mark lives in Cape Town with his family.

ACKNOWLEDGEMENTS

*A good writer possesses not only his own spirit but
also the spirit of his friends.*
— *Friedrich Nietzsche*

*E*very publication is the result of a team effort, and none so more than this. Special thanks to Nick Mulgrew and Karina Szczurek whose tireless efforts, keen eyes and dedication helped these twenty-one writers improve their stories and their craft. Nick's many talents do not begin and end with his editorial skills. He is responsible for the astonishing cover collage and the page design and layout.

Arthur Atwell and Electric Book Works formatted the e-book, while Worldreader once again supplied the seed funding to cover the cost of editing and designing the anthology. Colleen Higgs and Emily Buchanan of Hands-On Books continue to offer support and publishing advice. As our publishing partner, they have taken our small project under their experienced wings and allowed us to grow. Thanks to Hands-On Books, new publishing partnerships have been formed with Cassava Republic and New Internationalist.

Special thanks to Abubakar Adam Ibrahim, Billy Kahora and Mary Watson for judging the *Water* competition.

Thanks too to the team of readers that helped us whittle down the long list, and thus played a vital role in shaping this anthology: Andrew Peter Rex Salomon, Anesu Chigariro, Ayesha Kadjee, Ayodeji Balogun, Bontle Senne, Crystal Warren, Dave de Burgh, Drew Carleton, Ester Levinrad, Gail Schimmel, George Okeke, Iain S Thomas, Isla Haddow-Flood, John Schaidler, Julie Bracker, Karina Szczurek, Kelly Tarmwa, Kerry Hammerton, Kyle Aiden Cowan, Laura M Kaminski, Louise Umutoni, Mack Lundy, Mandy Thomas, Margot Bertelsmann Doherty, Mary Ajayi, Nick Wood, Rahla Xenopoulos, Samantha Costanzo, Sharleen van Zweel, Sheryl Kavin, Sima Matal, Sumayya Lee and Tolu Awobusuyi.

Funding assistance from ANT ProHelvetia helped Short Story Day Africa run Water Flow Writing Workshops in Botswana, Malawi and Zimbabwe. As a result, we received several entries from these three countries into the Short Story Day Africa Prize.

The online writing courses the winning writers receive were donated by All About Writing. Funds for the monetary prizes came from ANT ProHelvetia, Books Live, Worldreader, and Gidon, Tallulah and Samuel Xenopoulos of Generation Africa.

And without the sponsorship, financially and in kind, of the following organisations and individuals, our scope would have been much smaller:

Alex Latimer • Alison McQueen • Amy Heydenrych • Andrea Nattrass • Arthur Attwell • Ben Williams • Bontle Senne • Bruce Hooke • C.A. Davids • Candace di Talamo • Cara Steyn • Caryn Gootkin • Catherine Shortridge • Cedric Downard • Charles Nfon • Christine Coates • Claire te Riele • Claire Robertson • Cristy Zinn • Darlington Richards • Dennis Reed • Deon Durholtz • Dewi Prichard • Diane Awerbuck • Dianne Stewart • Dorothy Dyer • Ekow Duker • Erica Lombard • Ester Levinrad • Edyth Bulbring • Fiona Davern • Fred Carleton • Helen Moffett • Henrietta Rose-Innes • Iain S Thomas • Isla Haddow-Flood • Jared Shurin • Jayne Bauling • Jenna Shively • Jennifer Malec • Jennifer Jacobs • Jess Hindley • Joanne Macgregor • Judy Smee-Dixon • Judy Croome • Karina Szczurek • Katherine Graham • Katie Reid • Katie Smuts • Kerry Hammerton • Lauren Beukes • Linda Mannheim • Lindsay Callaghan • Lionel Ntasano • Lisa Lazarus • Louis Greenberg • Mack Lundy • Máire Fisher • Manu Herbstein • Manuel de los Reyes • Margot Bertelsmann Doherty • Marius du Plessis • Melanie Donaldson • Mehul Gohil • Michelle Preen • Mike Sweeny • Mignon Hardie • Nick Wood • Nozizwe Cynthia Jele • Paddy Esselaar • Paige Nick • Pilar Ramirez Tello • Rahla Xenopoulos • Richard de Nooy • Robyn Goss • Saaleha Bamjee • Samantha Gibb • Sarah Lotz • Sarah Woodward Sonica Kirsten • Stephen Embleton • Steven Lottering • Subhas Shah • Sylvia Hall • Vanessa Beautement • Yana Stajno • Yewande Omotoso.

We are grateful to the members of our board, Helen Moffett, Isla Haddow-Flood, Karina Szczurek, Mary Watson, Rahla Xenopoulos and Sheryl Kavin for their support and dedication; especially to Isla Haddow-Flood for the expertise and time she gave to secure funding for the Water Flow Workshop Series, and Rahla Xenopoulos for recruiting her wonderful,philanthropically-minded children to raise prize money.

And to all the writers and readers of African fiction: we thank you.

RACHEL ZADOK, TIAH BEAUTEMENT & NICK MULGREW
THE SHORT STORY DAY AFRICA TEAM